CONVINCING YOU

SENSING SERIES 2

J.M. ADELE

Edited by CREATING ink
Proofed by Fiona Dreaming
Cover by Tall Story Designs
Formatted by Book Flare Publishers

Print Edition
ISBN: 978-0-6487360-0-4

For my B.

I wish you could understand that I will love you for eternity no matter what you do or say, or how far you roam. No matter your achievements or failures.

There is no stopping this love.

I wish you would believe you deserve it.

I wish it was enough.

Titles by J.M.

Coming Home Series

Shattered Home
Remembering Home
Finding Home
Leaving Home (TBA)
Coming Home (TBA)

Sensing Series

Sensing You
Convincing You
Indulging You (TBA)

Bloodlust Series

Ashes and Dust
Ember and Flame
Bone and Blood (TBA)

Contents

Aussie Glossary

Agro – Aggression

Bags – Call dibs. To claim something as yours before anyone else can.

Barbie – Barbecue. Grill.

Blow chunks – Vomit

Bogan – An uncouth person

Bomby – A dive where you curl into a ball to make a large splash

Chippie – Carpenter

Dacks – Pants

Dunny – The toilet

FIFO – Fly in, fly out. An acronym used to describe workers who are flown on-site to work, and flown back home at the end of their block of shifts

Galah – Australian species of bird

Glove Box – Glove compartment or jockey box

Gob – Mouth

Goldy – The Gold Coast in Queensland, Australia

Grog – Alcohol

Grub – Food

Idiot Box – Television

Jackeroo – Young man working on a sheep or cattle station. The female equivalent is Jilleroo.

Knackered – Exhausted

Let one rip – Fart

Macca's – McDonald's

Maggoted – Drunk

"Nah, yeah" – Yes

Op shop – Thrift store

Portaloo – A portable toilet often used on a worksite

Pulling someone's leg – To tease them

Ranga – Redhead

Rocky – Rockhampton, Queensland, Australia

Shirt-front – To push your chest into another person's. Usually an aggressive move

Smoko – Morning tea or afternoon tea break

Sneakers – Running shoes

Sparrow's fart – Before dawn

Stubbies – A brand of workwear. Refers specifically to shorts

Squiz – A glance or a look

Taking the piss – Having a laugh

Thong – Beach footwear. Flip flop.

Tool – Idiot

Tucker – Food

Uni – University

Ute – Utility vehicle or pickup truck. A car with a tray on the back for hauling loads

Veg – Relax

"Yeah, nah" – No

Disclaimer

The following story contains scenes that may be of a disturbing nature to those sensitive to triggers. Please do not proceed if you feel you may be at risk of emotional or psychological harm in doing so.

Please reach out for support should you need any. You don't have to suffer alone.

Prologue

Call me John Doe

Rockhampton, Australia
26th June, 2006

They sashayed around in their short skirts, flashed their cotton underwear as they bent over. And then pretended they didn't want a man's dick buried deep inside them.

Fucking schoolgirl cock-teasers, playing a dangerous game.

They asked for it and I was ready to give it. Girls wanted me to get them alone so I could fuck them raw. I had them begging for it just with a look. And when I caught one of my little does, they were always bucking for a fucking.

My cock lengthened in readiness as my brain teased out a scenario.

All I had to do was choose who the next doe would be.

A young blonde jogged over to her brunette friend, perky tits bouncing all the way. I reckoned she'd be about fourteen. Just the right age. Not too young to be completely naive to female power, but not old enough to know how to wield it as a weapon. Fourteen was the perfect age for me to make a girl believe her self-worth was under my control.

I couldn't decide which one I liked better. The brunette was taller, but she had less meat on her bones. Her hair only just reached her shoulders. That was a shame. I liked to wrap a good length around my wrist when I pounded their flesh. Two more girls joined their group. A plump, auburn-haired beauty, and another blonde—this one flat chested. *Wait.* I looked closer. *No.* I could just see the outline of swollen nipples. She was just developing. *Perfect.*

So many girls ripe for the picking. Which one will it be?

Chapter
1

Andrea

Brisbane, Australia
19th December, 2016

A cracker loaded with brie and quince paste was passed in front of my face as Lee handed it to Ronnie.

Brie. Sweet, sweet, unpasteurised, soft, bacteria-ridden cheese. *Oh, how I've missed you.*

I licked my lips, sucking in the smell as my nose followed the delicacy.

"Are you sniffing my food?" Wrinkles carved grooves into Ronnie's cheeks.

"It has been nine months. *Nine. Months.* Yes, I'm sniffing the brie. I *miss* it." My statement came out as a whimper.

Ronnie took a small bite before asking, "Can you still have soft cheese if you're breastfeeding?"

"I don't think so," Lee answered, scrubbing the back of his freckled neck.

I arched my sore back. "What? Of course I can. Don't tell me that."

Ben wrapped his fingers around my ponytail and stroked its length. "I dunno. I think it might be too risky for the baby."

I twisted to look at him. "Bullshit. You're wrong." I searched his serious expression for any hint of a joke. A twitch in the corner of his mouth. A change in his eyes. Nothing. He was stone-cold sober. "Don't tell me I can't eat the cheese. I want the cheese. Babe, you know I can't do without the cheese."

Ronnie rested her forearms on the table and leaned forward, her gaze glued to mine. "I read an article last week about this woman who did all the right things during the pregnancy and as soon as the baby was born, she gorged on all the cheese. Brie, camembert, blue vein—she went to town. She fed the baby a couple of hours later. The poor thing ended up in hospital with a nasty infection."

"Are you shitting me?" I dropped my chin, mouth agape. If this was a joke, she was no longer my friend.

"Yes. Yes, Andy, we're shitting you." She leaned back with a huge grin on her face as Lee and Ben sniggered. "It's way too easy."

"I hate you."

"Not true."

Ben tried to tuck me under his arm. I pouted and inched away. "You're so mean to me in my vulnerable state. You know it's my due date and I'm still fecking preggers."

"He'll be here soon. He's just way too comfortable inside there." Ben nuzzled my neck, whispering in my ear, "I don't blame him. I wanna be inside you right now."

I wriggled in my seat as a choking noise came from across the table. "Jesus, I heard that." Ronnie scrubbed her hands over her ears, masses of dark curls bouncing as she did.

I didn't give a shit that she'd heard what Ben said. I loved that he still found me desirable despite the fact that I'd swelled to twice my normal size and couldn't see my toes, let alone touch them.

The loud clap of Lee's hands made me jump. "Who wants prawns? Not you, Andy. I did a rolled turkey roast for you. Sorry."

Prawns. Another thing I couldn't eat. *Yet.* After this kid was out, I was going to fill myself with all the pre-prepped salad, shellfish, soft cheese, and wine I could get my hands on.

Lee dragged his chair back as Ronnie jumped to help him.

I rested a hand on Ben's thigh. The delicious smell of our early Christmas dinner wafted from the kitchen. "Do you mind if we exchange gifts first? I can't wait. We might have to run off to hospital at any moment."

"You can't hold off for another half an hour?"

"Nope."

Ben pushed his chair back.

"Babe, can you grab the presents for me please?"

"Already on it."

He was the best.

Lee stood behind Ronnie with his arms around her teeny tiny waist, one palm spread over her stomach. They presented such a contrast. Her with sultry, dark features and caramel skin, and Lee with freckles and auburn locks. He was only just taller than her. She and Ben were eye to eye, but he was twice her girth, although they were both solid muscle. All three of my dinner companions could've done a Nike ad, while I was the Oompa Loompa in the background.

Not for much longer hey, baby boy?

Our hosts watched me from the kitchen. Something silently passed between them, evident from the way they held each other.

"Are you coming over here, or are you going to make me get up?" I raised a brow.

They returned to their seats with matching smirks.

Ben slid in beside me, placing down an envelope and a box wrapped with multi-coloured braided ribbons and topped with a pretty bow.

"Thanks." I handed the envelope to Ronnie. "Merry Christmas!"

Lee had given Ronnie tickets to Sydney for her birthday two weeks ago. They were going before uni started back in March. As soon as I found out what he'd planned, I'd known what I wanted to give her for Christmas.

A smile tilted her mouth at one corner as her eyes flitted around the table. She ducked her chin and used her knife to open the present. Slipping out a piece of paper, her eyebrows scrunched before popping high. "A private ghost tour of Sydney." Her shoulders kissed her earlobes. "I'm shitting myself. Thanks."

"All the oldest buildings are haunted, but you already know that. I figured you could kill two birds with one stone. Face down your fear of spirits and get an inside view of some beautiful old buildings."

"You'll be with me. I'll protect you, babe." Lee kissed her cheek and she responded with a roll of her eyes.

He knew damn well she didn't need protection. They were cute together. It was nice to see them both happy after the fucked-up shit that had gone down earlier in the year. She'd nearly died trying to save her friend from an underground sex cult. Nothing would ever clear those images from their heads, but they could create new memories—happy Polaroid moments, shining light into the darkest corners of their minds. Not that ghosts would provide particularly happy snaps necessarily, but Ronnie could handle anything that was thrown at her now. She was a badass.

"Your turn." Ben pushed the box across the table to his mate.

"Did you wrap this?" Lee tried to hide a smirk.

"That's all my handiwork, mofo. You know I'm good with plaits."

My eye twitched as Lee fiddled with the ribbons, trying to delicately untie the bow. "Just rip it."

"You sure?"

"Yes! Jesus." I almost dragged my hands down my face.

He yanked at the paper, tossing bits on the table. "Do you know what you're gonna call Benny junior?"

"Sebastian." I answered without thinking.

"Hell, no." Ben frowned.

"Why not?" I thought we'd discussed this already, but maybe that had all been in my head.

His blue eyes pierced mine. "Sebastians don't play rugby."

I wracked my brain trying to remember if there'd been any players named Sebastian. Surely there were. I shook my head. "What if he doesn't wanna play?"

Ben paused, his Adam's apple bobbing as he blinked at me.

"Are you going to make him?" I asked.

"No?" It sounded like a question.

I took it as a definitive answer, rubbing my belly. "I'm relieved to hear it."

"Is Stewart gonna make him play league?" Ben narrowed his eyes.

"Not if he knows what's good for him." My brother wouldn't dare. I'd slap him if he tried to influence my child in any way.

He scoffed. "He has never known what's good for him. I still can't believe they let him into the police force."

I couldn't get over that one myself.

"Why Sebastian?" Ben frowned.

"I don't know. I just have a feeling." The moniker had been rolling around in my thoughts more and more lately. There was something attached to it, tangled strings that needed unknotting. Unfinished business. I'd never known anyone with that name, but it wouldn't leave me alone. Our son *had* to be called Sebastian—I knew that much. I just didn't know why. "It'll grow on you. Trust me on this one, okay?"

Ben pushed a breath through flared nostrils. "Do I get to pick the middle name?"

"Absolutely ... as long as it's Ben." I smiled with all my pearly whites on show.

His lip quirked. "Sebastian Ben Locke." Running his tongue along his teeth, he looked at me. "Seb for short. That's okay."

"Cute." Lee added. "And he's going to play league. Is anyone interested in my critique of my present?"

Ben and I twisted our heads and found that Lee had opened the box and was wearing his present on his head. A fluffy wallaby with a baby in her pouch sat atop the brim of his Australian national rugby union official team cap. I'd made the alterations myself.

Ronnie gave him the side-eye while leaning away.

"I love it." Lee grinned.

I snorted. I couldn't help it. He looked ridiculous.

Ben, Lee, and I were laughing so hard I didn't realise at first that we were the only ones. Ronnie had a smile on her lips, but her worried eyes were on my stomach. She almost appeared sick. Or spooked.

Sebastian rolled. I shifted in my seat, holding my side. Her gaze tracked my hand. She grimaced before turning away.

What is that all about?

The only answer I got was a sinking feeling in my gut that had nothing to do with Seb's movements and everything to do with the way Ronnie stared at my baby bump.

I take it back. I don't want to know.

Chapter
2

Andrea

Brisbane, Australia
24th December, 2016, 3:23 p.m.

Have a baby, they said.

It'll be fun, they said.

Lugging this stomach around a shopping centre on Christmas Eve was not my idea of fun. I squeezed out of the car, swearing at my husband's tool benches and the equipment crowding the other side of the garage. He could do whatever he wanted with his space, but he wasn't allowed to infringe on mine. The trouble was, I needed more now that I was pregnant. And I'd still need to expand after the baby was born. The man needed a shed.

Making my way through the laundry to the open living area, I switched on the air conditioner before hauling my bags onto the kitchen bench. A sigh rushed from my mouth at the sweet relief of getting rid of the weight. "Oh, thank you, Jesus." Yanking my arm away, I rubbed the sting from where the bags had dug in.

Bang. Pop.

Cool, fizzy liquid sprayed my legs and up the back of my dress. I jumped, my head snapping around in shock. "What the shit?" I croaked in dismay as a bottle of soft drink spun, dousing every friggin' surface in a fountain of red, sticky hell.

It finally ran out of pressure, rolling to a stop beside the fridge. My shoulders dropped, eyelids falling to half-mast in mourning for the floor I'd cleaned only yesterday. I screwed my lips, snarling, "You bastard," at the bottle.

How. Dare. You.

I wasn't cleaning that. Not now. Not ever. I was done. My energy levels were about equal to the level of liquid remaining in that bottle: fuck all.

I unzipped my dress and dropped it in the puddle. Carefully stepping out of the wet fabric, I headed to the living area and took a seat on the couch. I hissed in pain as I kicked off my thongs—the only shoes that currently fit me—and put one foot on the coffee table so I could see it. Speckled droplets of red decorated my skin. The rubber straps had cut into my swollen flesh, leaving deep indents. I would've rubbed them if I could reach them. Lip quivering, I returned my foot to the cool tiles and rested back on the cushioned leather. I could already feel the grip of stickiness under the backs of my legs and on the soles of my feet. I needed a shower. I needed a cleaner. I needed Ben.

I checked the clock. 3:33 p.m. Another hour and twenty-seven minutes until he'd be finished. And another hour after that until he'd be home because he was working on a project in Redland Bay.

The sting in my tear ducts amped up, but I squeezed my eyes shut, holding back the deluge. *Fuck it.* I was going to have a nap until he got home. Propping my legs on the leather, I rolled to the side and made myself as comfortable as I could. I searched for the cushions, spying the kitchen bench in my peripheral vision.

"Ah, shit." I hadn't put the food in the fridge. My head flopped back and I filled my lungs. "Ssshhhhiiiiiiiiiit!" I yelled to the empty room like it was going to solve all my problems. The baby gave me a couple of kicks to the ribs, as if to say, "Shut up. I'm sleeping here."

I'm not budging from this couch.

It seemed we would be having tinned soup for Christmas Eve dinner.

I let my eyes fall shut. My ankles had stuck together, but it was okay. I could ignore it. My breathing evened out.

My mind started to wander to the future and what our baby would look like. He'd have blue eyes, for sure. But would they be denim blue, like mine? Or summer-sky blue like Ben's? Would he be blond—like me—or dark like Ben? Ben's hair hadn't been as dark when he was a kid. I'd pored over his baby photos the first chance I got.

I imagined Ben's eyes with a darker shade of wavy blond hair.

All those years ago when Ben and I met, who would have thought that we'd end up bringing a new life into the world?

I had. I'd thought it. I'd known we would be more, even though I hadn't let myself believe it at the time. I remembered meeting him like it was yesterday ...

———

Rockhampton, Australia
18th March, 2006

I took a running leap, hugging my knees into my chest as I yelled, "Geronimo!" before landing a bomby in the pool.

"Shit! You got nasty pool water in my Coke." Stewart's words dove under the surface to reach my ears.

I grinned. *Suck it, bro.* My body was small, but I could send up a decent wave if I landed just right.

Kicking off the bottom, I almost reached fresh air, but my big brother was too quick, shoving me back under. *Arse wipe.* Sometimes I hated him, even though I loved him.

I struggled to break free, but his hands locked on my shoulders in punishment. My lungs started to burn. His taunting cackles speared the water like fingers poking into my deflated air sacs. I thrashed at the pain, panic rising.

He was twice my size, but only two years older. I was screwed.

"Benny-boy! Lee Major! You made it." He didn't let me go, even though he apparently had visitors.

Wait a minute. Visitors! I'm saved.

"Is that your sister?"

"This? Nah, it's just a drowned rat." Stewart punctuated his insult with another cackle.

I was only seconds away from dragging in a lungful of water. I stopped kicking. Twisting my arm enough to reach the tender flesh inside his biceps, I pinched as hard as I could. He yanked his arm away and I shot to the surface, delivering a knee to the groin for extra points.

"Fuck! You little cow."

My chest ached as I dragged in some air. Flailing my arms and legs, I managed to put some distance between us. I clung to the opposite side of the pool. It took me a solid minute to regain my breath. When I was in the safe zone, I turned on him. "You dickhead! I almost drowned."

He rubbed the skin under his arm, his nose screwed up. "Nah, bullshit. You were fine."

Behind me, the screen door opened with a squeal of its hinges. "What's going on out here?"

Dad.

Spewart was in so much shit now. I raised an eyebrow at my big brother and crossed my arms.

His face rearranged into what I called his Little Boy Blue. "Nothin'."

The big eyes and guileless pout might've worked when he was six, but now that he was ten years older and growing bum fluff on his pimply face it didn't have the same effect. I kept my death stare cemented in place. I wasn't gonna say anything. I wasn't a snitch.

"Don't be an idiot, Stewart. Leave your sister alone." Dad's feet came into my peripheral vision as he stood right on the edge near my head.

Righteous indignation replaced the Little Boy Blue. "She started it."

Real mature, Spew. My eyes played rollerball in my head.

"You say that every time and I haven't believed you once," Dad barked. "If you can't play nice, your friends are gonna have to go home."

I smiled as my brother's jaw went slack. *Suck it.* Were his mates even still here? Neither of them had bothered to come to my rescue. I hadn't set eyes on them yet and already I didn't like them.

"That's not fair! Why can't *she* go inside?"

No. I gasped, craning my neck to catch Dad's reaction. *Please don't make me go inside.*

Dad swiped a finger across his sweaty forehead, before drying it on his shorts. "Because it's hotter than a Holden's dashboard in January."

"Then why aren't you out here?"

He'd been inside drinking beer and re-watching the season-opener of rugby league, that was why. And Anna—his second wife—had gone out with our little brother, Will, and Dad was taking advantage of the peace and quiet—which we were ruining, but whatever.

"Stop arguing and look after your sister or I'll tell your mother. She won't let you come back here."

Dad always used Mum as a threat. He didn't realise that he was the only one afraid of her. Her and her lawyers, that was.

"Do it." My brother dared.

"One more word and you won't be borrowing the car anytime soon."

Ooh, snap. Way to go, Dad. Hit him in his weak spot—freedom.

Spewart clamped his lips together and I heard snickers from behind me as the screen door slapped shut.

They are still here.

"Burn, bro." One of his mates finally spoke up.

I turned to see who it was. A gangly, freckled redhead had one side of his mouth quirked in amusement. Next to him—*hell ... oh. Who are you?*

I sank into the water, my eyes level with my fingertips as they gripped the tiled edge. Dark hair framed a gorgeous face. Blue—the bluest—eyes stared back at me. His gaze shifted to Spewart, a line creasing between his brows. He wasn't as tall as the other guy, but he was built like he lifted hay bales all day. Something in me roared to life. For the first time, my entire body tingled.

And then he spoke.

"You took it too far, idiot. I was about to jump in."

He hadn't been the one to speak before. Deep, soulful tones sashayed off his tongue. *Oh, damn.* Now I was thinking about his tongue. If only he had jumped in. He could've given me mouth-to-mouth.

I'd only kissed two boys so far. My first kiss had been another near-drowning incident—nearly drowning in spit. Jonathon White had pulled me aside after phys ed class and laid one on me for five minutes straight. I hadn't known how to stop it. The guy had been determined to check thoroughly for cavities. I'd managed to avoid him for six months afterwards until he cornered me one day after school and I had to tell him that he was a sloppy Joe. Or sloppy Jon, in his case. My second experience had been with a peck and retreater. Even after we'd chased each other for a whole year. So disappointing.

I sized up Spew's friend again, feeling hopeful for a passionate encounter in the near future.

"Are you here to swim, or not?" Stewart snapped.

The redhead copied my move and bomb-dived, sending up a huge splash. *Hmph.* I bet Spew wasn't gonna drown his *friend* for spiking the Coke with chlorine.

The big guy sat on the edge a couple of feet away, sinking his legs into the water. He smiled at me before sliding into the pool and gliding to the middle. I swam to the steps so I could sit and watch. I never wanted to look away.

"Who are your friends?" I figured I'd ask, since nobody was offering introductions.

The redhead raised his hand. "I'm Bradley." He pointed to my crush. "That's Ben. Are you Bree or Andrea?"

Stewart butted in before I could answer. "Bree has a different dad. She doesn't come here."

And Bree is only nine, but whatever. I wished she *was* here. There was a little too much testosterone in the waters. Which normally would've been fine with me, but I shared chromosomes with one of them and he was pissing me off. I needed backup.

Bradley nodded. "Oh, right. Sorry. So this is Andrea."

"The one and only." I put my hands on my hips and gave him a toothy smile.

"I see shyness runs in the family," he joked. "I have a younger sister. I should introduce you."

"Yeah, you should. What's her name and what year is she in?"

"Letitia. And she's in year six."

"Did she get the redhead gene?" I straightened out one leg and wiggled my toes above the surface.

"Not exactly. She's a strawberry–blonde."

My foot sent up a splash as I dropped it back in the pool. "Then she's awesome!"

Ben's eyes focused on me, a hint of laughter in the tilt of his lips. He didn't say a word. *Mm, mm, mm.* He was the strong, silent type. *Me likey.*

Throwing my chin out in Stewart's direction, I asked, "How did you two get mixed up with this idiot?"

"Hey!" Big bro swung his arm, sending a spray of water my way.

Ben flashed his teeth, but still kept his silence.

Bradley jumped in with the answer. "I'm playing with the under-sixteens at the North's Knights this year. Stew and I are teammates."

You poor bugger. I sent him a look of sympathy before turning back to Ben.

"What about you?" *Delicious, scrumptious, male—please tell me you're just tagging along because of Bradley.*

"I play union with the Colts."

Union, hey? Dad wasn't gonna like that. That didn't explain how he could possibly be friends with my brother.

Bradley, I understood. He was kinda like a Golden Retriever from what I could tell. Eager and friendly with just about everyone. But Ben ... he seemed more like a wolf. More discerning about who he let into his pack. "So, how do *you* know Spewart?"

His eyebrows popped before he choked on a laugh. "I met him through Lee."

"Lee?" It took me a second to figure it out. "You mean Brad-Lee?"

"Yeah."

My thoughts rewound to the moment underwater. "That's right, Spew called him Lee Major."

Ben dipped his chin in affirmation.

"And you were Benny-boy."

His mouth turned down at that.

"I think I'll call you Benji. And Bradlee shall be Lee Lee."

"That's what my Mum and sister call me." Lee smiled.

I shot to my feet and clapped my palms together. "Excellent!" Putting on a British accent, I added, "I hereby declare, from this moment forward, you shall be known as Lee Lee and Benji." I sliced my arm in the air as if I were the queen wielding a sword.

Big brother screwed his nose up at me. "You're such a friggin' fruit cake."

"Fruit cake is sweet and loved globally, so I'll take that as a compliment." I got out of the water and backed up, ready to show Lee how it was done. "You better cover your drink, Spewart, unless you want it diluted some more. I'm about to unleash a tsunami."

"Jesus, you're embarrassing."

"Not as embarrassing as your face." Seriously, the bum fluff was so bad. And to think we used to look like twins. *Ew*.

I loved him. I really did.

Sometimes.

Chapter
3

Andrea

Brisbane, Australia
24th December, 2016, 4:04 p.m.

A rumble of thunder interrupted my reverie. I blinked my eyes, disoriented as to where I was and why I was all sticky. Shivers tracked along my skin as I looked down. Why was I only wearing underwear? My gaze found the clock. 4:04 p.m. More thunder shook the house with a massive crack of lightning.

A thought constricted my throat, trapping a gasp. I peeled my legs apart and slid them off the couch, pushing my body upright. I'd left the bloody washing on the line, hadn't I? "Ssshhhhiiiiiiiiit!"

"Andy?"

My gaze shot to the doorway, finding Ronnie standing with a basketful of washing and a bucket of pegs dangling from one wrist.

Oh, I'm saved! "You are an angel! How did you get in?"

"You left the garage open."

I grimaced. "Crap. Whoops."

"Why are you almost naked?" She dumped the load on the table before copping an eyeful of the kitchen, freezing on the spot. "What the fuck happened in here?"

"Runaway bottle of red creaming soda."

"Bastard," she snarled.

"I know, right?"

"In my head, I saw you covered in blood, passed out on the couch."

Sometimes Ronnie's psychic gifts came in handy, although she'd tried to deny them for so long. Being able to remote view must have its uncomfortable moments. And that was just one of her talents.

"You weren't far off."

"Um, do you need help getting in the shower?" She cringed like she'd rather pull a tooth than see me naked.

"No, I'll manage."

Her face relaxed into a smile. Clasping her palm to mine, she gave me a boost off the seat before shooing me down the hallway.

I had a quick shower, hoping the soapy water running down my legs would be enough to wash away the stickiness because I wasn't going to bend or lift anything unless I absolutely had to. This body didn't feel like mine. Everything was puffy and sore. My boobs had their own postcode. Each. I had no chance of being able to fold my arms. My cheeks looked like I'd been storing nuts for the winter. I couldn't bear my reflection.

Not bothering with underwear, I threw on a stretchy sleeveless dress and made my way back to the living room.

Ronnie watched me as I entered the room. "Hey. How many days overdue are you now?"

She knew the answer to that, but I said it anyway. "Five."

"Yeah. It shows. The couch is clean if you wanna beach yourself."

"Har-de-har. Bitch, wait your turn." I playfully bared my teeth, watching her face drop. She averted her eyes and got back to work.

Cocking an eyebrow, I did exactly as she'd suggested and stretched out on the leather. I wasn't good for much else. The kitchen cupboards were all clean and the shopping had been put away. She'd tied her dark hair into a messy, high bun and was working the mop like a champ. She really was an angel.

My throat got tight again. "Thank you. I couldn't face it."

"Fair enough." She acknowledged with a nod. Ignoring me, she flicked the mop back and forth, seemingly engrossed in the task. But I knew her better than that by now. Her synapses were always firing, and her senses were on alert, picking up messages and vibes about the people in her life almost constantly.

Ronnie kept things close to her chest. She had sharp edges that came with a warning, but we understood each other. I'd had my doubts when she'd moved in with our friend, Bradlee, but they'd worked their shit out in the end.

"How's Lee?" I asked.

Her shoulders twitched for a second. "Why the fuck wouldn't you use the dryer?"

Avoidance. *Hm.* "Because it's bad for the environment."

She glanced at me, rolling her eyes. "So are disposable nappies."

"I won't be using disposables."

"You're going to kill yourself washing nappies?" Her brows jumped.

"No. Parents managed for millennia before disposable nappies were invented. I'm sure I'll survive."

"Bleach is bad for the environment, too." She mopped the same spot repeatedly, her distant gaze fixed on a point on the wall.

My forehead tightened. Something was off. "How's Lee?"

She blinked before dunking the mop in the bucket. "He's fine."

"Fine?"

A streak of lightning lit up the sky and the wind tossed dead leaves and dust into the air as if warning me not to stir shit up.

"That's what I said." Her foot slammed on the bucket's pedal and she yanked at the mop a little too forcefully. *What the hell is going on?*

I decided to change the subject, but something inside me probed around for the answer.

"Are you seeing your sisters over Christmas?"

The tension around her evaporated and she looked over with a grin. "Yep. On Boxing Day we're taking them up to Noosa."

Okay, so the family were fine. Lee was definitely involved in whatever heaviness she was carrying. "The beach will be packed."

"Not where we're going."

Baby.

The word pressed into my head from somewhere *other*. I'd always imagined a force reaching down to stamp its mark on my stream of thought. A reminder that I possessed extraordinary abilities and had a responsibility to use them to help people. But it didn't matter how many times I'd experienced the intrusion, I still had trouble trusting and deciphering the messages.

My hands flew to my stomach and I received a reassuring bump on my hand. *No, Ben Junior is fine.* "What do you mean?" I voiced the question, although it wasn't intended for Ronnie. It was directed to the source of the message. Whomever or whatever that was, I didn't know.

"We're going to A Bay."

"Alexandria Bay? Isn't that a nudist beach?"

Baby*.* The message persisted. *My baby? Whose baby?* Be more specific, damn it.

"Not anymore," Ronnie answered.

Rain pelted the windows in a sudden downpour as the thick clouds had night crowding in prematurely.

Veronica*.*

Ronnie? Wow, really? I had to ask. "Uh, you might want to check it out first or your sisters could cop an eyeful. Are you pregnant?" I didn't bother pausing before I threw the question out. If she didn't want to tell me, she wouldn't.

Her face screwed up, her caramel skin taking on a grey hue. "What!? Fuck, no."

"Are you sure about that?"

Scowling, she shoved the mop back in the bucket, dirty water splashing over the sides.

The front door swung open, briefly letting in the roar of the rain and wind. *Ben!* He was home early. "Babe, you okay?" His voice echoed from the entryway.

"Yeah. Ronnie's here."

He moved into view, but didn't come closer. The contours of his chest were visible through the saturated fabric of his dress shirt. "Yeah, I saw her car." His feet squelched on the floor tiles as he proceeded towards the hallway.

Not so fun having to park in the driveway, hey, Benny-boy?

"Hey, Ronnie." He lifted his chin at her before his gaze shifted to me. "I'm just gonna grab a hot shower and change into dry clothes." He disappeared behind the wall.

"Okay," I shouted.

Ronnie wheeled the bucket towards the front, mopping away the trail Ben had left in his wake. She traced his steps and I lost sight of her for a minute. Metal clanged against metal and water gushed and gurgled before she reappeared without the cleaning equipment. "Now that you're all good, I'll head off."

"In the middle of a storm?"

"Yeah, I'll be fine. It's not that far."

"Just wait it out a bit longer."

"No, it's going to be like this all night."

What? "Hand me my phone, please."

Rolling her eyes, she fished it out of my bag and passed it over. I tapped the screen, opening the Bureau of Meteorology app. "The radar shows it's moving pretty quickly. Should be cleared within the hour."

She propped her hands on her hips and raised her eyebrows. "Nope. The storm is intensifying. If I don't go now, I'll have to stay the night."

Okay, I know that look. If I had to bet on the bureau versus Ronnie, I'd pick Ronnie's predictions every time. "Alrighty, then. Gimme a hug goodbye and don't forget to text me when you get home."

I pushed on the cushions in an attempt to sit up, but she shook her head. "No, don't move. You're good where you are." Leaning down awkwardly, she patted me on the shoulder and pressed her cheek to mine. "Merry Christmas. See ya on the flip side."

Flip side? She'd been saying goodbye to me like that for the last five days—since I'd hit my due date. Whether the flip side was motherhood or not, I didn't know. I always hoped it was her way of telling me the baby would be here soon. But I was still pregnant, so ... I had an awful feeling the flip side was something more final.

Ronnie straightened, her hand brushing my belly. She froze. All colour drained from her face. She almost could've impersonated a sheet of paper. Her throat moved like she had something stuck in her pipe as she whipped her hand away. That dark gaze collided with mine for a fleeting moment and she mouthed, *"Bye,"* before she practically vanished.

What the hell was that?

I was left blinking at the empty space she'd left for five minutes while I rubbed my belly, more to reassure myself than because the baby was doing gymnastics.

"Hey, babe." Ben pressed a kiss on my lips. He cupped his hands around my stomach and using them like a megaphone to speak to the baby. "I got you a present today, little man, but you've gotta come out to get it."

"Ooh, what'd ya get?"

"His first rugby ball." Ben pulled out a fluffy blue and yellow ball from a paper bag. Embroidered on the side it said, *I wanna be a Wallaby*. "I think it's a knock-off, but it's the fluffiest one I could find. I got him a Wally the Wallaby, too. And for you, I got Häagen-Dazs, Caramel Biscuit and Cream Speculoos."

Saliva pooled in my mouth and I had to swallow. "Oh my God. I love you. You stopped on your way home in a storm to bring me ice cream?"

"Yes, I did."

"You're crazy."

"Possibly." He crossed his eyes, grinning. "You look exhausted. Why don't you have a nap before dinner?" I opened my mouth to speak but his finger landed on my lips in a clear *shh* signal. "And you've slept through plenty of storms, so don't give me that excuse. You know it's going to be me waking up to the baby. You sleep like the dead. Don't worry. I'll teach him how to latch on. You won't even have to move."

"I already had a nap, dirty bugger." I spoke against his finger before kissing it.

My dirty bugger. There were so many reasons why I'd married this man. Why, despite all the signs telling me that it was impossible for us to be together, I never gave up hope. He was mine and I was his. I would never regret a thing that had happened between us, good or bad. It all had to happen the way it did.

Even the near-drowning. And the pain that came after it.

I'd go through it all again for him.

Chapter
4

Andrea

Rockhampton, Australia
20th May, 2006

Leaning against the chain-wire fence, I released a sigh. It was Dad's weekend to have us. That meant at least one day spent at a rugby field. Today, Stewart's team had a home game. It was now three months into rugby season and I hadn't spotted Ben at any of the games. But why would I when he would likely be elsewhere playing union? Still, the anticipation of seeing him had my nerves buzzing every weekend.

We went to the same high school, I discovered, but I'd only caught glimpses from afar. Seriously, how had I not found out sooner? Probably because a gaggle of lusting females surrounded him everywhere he went. Ben was in year eleven and I was only in year nine. The seniors didn't mix with the juniors. It was an unspoken rule, if not encouraged by the school with their separate areas for each level.

I'd seen plenty of Lee, however. Almost too much at the last game when the opposition used his shorts as a handle. I learned that his freckles didn't stop at his tan line. When had his butt been exposed to the sun in order for the freckles to form?

Today I *would* see Ben. How did I know? Well, I didn't *know* exactly. Nobody had told me. I just felt him near. It was this tug in my chest, and a trip and tumble in my pulse. It was hard to explain. Okay, maybe I *am* a fruit cake. Maybe I was making fairy dust and unicorns out of dirt and desperation. Rockhampton *was* the cattle capital of Australia. And where there were bulls, there was plenty of shit to go with them.

Shake it off. It's all in your head.

Clouds spread a splotchy blanket of shade over the grounds. I wore my raincoat, just in case. Dad set up his folding chair in his usual spot on the sideline and pulled a beer from the esky before using it as a footrest. He only ever had one per game and it was a light beer. The limit on alcohol had been introduced since he'd married Anna. When he was with Mum, he used to come home with a six-pack of cold ones almost every day. If a guy has to anaesthetise himself with alcohol on a daily basis, he isn't happy where he is. Just sayin'.

Will crouched a few feet away, drawing pictures in the gravel with his umbrella. His vibrant yellow raincoat presented a bright spot on a dull day. He loved rugby, but he found being a spectator boring. I wholeheartedly agreed with him. Spending more than an hour watching my big brother was not my idea of fun.

I squatted to Will's level. "Do you wanna go to the canteen?"

Light brown hair fell across his eyes as his head popped up. "Yeah. Can I have lollies?"

Maybe not lollies, but I wasn't going to tell him that. I needed to be a responsible big sister and it was only ten in the morning.

"Dad, can we have some money, please?"

"What for?" He looked at me like I'd slapped him. "I've got drinks and snacks in the esky."

"Aw, come on. What's a game of rugby without a trip to the canteen?"

Grumbling, he pulled a five-dollar bill from his wallet.

"Thanks." I grabbed it and motioned for Will to follow me.

Lee trotted past, a grass stain colouring the back of his light blue shirt. "Hey, Andy."

"Is your drawstring tied nice and tight today? I don't wanna see your plumber's crack." I wasn't going to let him live down the freckle display.

He ducked his head, mumbling, "Yeah, jeez."

"Is your sister here?"

"Yep." He pointed to the opposite sideline from where we were camped. "She's not staying, though."

"Alrighty, well, you and your freckles have fun out there." I gave him a wink, grinning.

We made our way around the pitch, stopping to chat several times as we got closer to the little shed that was the canteen.

Will tugged on my arm. "Would ya stop talking? I'm hungry."

"Okay, monster."

By the time we got there, the line had dispersed. Every weekend I was guaranteed to find Mel, a stout woman with maroon hair, behind the counter. If the canteen wasn't so tiny, I would've sworn she lived in there. I bought Will a chocolate brownie. That was better than lollies, right? "Thanks, Melly. Let me know if you need help next fortnight."

"I can always use a hand, darl." She waved us off just as the whistle blew for kick-off.

"Okay, I'll see you then." I turned to hand Will the food, glancing up to watch the game. My hand went limp, nearly dropping the paper bag as I did a double take. "Shit. I was right." Ben's buns were on display in rugby shorts a size too small just metres away. My heart tripped over itself. What was he doing playing league? And for the opposition?

"Swear jar," Will absently commented before breaking off a piece of the dessert and shoving it in his gob.

Crap. I said that out loud. I screwed my mouth up and pinched a chunk of the choc delight.

"Hey, Ben's here."

My eyes shot to my little brother. "You know Ben?"

"Yeah. He's Adam's big brother."

"Adam, your friend from class?" Will always talked about Adam like they were joined at the hip.

"Yep. I wonder if he's here, too." Will's neck craned, as he scanned the crowd.

Interesting. Ben had a little brother the same age as Will. I tuned out, my mind wandering to a fantasy world of possibilities. I stopped myself from imagining Ben as the father of my children. *Just.*

"So Adam is eight years younger than Ben?" I shamelessly picked Will's brains.

"Yeah. They have different dads."

Is that right? Had his parents split, or was Adam a love child and the parents had decided to stay together after the infidelity?

A drop of rain landed on my cheek. This game was gonna get messy. So was my probing if I wasn't too careful. Will was a smart kid. If he figured out I had a crush on Ben, he'd go and tell Adam, if not Ben himself.

My fears didn't stop me from asking more questions, though. "Does he have any other siblings?"

"Nope. Just Ben."

I had to pause. I had been asking about Ben because that was where my mind had gone, but I hadn't explained that to Will. He'd still been talking about Adam. I could ask *all* about Adam and find out the same info without incriminating myself. Win, win.

"So, his mum and dad split? Did his mum remarry?" *Okay, slow down. One question at a time.*

"No. His parents are married."

Oh, shit. That's right. I was supposed to be asking about Adam. *Shut up, Andy. Just shut up.*

"Do you know if Ben's dad remarried?" I immediately bit my tongue. *Fuck.*

"Go, Stew!" Will's attention had diverted to the game.

Thank God. Why couldn't I control my mouth?

"What?!" He threw his arms in the air as the whistle blew.

I didn't see what had happened, but the ref gave possession to Ben's team and Stewart's face twisted in anger as his mouth flapped.

"The ref has his head up his arse," Will spat.

My eyelids peeled back. "I beg your pardon?"

"What? Arse isn't a swear word. Dad says it all the time."

"Dad says a lot of words that you shouldn't be saying. Now who owes the swear jar?"

"You won't dob on me."

I jammed my hands on my hips. "Is that right?"

"Yup." He nodded.

"Why's that?"

"'Cause if you do, I'll tell everyone you like Ben."

My jaw hit the turf. *You, manipulative, perceptive little shit.* I clamped my teeth together before turning away to walk back towards Dad. There was no point denying it. My face couldn't lie for shit.

"I'm going to see what snacks Dad has. You coming?"

"Yeah." His eyes widened. "Are you angry with me?"

"No. I'm just hungry." I may have stomped rather than walked behind the scattering of spectators. I wasn't mad at him for calling me out. I was pissed at myself for being so tragically obvious.

"You talk about him in your sleep."

I pulled to a stop. *What? Oh, my God.* It was worse than I thought. Narrowing my eyes, I stared at the ground. Will walked on ahead for a few more steps before searching for me.

"What do I say?" I chewed on my lip.

"Ben, mumble, mumble. Baby, mumble, mumble. I dunno. It was gibberish." Will paused to lick his fingers. "You also said M. E. Line."

What the hell does M. E. Line mean? I rubbed my hands on my denim-covered thighs before hiding them in my raincoat pockets. Had I always talked in my sleep? What else had I been saying?

I made my feet move as my head tried to sort through his revelations. Glancing back to the game, I sought out Ben's dark hair. What was it about him? Why was my attraction to him so strong that he was invading my dreams?

Ben's teeth bared in animalistic rage as he hunted his prey—the ball. His arm hooked around the waist of a player from our team, felling him so he couldn't dispose of the ball. I searched all the faces. Every player had transformed from son and brother to hunter and the hunted. I half expected to see fur, feathers, and scales catching on the wind. Why did everyone like this game so much? Why was this brutality celebrated? Did I really want to be with someone who loved smacking down the enemy on his days off? I listed the cons and laid them out like stepping stones leading in a whole other direction. A path that was safe and stable and wouldn't make me feel as off balance as I'd felt the moment I'd set eyes on Ben.

Yeah, my heart was playing tricks on me. *I'm good. We're good. It's all good.* I let out a breath.

"Hey, Adam," Will chirped.

I found my seat, smiling as my little brother dumped the paper bag on his chair and ran off with his friend.

Adam's hair was just as dark as his brother's. His eyes were brown, though. Maybe it was too early to tell, but he wasn't going to be as big as Ben. Will was at least two inches taller than Adam.

They came running back as Dad jumped out of his chair, yelling and whistling.

"Did Stew get a try?" Will asked.

Dad reclaimed his seat and picked up his can. "Nah, but he set it up."

Will's shoulders shrugged, like that wasn't impressive enough for a show of enthusiasm. "This is my sister, Andy. And my dad." He told Adam, pointing a finger at each of us in introduction.

"Hey, Adam. Nice to meet you." Oh, he was a cutie. He gave me a shy wave and glanced at the back of Dad's head. Dad was too enthralled in the game to notice we had a visitor. I felt sorry for the kid, but he wasn't going to get much out of Dad until the final siren.

I knew just how to keep the boys' minds occupied and their energy spent.

"Do you guys wanna race?"

"I bet we can beat you to the try line." Will wore a cheeky, gap-toothed smile.

"I bet you can, too, but I'm gonna give you a run for your money. What's your wager?"

"My way—what?" He scrunched his blond brows and pointed to the end of the field. "That way ... duh." Rolling his eyes like I was an imbecile, he crouched in a racing stance.

I had to giggle under my breath. He liked to think he was the same age as me—fourteen—rather than the reality that was six years shy of his ambition. Adam followed his lead, lining up to go.

"A wager is a bet. You said you bet you can beat me. So what do I win if you lose?" I tapped my finger on my chin and gave him my most serious face. "I know. If I win, you have to draw me a picture of my favourite person. What would you like if you win?"

Adam's eyes squinted and he bit his lip, mining for the answer.

"Easy. An ice cream. Double scoop. Chocolate." Will grinned and rubbed his palms together.

"Ice cream. Yeah, I want that, too." Adam's head bobbed as his decision was made.

Will smiled at his friend. Watching his freckled face, the centre of my chest tugged just like it did every time we saw each other. I loved this kid to bits even though he was a pain in the butt sometimes. I hated the inevitable parting of ways every second Sunday. I was so glad he'd found a friend.

"Okay, but only if Dad agrees to drive us. I'm not giving you a piggyback into town."

Holding out my hand for him to shake, he took it like we were sealing a billion-dollar merger. "Deal."

I shook Adam's hand too, not knowing how I'd deliver if he won, but I'd figure something out.

The game on the field continued, with the shouts of the players and referees not quite as loud as the spectators' shows of enthusiasm. My father included. "Ca'arn, Stewart! Get in there, son."

Such a bogan.

A race was a great excuse to put some distance between his air-horn voice and my ears.

I positioned myself between the boys just as the rain started to pour. After reaching over to pull up the hood of Will's raincoat, I did the same with my own, smiling and nodding to the end zone. "Game on, little bro. A few drops of rain isn't gonna stop me."

"Three, two, one, go!" He counted down and sped off on the 'one', rather than the 'go'.

Cheater.

Little legs kicking up wet grass, he pushed his body at speed. And he *was* fast. I had to pump my legs to catch him. Adam lagged behind me. Grimacing as a stitch stabbed me under the ribs, I faltered and clutched at my side, handing Will the victory, with Adam coming a decent second. *Damn it.*

I laughed at my little brother jerking and shaking what his mamma gave him in a forming puddle of mud. "I won. I won. You'll have to pay up, Andy."

"Yeah, all right. No one likes a smug winner. Congratulations."

"Aw, it's okay. I'll still draw you a picture."

"You are so sweet. But only if you want to. Thanks, Mr. Matey."

"Ugh. Don't call me that."

"Sorry. I forget how much you've grown up. Every time I see you, you've added another hair on your chest." I grabbed for his coat, pretending to open it. "How many have you got in there now? Ten? Twenty?" He writhed away, cackling at my antics.

We jumped clear, interrupted by the oncoming collision of flesh hitting flesh as six teenage boys skidded across the touchline, landing in a heap. The rugby ball flew over their heads, drawing a few swear words off loose tongues. It whacked me in the side of the face and dropped at my feet.

"Shit!" I wiped the mud off my cheek, rubbing the sting away. On the surface, at least.

Fighting off a fit of laughter, Will added, "That's another dollar for the swear jar," before he and Adam ran back to the chairs.

Bugger the bloody swear jar.

Stewart's mud-slathered mop of hair poked out from the bottom of the pile of people. Of course. He was always at the root of any trouble. His tongue was the loosest of the bunch. Apparently his fingers were, too.

"Nice intercept, sis. Told ya your head was too big."

"Shut it, Spewart."

The ref blew the whistle, jogging over. The hood of my raincoat formed an amphitheatre around my head and let the heavy raindrops add their applause to the shrill sound. The referee motioned for the players to form a scrum. I stood there like an idiot waiting for someone to take the damn ball. Our team had lost possession so it had to go to the other team.

"No worries, Andy, I've got it."

I flicked my gaze up, copping an eye-full of drenched dark hair and splatters of mud sticking to a perfect face.

Ben.

My heart started to flap.

Okay, the brutal, animal, hunter thing—totally sexy. I loved this game.

I swallowed, smiled, and ducked my head before retreating to my folding chair. Behind where we sat, the boys had moved on to kicking a kid-sized rugby ball.

"Pity." My father sniffed.

"Huh?" I turned to him, huddled under an umbrella, tiny droplets of rain clinging to his silver beard.

"Pity Ben doesn't wanna switch codes. He's got instinct, that kid. Natural hooker. We want him on our team. Plenty of players have switched from union to league. Elsom. Cross. Lewis." He swiped his nose with the back of his hand. "They shouldn't have let him play on their team. It must be against the rules."

"Would you be saying that if he was playing for our team?"

He grunted, hunching his shoulders.

I'd known the union thing would be an issue.

Despite the unrelenting rain, only a few people left the grounds. The rest of the half-drowned onlookers stayed, staunch supporters for their boys. En masse, people jumped from their seats, cheering as our team intercepted the ball and made for the try line seconds before the siren sounded.

I didn't bother watching the play. My eyes were glued to Ben as he clapped his hands together, congratulating his opponents on their narrow victory. Most of his teammates weren't so gracious, kicking at the soggy mess of mud at their feet as they sulked off the pitch.

"All right, kids, grab your gear. We'll go home and get cleaned up, and then how does some Macca's sound?"

Will threw a fist in the air, shouting, "Yes," before turning back to Adam. "Can Adam come, too?"

"Only if it's okay with his mum. Gimme a sec to pack up and then I'll walk you over to ask. Okay, Adam?"

The little boy nodded, enthusiastically.

My father stood, struggling to fold his chair while holding his umbrella. I took it from him and held it over his head so he could get the job done quicker. The rain pelted so hard, it pressure-washed everything in its way. I would've happily stayed in it if it meant watching Ben a bit longer.

We trudged back to the ute before throwing the chairs in the back. Will and I jumped inside, out of the downpour, while Dad secured the cover over the tray. The air in the car was rife with stale sweat and energy drinks. Dad was a plumber, so he didn't care that we were covered in mud when he'd sat in this car with way worse all over him. On the downside, I really hated sitting in here when I was actually clean.

We watched the blurry outline of my father talking with Adam's mum through the rain-drenched windshield. A whimper escaped my little brother's throat when his friend disappeared inside his mother's car and Dad headed back empty-handed.

I sat up straight, my gut dipping with excitement from a pressing nugget of information. "Relax, Adam's coming." *And he's bringing his brother.*

"How do you know that? It doesn't look like it."

"I just do."

It's complicated.

With a protesting squeal, the driver's door opened, moist air rushing in to greet us. Will's head bumped my shoulder, the whole car shaking as our father hefted his weight into the driver's seat before slamming the door.

"She said no?" Will whined.

"Nuh. They're gonna meet us there."

Will's gaze darted back to mine, his smile infectious. "Cool."

Yeah. Kinda.

Taking in my mud-soaked jeans and shoes, I wiggled my toes against the squelchy feeling. Desperate for a shower, I curled my lip at having to wait around for Stewart. We'd better go home first. I didn't want to eat lunch in front of Ben looking like I'd had a bath in a pig pen.

The car swayed again as Stewart opened the door and took a seat in the front with Dad, bringing noxious gases with him.

I slapped my hand over my mouth. "Even Mother Nature isn't strong enough to wash away your pong."

"Nah. I know how you love my smell. Blends in with the shit wagon, hey, Dad?" He slapped the dash, baring his teeth in a grin.

"You're disgusting." I rolled my eyes, frowning at the passing scenery.

"Watch your language, and don't insult the Plumber Hummer." My dad tried to pull the authority card, but his smirk made it worthless.

"Hey, if it's not pissing down tomorrow, are we still going fishing?"

Dad white-knuckled the steering wheel. "Stewart!"

"Oh, come on. Are you telling me you never swear in front of Will?"

"Anna doesn't like it." Dad stared hard at the road ahead, his tone gruff.

Swearing. Another concession for Dad's second wife. He was so concerned with her feelings and eager to keep her happy. When he'd lived with us, he'd swung between angry and absent. I guess part of being truly in love was being motivated to be the best version of yourself.

"You're a sixteen-year-old boy. You shouldn't be talking like a ... forty-five-year-old plumber. Apologise to your brother."

"Sorry, bro." Stewart reached behind to give Will a fist bump.

That was the thing about Stewart. He made mistakes all the time, but he was happy to own up and ask for forgiveness. He wasn't trying to do anyone damage. He just ... didn't use his brain.

———

After a production line of showers in our one bathroom, and a change of transportation to something sanitary, Anna's car, we descended upon the golden arches. Dad and Stew aimed for the lunchtime line-up at the counter, while Will and I headed straight for the play equipment. I raced him to be the first one up the colourful tubes. His squeals echoed in the hollow plastic space as we climbed to the top. I didn't care that I was supposed to be too mature to want to use a slide. Who said growing up meant you couldn't have fun?

I crouched at the top of the slide, twisting my neck to see Will waiting eagerly behind me for his turn. "Do you want to go together?"

He frowned, almost looking insulted. "No. I'm big enough to go on my own."

"Fair enough. You go first then." I pretended to back out of the way. He tried to move past me, but I blocked him, getting my legs in place. "Too slow!"

I laughed all the way down with his complaints chasing me.

I only had a second to register that there was an obstacle blocking the exit before I crashed into a pair of hairy, muscled legs. With my crotch. Heat rushed to my cheeks. *Kill me now.*

Limbs splayed either side of his, I reluctantly lifted my head to find Ben, his eyelids peeled back in shock. He side-stepped, turning away as he coughed. Or choked. Or maybe he was laughing. I dunno. I didn't have a chance to figure it out as Will landed on top of me, followed closely by Adam.

"Shit!" *That hurt.*

"Another dollar for the swear jar," Will sang, rolling away before he sprang to his feet.

Fucking swear jar.

Ben offered a hand to pull me up and I grabbed on, twitching as warm tingles rippled along my arm.

Oh, yeah. The slide had nothing on the slippery slope that offered itself to me in his blue eyes. If I decided to take the ride, I was definitely gonna end up hanging by my fingernails. And I'd love every second of it.

I gave him a grin, only just stopping myself from adding a wink. 'Cause that would be wrong. He was my brother's friend. If I should be avoiding anyone, it was a person who actually thought Stewart was funny. But it was endearing that he humoured Stew. Most people got pissed off and offended by him within the first hour of meeting him. And if Ben and I were going to spend the rest of our lives together, it was important to me that he got along with my family.

Ben was going to be my husband—he just didn't know it yet. Don't ask me how I knew. I just ... did. Did I understand it? Nope. Did I trust my knowing? Sort of. Kinda. No. Not really. I wanted to. So badly. But every time I pictured walking down the aisle to meet Ben at the altar, I felt completely insane.

He let go of me before I let go of him. I was shameless. Any opportunity to touch him, I'd take it.

Adam launched himself at the gate until he'd monkeyed up high enough to raise the latch.

"Wait up, champ. You'll break the gate and they'll refuse to feed you."

"What!?" Adam's feet dropped so fast he lost balance, stumbling back into his older brother. "Really?"

Ben unlatched the lock and the boys and him made their way through to the outdoor eating area. He guided the younger two, teasing them as he led them to their seats. "Yes, about the gate. No, about the food. Of course they'll feed you. They haven't booted Stewart out yet and he's done way worse."

Tall and broad, way too big for his sixteen years, Ben's presence alone could have parted the tables even though they were bolted down. Those boys hung on his every word. Chaos churned my insides as Ben threw a grin at me over his shoulder. I was still standing in the play area like an idiot. I scurried out and grabbed a seat two tables away. Leaning on my elbows, I dropped my chin to inspect the scratched tabletop, and prayed for the riot in my gut to stop. I expected Ben to go inside and join the others at the counter, but the chair beside me squeaked as he plonked his weight down.

"You've gone quiet. What's wrong?"

I flicked a glance at his nose, knowing that if I looked him in the eye he might see something I wasn't ready for him to see. Something I was trying to understand for myself before I admitted it to anyone else. I wouldn't be admitting it to him, that was for sure.

"Hm? What? No, nothing. I'm just hungry." I hid my hands under the table. *Way to play it cool.*

One of Ben's brows inched up.

Tapping a finger on the edge of my seat, I ignored the weight of his stare. The silence was like a wedgie that you couldn't get rid of.

I cleared my throat and aimed for casual conversation. "So, are you a league convert yet?"

He scoffed. "Never. I was only helping out a friend."

"If you hate it so much, why'd you do it?"

"I don't hate it. I'm just loyal to my code."

"Plenty of players switch." I picked my brain trying to remember the names Dad had said at the game. "Like, you know, that guy, The King. What's his name?"

"Wally Lewis?"

"Yeah, him." I think. He was the only player I could think of.

"Just 'cause The King switched doesn't mean I have to."

"Fair enough."

Ben stood by his convictions. I liked that. My eyes drifted sideways in a bid for some reprieve from his gaze. Two tables away, the boys were slapping each other's hands, doing some customised shake thing, and laughing like loons.

"They're good mates." Ben's comment brought me right back to those crystal blues.

"They are." I tilted my head. "Why are you friends with my brother? Seriously?"

His lips quirked. "Stewart's all right."

"He's different with his friends, I guess."

He hooked an arm behind his seat, twisting his chest towards me. "I know he can be a dick sometimes. He has a weird way of getting attention. He means well."

The fact that he was defending my brother endeared him to me even more.

"Do you play any sport?" Ben scratched behind his ear like he was uncomfortable talking about Stewart.

I was happy to change the subject. "I dance."

"You dance?" His brows rose as he leaned back a little. "Like ballet?"

"God, no. I'm not graceful enough for that. Hip-hop is my thang."

"Your thang?"

"Yeah. Like this." I jumped out of my seat and gave him a demo—legs popping, arms locking, all while Nelly Furtado and Timbaland sang about promiscuity in my head.

His mouth dropped open and his eyes bugged out.

Am I that bad? I slid back onto my seat, heat infusing my cheeks.

"You're good."

Pulling my shoulders back, I puffed out my chest. "Thank you."

"No, I really mean that." He blinked, swallowing.

I relaxed against the back of my chair. *Sincerity.* Another tick on the list of his good characteristics. I was sure there had to be some negatives.

I already liked so many things about him. His commitment. His discipline. His arse. But if I told him, I'd scare him away. He wouldn't get it. Not for another few years at least. I wasn't sure how I knew that either. I just did. The thing was, I didn't understand how or why it was going to take a few years. And that worried me. What was about to go down that I'd have to wait so damn long to have him by my side?

The air grew so thick, my lungs had trouble dragging it in. I shuffled my butt, fighting against the unbearable tug urging my eyes to connect with his. "It was nice of you to help out the opposition, even though they couldn't find a uniform that fit you."

He placed his arms on the table, his elbow bumping mine. It was the final yank in the tug-of-war. My gaze snapped to his crystal blue stare.

A hint of a smirk played on his lips. "It's no biggie." Deliberately bumping my elbow again, he set his grin free.

He's laughing at me! My mouth popped open before clamping shut.

The rest of our group approached through the glass, trays in hand. Their arrival would mean the end of our conversation. *Last chance to make an impression.* "Yeah, you're right. Their team lost. You were no help at all. I don't know why Dad whinged that you're not a league player. Seriously, you sucked. Stick to what you know, Benji."

Ben's grin dropped off his face, and his eyebrows jumped high as he barked a laugh.

Like idiots, we grinned at each other, and something *more* passed between us. That thing that I couldn't yet define, but saw behind the gaze reflecting back my smiling face. It was so familiar. I'd seen it before. I knew it.

Unbelievably, his face aged ten years in ten seconds. Suddenly he was a man with the beginnings of wrinkles fanning from his eyes. And I was ... huge. I checked myself out. A wedding ring dug into my swollen finger. My stomach was round and full. And moving. We were both naked. Naked!

My gaze snapped back to his, finding his face in transition again. Light reflected off his bright blue irises, splitting into a prism of colour before swirling and blending into a muddy dark brown. A colour that could swallow you whole if you let it.

"Emmeline." I saw his mouth move, but it wasn't Ben. I was staring at a young man with scruffy brown hair, sweat and dirt smeared on his neck. "Emmeline," he pleaded.

Who was Emmeline? Who was he?

I didn't get a chance to find out. My body jerked as I was abruptly brought back to awareness.

I screwed up my face, recoiling at the sight before me. Spewart. *Fuck.*

"Space cadet. Hellooo. Where'd ya go?" He clicked his fingers in my personal space, his ugly mug pulling a stupid expression.

"Rack off, Spewart." I gripped my stomach and squeezed my legs together, feeling like I'd lost something. Where had my mind gone? *When* had my mind gone? I could've sworn ... Patting my flat tummy, I frowned. It just felt wrong. I chanced a glimpse around my brother's fat head. I wanted to sink under the table as the pinpricks of everyone's scrutiny bit into my skin.

Tiny bits of food sprayed from Dad's mouth as he barked at my brother. "Sit down, Stew. Stop being an idiot." Wiping a hand over his mouth, he turned to me. "Eat your lunch before it gets cold."

I checked the table in front of me. Sure enough, there sat my meal, steaming itself into a soggy, inedible mess. *Mm. Tasty.* "Thanks. Did you ask for minus the pickle?"

He nodded, speaking through another mouthful. "Yeah, but you know it's potluck."

I shoved a fry in my mouth, not wanting any more attention. Chewing was also a way to stop my mouth from scowling as I became painfully aware that Ben had moved to sit with Stewart, Lee, and a triplet of leggy wannabe WAGs. I should've been relieved at the waning of that swirling, sucking energy beside me. It was still there, but with his attention diverted I had space to breathe again. Adam and Will had moved tables to sit across from me, shovelling food into their gobs.

Downing a mouthful of fizzy drink, I gave myself a minute to recover. What the hell had just happened? It was like I'd been in another body. A much rounder body. I sized up my B-cups, ridiculously disappointed at their inadequacy. I was just shy of fourteen—they were perfectly decent. But they'd been huge. And my stomach ...

The tease of Ben's attention stroked the side of my face. It was as strong as the bump of his elbow had been. Unmistakable in its intention. Glancing in his direction, sure enough, his eyes darted away a second after our gazes collided.

My face flushed. *Oh, my God.* I'd just had a sex dream about my crush in front of my family and friends. Not to mention the star himself.

There he was with his mates—girls fawning all over him.

And here I was ... at the kiddie table.

Chapter
5

Andrea

Brisbane, Australia
24th December, 2016, 6:06 p.m.

Rubbing my hands across my face, I yawned before stretching my stiff limbs. *I fell asleep again?* The rain outside continued, but the thunder had died down to a distant rumble.

"Welcome back. What do you feel like for dinner?" Ben's face crossed my vision, albeit upside down from my reclined position on the lounge.

"Aw, are you offering to cook for your pregnant wife?"

"It's easier than hauling you off the couch." His dark eyebrows headed towards his hairline.

I released a gasp, more for theatrics than anything. "I cannot believe you just said that. You'll be sleeping on this couch tonight."

"Can't. There's no room."

This time I gasped for real. "That's just mean."

"You know I love you, babe. And I think your huge belly is the most beautiful thing I've ever seen."

Smooth talker. My heart skipped a beat as Ben shifted beside me, kneeling down and raising my tank dress so he could kiss my stomach. Our baby. I loved it when he did that. His eyes lit up every time. Lumps and bumps surged in waves across my stomach as the baby moved to the sound of his daddy's voice. It was freaky and beautiful at the same time. Even seeing the evidence, it was still hard to get my head around the fact that I was growing a human.

I grunted as the baby landed a kick to my liver. "Jeez, kid. There's not enough space for you and my organs. Get out, already."

"Behave yourself in there, Seb." Ben's hand rubbed circles on my tummy before going lax and sliding off the slope to land in my lap. His palm flattened over my bare pelvic bone. "You're not wearing any underwear." His nostrils flared. "You know, I've heard that sperm can bring on labour. So can orgasms. And if I suck on your giant boobs, I'm pretty sure junior is gonna come out and tell me to back off. Wanna try?" A wicked glint shone in his eyes as they crinkled at the corners. One side of his mouth tipped up before he buried his face in my cleavage.

I let out a sigh as he kissed and sucked his way along the neckline of my dress. "Do what you gotta do."

He tugged my dress higher until my chest was bare. "Fuck, I love these." He pushed his face between my boobs and dragged in a deep breath. "I can't wait to watch our son feed, but I wanna taste, too." His hands wrapped around each side, gently pushing the mounds together. "You should go topless all the time." The words were almost muted against my skin. Suddenly his head jerked up and a line creased between his eyes. "But only at home. I don't want any other dicks seeing these puppies."

I snorted. There'd be plenty of people getting a glimpse when I breastfed, but whatever.

Ooohh. My eyelids peeled back as he licked around one sensitive nipple before pulling it into the warmth of his mouth. The sensation shot straight to my womb like the two were connected by a tightrope. That was something new.

There were *some* advantages to being a human incubator. Like orgasms. My orgasms were definitely stronger. And hello multiples. I bit my lip and gripped Ben's hair, just thinking about what was to come. And I did mean come. This man could rocket me to the stars with a puff of his breath.

I writhed at the scratch of his stubble on my nipples. He didn't seem to notice as he was preoccupied with a face full of titties. He hadn't taken a breath in a while. I worried that he might asphyxiate before this really got going.

The baby landed a few more elbows to my intestines. I figured it was his version of banging on the bedroom door to ask what we were up to. Or maybe to tell us to be quiet 'cause he wanted to sleep. Junior was gonna have to learn fast that life wouldn't always revolve around him. Mummies and daddies needed their plaaayyy tiiimme. *Hoooly mother f—*

Hips surging forward, my wayward thoughts pulled back into line as Ben started stroking my centre.

Lifting his head, he watched me as he licked my slickness from his fingers. "You're dripping."

With a groan, my lids fluttered and my pussy clenched. This man. He knew every way to make me crazy. I was so bloody lucky. "When are you gonna get naked? I want you, skin on skin. Now."

"At your service."

"You'd better believe it, Daddy."

He stood, peeling off his shirt and unbuttoning his shorts as I stared with my tongue hanging out.

"Wait!"

Hands gripping the waistband of his pants, he raised his brows at me.

"Do this part slowly. I want the full strip-show experience."

My core pulsed at the display of muscles and the tease of his unbuttoned shorts, his tan line peeking just above the zipper. He was insanely beautiful, extraordinarily so, and I wasn't just talking about on the outside. Truth was, he'd still turn me on if he had a dad bod.

"Do that thing you do with your hips."

His face split wide with a grin. "You mean this?" He circled his hips like he was grinding the finest coffee and eased the waistband down another inch. *Hello, end of the rainbow.* Or end of the snail trail, more specifically. Another inch and I'd get a glimpse of his baby-maker.

I sang the chorus of "Pony" by Ginuwine as Ben slid closer and his shorts dropped a bit more. He spun away, showing me his half-bare arse before he shimmied side to side. *Yeah, baby, shake it.* With a thrust of his arms, his pants and jocks were at his feet. He peered over his shoulder at me as he clenched and relaxed his butt cheeks in a comical dance.

Giggling, I reached out to grab a handful, but he stepped beyond my reach. Slowly, he turned and my mouth parted at the sight of him naked with his cock in hand.

Dayum. This was exactly why I was the size of a house right now. He only had to pull it out and I was ready to come. Now I had Monifah singing in my head. Yes, I wanted to touch it.

"You know I can barely move, so you'd better bring yourself over here before I cry."

His smile vanished. "Cry? What?"

"Ben, give me your dick. I need it now." Sometimes men needed it spelled out for them. Jeez.

He scooped his arms under me and rolled me so I faced the back of the couch. Lifting my hair off my neck, he feathered kisses from my ear to my shoulder. Shivers chased the trail his lips made over my skin. One of his hands found its way to my breast before tugging and pinching the nipple as he crouched behind me. I dragged in a lungful of air when the tip of his penis slid through my folds, stoking my desire for him to painful levels. My breath quickened, sweat beading on my brow.

"Ben." *Don't be a tease.*

I didn't need to say another word. His shaft slid inside, stretching and massaging the walls of my core. I groaned.

He growled in my ear, "You're squeezing my cock so tight. Fuck. I need to go slow."

I gritted my teeth. He was going to torture me. *Arseho—*

Before I knew what he was doing, my right leg was propped up on the back of the couch and his fingers were playing my clit like a cello. Plucking and pinching, sliding and flicking. I exploded. I screamed so loud there was no way the neighbours didn't hear, even over the rain. Did I give a shit? Hell to the no. Ecstasy gripped my body, seizing my nervous system and heightening my awareness of everywhere Ben and I touched.

I slowly came back into my body. Or somewhere just above it because his fingers were still right on the button—barely moving—but still, the anticipation prevented me from landing fully.

His teeth nipped at the shell of my ear before he whispered, "One."

Holy shit.

Grunting, he pulled out. My lip popped in a pout. *Where the heck do you think you're going?*

"Can you get on your knees and lean over the backrest?"

Oh. Uh, yes and yes. Alive with energy, I manoeuvred into place. He pulled my hips back and down so my stomach was resting on my thighs and my arse was hanging over the edge. I turned my head, resting my cheek on a cushion so I could watch my beautiful beast. He sat on the floor, facing away. *Huh?* Head resting back on the seat, he tilted his neck until his mouth found my centre. *Oh.* His hands grabbed my butt, guiding me to where he wanted me.

I jerked when his tongue plunged into me before dragging over my engorged clitoris. He did the same move a few more times before sucking on the sensitive bundle of nerves. I wanted to move my hips but he had me locked in place. It made the teasing all the more unbearable. He swirled and flicked his tongue before pushing his fingers inside, finding the spot he knew drove me crazy. Before long, the second orgasm barrelled through my body.

"Two," he grunted, freeing me from his grip and lurching to his feet.

My muscles were still pulsing as he lifted my hips, burying his cock deep.

"Fuck, I can't." He held still for a second before his desire took over.

He pumped in and out with fierce abandon, his face twisted in painful ecstasy. I held onto the backrest for dear life, unable to do much else. I loved it when he let go. I loved that he could do that with me. That I could be the key that released his grip on control. My chest cracked open, unable to contain the mass of love that I had for this man. Every muscle shook with the force of it. Our truth was undeniable. We were made for each other.

Overwhelmed with joy, I reached the third precipice, my body coiling tight. With a long groan, Ben thrust deep a couple more times, releasing his orgasm. His hands covered mine on the seat, our fingers threading together as he planted kisses down my spine.

"I love you." His breath tickled the curve of my lower back.

"I love you, too." Tears pricked my eyes at the insufficiency of those four little words. But our bodies articulated it with more clarity than any words could express. Words had a limit that love surpassed by far.

"Did I wear you out? Lie down, babe."

He pulled away and a waterfall gushed between my legs.

"Oh, shit!" Ben jumped back to avoid the tsunami.

I was too scared to move. *Fuck.* The couch was cactus. "Um, I think we broke my waters."

My legs turned to jelly, collapsing underneath me. I managed to twist sideways into a sitting position. The fluid kept running. I wanted to cry. All I could do was surrender.

It's only a couch. It's only a couch.

Our baby is on his way.

Giggles bubbled up from my gut. Our baby was on his way! My head snapped to Ben and the laughter swelled to a raucous cackle. He'd gone as pale as Ronnie had, was naked, semi-hard, and sporting a petrified mask.

Well, he was right about his sperm bringing on labour.

Here. We. Go.

Chapter
6

Andrea

Rockhampton, Australia
23rd June, 2006

Crows beat their wings in a hasty retreat as we all barrelled out of our classrooms and made for the exit. The pitch of the crowd's noise seemed to double in proportion to our excitement about school holidays. Two weeks of no school. *Yeah, baby.*

On tippy-toes, I searched the bodies for the object of my obsession. I only succeeded in glancing backpacks and school emblems on shirt pockets. *Damn it. I need some stilts.* Sometimes it sucked being a short-arse.

I hadn't seen Ben for more than a week. *Where is he? How is he?* I wanted to know everything about him. I wanted to be in his life, and I wanted him in mine.

I swivelled my head like a puppy sniffing for a treat. I was beginning to piss myself off. My attachment to him wasn't healthy. I was always aching for the next glimpse, the next word. Any scrap of attention he'd give me was like a hit from the most addictive drug, and I wanted more, more, more.

I groaned and sank onto my heels. *God, just stop it.*

If only it was as easy as deciding to stop.

Turning, I spotted my friend. Her head stuck out above most of the chaos. "Hey, Pauline, wait up!" I jogged over as she paused just inside the school gates. "Are you dancing this arvo?"

"You know me. I wouldn't miss it." She bounced on the balls of her feet in a move called the running man, her dark hair sweeping her shoulders.

Pauline spent hours practising in her bedroom every night. She was ridiculously good. She could lock and pop like the pro dancers in an MTV video.

She came to a stop, pocketing her hands. "What are you up to these holidays?"

Oh, you know. Pining. Obsessing. Wasting my life. That sort of thing. Ugh. "Not much. How about you?"

Goosebumps spread like vines up the back of my neck and curled over my ears. I spun around to find another two members of our dance crew, Jess and Kate, approaching. "Hey." I offered the distracted greeting as I searched behind them, picking through the thinning crowd for the source of the bad vibes. My senses kept drawing me back to my friends. Worry had my mouth drying up. Goosebumps weren't good. And there was no cold breeze to blame.

Sweeping my eyes over the playground again, I only found students, a couple of teachers, and the groundsman with a blower vac. Again, I was drawn back to our little group. *Shit.*

Kate brushed auburn tendrils away from her face, watching me with a frown. "Hey. You okay?"

Nope. "Yeah, I'm fine. Do you mind if we walk and talk? I gotta go get Bree and Will." *And I want to move to see if the feeling follows us.* We headed out the gate to the primary school next door.

Kate trotted to catch up to me. "Are you at your dad's this weekend?"

"No. I just have to walk Will to Dad's before I go home. He's only eight, remember?" I always thought it was sad that the only time I spent with all my siblings together was the walk home from school. Before Stewart chose to ride home, that was. Bree never went past the front door at my dad's house and Will never came to Mum's. That was just how it was.

"Oh, yeah." Kate scratched her freckled nose before shooing away a fly. "You're lucky, having two houses."

"Are you kidding? It's a pain in the arse." I curled one corner of my mouth.

"You got that right," Jess added. She knew all about growing up in a broken family.

Kate held up a hand. "You get a break from each parent, though. You always have somewhere else to go when things are turning to shit. And you don't have to walk on eggshells, knowing your parents hate each other and could start arguing at any minute."

Aw, Kate.

I hooked an arm through hers, leaning my head on her shoulder.

She had a point. I didn't miss living in a pressure cooker of tension. Parents who thought it was a good idea to stay together for the sake of the children were kidding themselves. Plus, Dad had an Xbox and Mum had a PlayStation, so I got the best of both worlds.

"You don't get a break if one of them takes off," Jess muttered. With her arms crossed and her chin touching her chest, it didn't look like she'd spoken at all.

My throat closed off as I studied her. Under my feet, I expected the concrete to crack with the force sucking me down. *Jess. What's going on?* I needed to talk to her. But not here. I'd make sure to grab her after dance class. Something shrouded her. A thick cloak of burden that wanted to drag her and me under.

"Isn't that your brother and sister?" Pauline pointed down the road.

Dragging my eyes away from Jess, the pressure immediately eased. About twenty metres ahead, I could see my siblings leaning against the fence, talking to ...

There he is. Ben had Adam with him. My legs were drawn towards him without me having to tell them where to go, the pull between us a palpable force. The tug took hold, permeating my body with a thrill that fed my soul. I didn't want to fight it. I couldn't fight it. *Did he feel it, too?*

Lee was waiting with them and a younger girl. Probably his sister. He'd said Letitia was a strawberry-blonde.

"Where's Stewart?" Kate sounded almost disappointed. And she was pouting.

Aw, no. Girl, don't do it. He was nowhere near good enough for any of my friends.

"Spew never sticks around anymore. He's on his bike and outta here, ASAP. Especially on Fridays."

Oh, my God. My lids peeled back as I had a realisation. *I wonder if Spewart thought the same about me?* My gaze shot to Ben. I was a catch. Any of Spewart's friends would be *lucky* to have me. But I only wanted one of them.

Those blue eyes skimmed over my friends before landing on me. I stumbled a step. It was totally because of the stupid gumnut under my shoe—the damn things were lethal—not because my legs went a little weak at the smile he sent my way.

Straightening my shirt, I cleared my throat. *Nice recovery.*

"Hey, Andy. Did you enjoy your trip? Take any photos?" Lee called out as we approached.

"Har-de-har, smart-arse." I couldn't stop the blush. *Stupid gumnut.*

"Swear jar!" Will stretched on his toes as he cried out.

Ugh. I glared at my little brother before I gave him and Bree a hug. Why did my most embarrassing moments have to happen in front of Ben? Was it some scheme the universe employed to turn him off?

I spun around to Lee's sister, willing the heat to drain from my cheeks. "Hi."

"Andy, this is Tish. Tish, this is Andy." Lee waved his hand between the two of us before turning to his sister. "Now you can stop bugging me to introduce you."

"I wasn't bugging you," she grumbled.

They launched into a squabble as I snuck a peek at Ben. He tousled Adam's hair while his brother tried to fight him off. My heart did somersaults, as if he'd plunged his hand inside my ribcage to tousle my heartstrings.

Clearing my throat again, I interrupted Lee and Tish's argument. "Lovely to meet you."

Flustered, she clamped her mouth shut and looked away, huffing.

"Do you like to dance, Tish?"

She shrugged. "Maybe. I don't know."

"Ooh, you should come. It's fun." Bree bounced on her heels, dark blonde curls bouncing.

My friends echoed her sentiment, talking over the top of each other.

"Come and watch our class tonight." I hooked a thumb in my friends' direction. "This is Pauline, Kate, and Jess. We dance every Tuesday and Friday afternoon. Bree's class is on Friday before ours." My eyes flicked to Ben again. He wasn't paying any attention. At all.

The fragile dreams I'd constructed from fleeting things like a glance or a smile vaporised into nothing. The fire inside me dimmed to a flicker. It didn't go out completely, though. There was something there. I couldn't shake this soul-deep knowing. I wasn't sure if I believed in God, but I thought maybe we'd met for a reason. The only thing I knew for sure was that it would drive me nuts if I kept thinking about it.

I turned to the girls. "Guys, these are Spewart's friends, Bradlee and Ben." My throat clamped on his name and I had to cough. "And Ben's brother, Adam."

"Hi." Lee leaned forward, shaking all their hands.

What a gentleman. I loved him. He gave me the warm and fuzzies.

Ben, on the other hand, he gave me the hot and heavies. He just nodded as his brother tugged on his shirt, Adam's attention aimed down the street.

Time to go. "Well, it was lovely to meet you, Tish. We might see you tonight. Or at a game sometime."

"I can't come tonight, but I'll definitely come say hi at the next game."

"Sounds like a plan."

A silver Volvo pulled up to the curb. I hadn't registered that the tingle on the back of my neck had stopped until the car arrived and the sensation returned with a vengeance. My shoulders jerked as a shiver raced down my spine. *What the heck is going on today?*

"Here's mum. Come on, midget. Gotta go." Lee opened the back door for his little sister before hopping in the front.

Midget. Cute.

"We'd better go, too. See you in dance." Pauline strode off with Kate and Jess, waving as they went.

"Bye." I spun back and smiled at Bree. "You ready?"

She nodded.

I tapped Will on the shoulder. "Mr Matey?"

His grin vanished. "You said you wouldn't call me that anymore."

Shit. "Aargh, sorry. I forgot."

Adam snorted. "Mr Matey."

Ben tapped the back of Adam's head. "Don't start, bug."

"Bug?" Will laughed. "Bug!"

I rolled my eyes. *Jeez, eight-year-old boys.* "Okay, okay. Enough. Let's go."

Ben stepped beside me. "Do you mind if we walk together? Your dad's place is on the way to ours."

There was a God. *Sorry I ever doubted.* "No worries."

It's cool.

We're cool.

I'm cool.

Breathe in, breathe out.

I licked my lips and wiped the sweat off my brow. The acrobat in my chest had recruited a buddy, my small intestine, and they were practising their trapeze act right about now. *Oh, my God. Do. Not. Vomit.* I wrapped an arm around my middle.

"Are you okay?" Ben eyed me with concern.

"Huh? Oh, yep. Just indigestion."

Will and Adam took off running and my gut surged for a different reason. "Boys! This isn't a playground. There are cars everywhere. Slow down and stay close."

They both stopped and looked over their shoulders, laughing before speed walking ahead.

"I'll go after them," Bree offered, skipping away.

"Thanks." Grunting, I clutched my stomach as a cramp set in. *Ow.* It wasn't that time of the month. What the hell?

"You're not a fan of rugby, are you?"

I tilted my head, eyeing Ben sideways. "Why do you say that?"

"You didn't seem happy to be at the game the last time I saw you."

"It's more to do with being forced to watch my brother do anything for a couple of hours." I braced my hands on my hips and clenched my teeth through another cramp. "It's not my idea of fun."

"Obviously. Are you sure you're okay?"

"Y-ep. To-tally fine." I clamped my mouth shut and blew out through my nose as the vision of me with a huge stomach flashed back in my mind. It was like I was pregnant. Either that or I'd eaten fifty-dozen doughnuts.

My hands fell loose at my sides as the pain eased. *Ah, much better.*

Ben pursed his lips, narrowing his eyes. "Okay." Hooking his thumbs under his bag straps, he turned his focus forward.

Okay? Maybe he didn't believe me? Maybe he was letting the white lie slide and giving me time to recover. He wasn't walking off ahead. He could've caught up to the boys, but he matched me step for step. Why?

We turned the corner, silence our awkward companion. Fifty metres. One hundred metres. Jesus, I hadn't been this quiet since I was a baby. Actually, scrap that. Mum told me that I constantly babbled from day one.

"I'm fine. Really."

"I know." His hands flexed, but his gaze didn't deviate.

Okay. "You're a great conversationalist. I haven't been this stimulated in a long time. I think we should talk more often. Why don't we exchange numbers? That way we can tell each other all about our day before we go to sleep and I can dissect yours and you can dissect mine and we can learn and grow from each other. It'll make us better people. What do you think?"

"I think your indigestion has gone." He watched me, reining in a smile.

I did a double take. His eyes were brown. My jaw loosened. *What?* I blinked. *Nope, they're blue.*

Turning away, I licked my lips. *I am losing my shit.*

"Are you looking forward to tubing on the river tomorrow?"

Come again? "Uh, am I s'posed to be?"

"Yeah, didn't Stewart tell you?"

I am going to kick his arse. "Spew and I only exchange insults. You'd know this if we talked more. Seriously, what's your number?"

"It's in the phone book. We're taking Geoff's boat out tomorrow. You, Stewart and Bree, and Lee and Tish are coming too. I don't know if Mum got permission from your dad for Will to come. I thought if he was home now I could ask him myself. Adam would love it if he came."

Why hadn't Mum told me about this? Now it made sense why Ben had decided to walk home with us. He wanted to talk to my dad.

"We only just organised it last night. Your mum said it was cool." He looked unsure.

"Oh, nah, yeah. It sounds great." *Crap, I hope my togs still fit. Which ones should I wear? The pink two-piece with the frills? Or the green one-piece that rides up my butt crack every time I move? I'll either flash my stomach or my arse. I choose stomach. Pink it is. I'll wear a T-shirt on top. What about food? Are we bringing our own lunch? What time are we meeting and where? Which boat ramp? Why isn't it just the boys going? Oh, because Ben's little brother needed a friend. And if little brothers are going, little sisters have to go too. I get it.*

"You're thinking. What are you thinking?"

"Does Mum know all the details? I have a list running through my head."

"It's all sorted. Don't stress." He squeezed my shoulder.

My head wanted to loll forward on my neck. He'd sapped the tension right out of me. There was something about him. A resonance felt between two that almost merged us as one. I really was losing my shit.

Maybe it was because we both came from split families. His mother had remarried. My parents had both remarried. What about his dad? Where was he? Did he spend every second weekend with him?

"Do you see your dad much?"

He huffed and scratched his nose. "Rarely. When he's in town and not too busy with his latest woman."

Oh. Bummer.

We crossed the street, Adam, Bree, and Will safely crossing five metres in front.

"Doesn't he live in Rocky?"

"He's a FIFO worker. They fly him out to the oil rigs in the Timor Sea. He's gone for three weeks and back for one."

"That's hard. Has he always done that?"

"No, he worked in Gladstone before. He stayed for his block of shifts and he'd come back for his days off. Just before Mum and Dad split, he drove there and back every shift. It was his way of trying to save the marriage. But it was wasted effort because he had other women in Gladstone the whole time."

Fuck. "I'm sorry."

"Yeah." He laughed without humour. "Me too."

"Why didn't he just leave if he wasn't happy?"

"He *was* happy. He wanted his cake and he wanted to eat someone else's cake too."

My brows scrunched together. "He didn't think your mum would find out?"

"He thought she'd understand that a man has needs and a week was a long time to go without getting some. Stupid thing is, now he has to go without for three weeks at a time."

"I think that may be what you call karma."

"Mm."

"Your mum is happy now though, right?" I shrugged. "She's got you and Adam, and Mr Hooper."

"Yeah, she's good. Geoff treats her well. They dissect each other's days, and learn and grow together."

I gasped, a big grin breaking free as I lightly punched him on the arm. "You *were* listening." *Damn, that arm is rock solid.*

"Did you think I wasn't?"

I pushed some hair off my face. "I dunno. You're quiet most of the time."

"Why talk when there's nothing to say?"

"Because silence is unbearable. Because communication is important. Because it drives your companion nuts if you deprive them of interaction."

"There are more ways to communicate than with words." He slowly reached out. The back of his hand brushed my forearm, stealing the breath from my lungs.

I lifted my eyes to his. We both stopped walking. He stared down through lowered lashes, his lips slowly curling up.

Oh, shit.

...

...

He'd blanked me with one touch. All my thought processes came to an abrupt halt and my senses took over. They bombarded me with feedback. His warmth, his smell, the tug and thrum between us. The trapeze act in my chest had fallen off their perches and were tumbling in a free-fall. I didn't know if there was a net to catch them. I didn't even care.

Ben took a step and I stumbled after him, picking my jaw off the ground. I checked to see where the boys were. They were nearly ten metres ahead now. We only had one more street until we reached Dad's house. Why couldn't he have bought a house farther away?

"You don't agree?"

"Huh?"

Ben laughed, adjusting the weight of his backpack. "You've gone quiet."

"You wiped my brain cells."

"Just like that, huh?"

"Yeah, just like that. Don't get a big head about it."

He chuckled, tugging on the waistband of his shorts. "I'll try not to."

"Do you wish your parents had stayed together?"

"Nah. Now that I see how two people are supposed to love each other, I realise what Mum and Dad had wasn't built to last."

I searched his eyes, not knowing what I was looking for. Sadness? Acceptance? "Do you think you'll ever find the real deal with someone?" *Like me, for instance?*

"Honestly, I dunno. I'm too young to be thinking about it anyway. And so are you. Don't let Stew know that you've got boys on the mind."

Okay, there was no net. My heart just slammed to the ground and turned to pulp. "What would he care?"

"He cares."

Yeah, right.

I walked ahead of him, opening the squeaky metal gate before following the garden path to our standard brick-and-tile.

Every house in the street appeared almost the same. The development was built in the eighties when brown was all the rage. Will knocked on the door, but if Dad wasn't home from work yet, nobody would be there. I had to wait until he arrived before I could leave. Anna didn't finish until five. Mum wasn't happy about the arrangement, but it meant I got to spend extra time with Will, so it was fine with me.

"He's not home," Will huffed.

"Great," Bree mumbled, lacking enthusiasm in her tone.

I took one strap of my backpack off, ready to dig out my keys, when the door opened.

"Keep ya shirt on. I was on the dunny." Dad peered at us, wiping his hands on his shorts. His *work* shorts.

My nose crinkled. *Such a bogan.* The remnants of his day clung to him in a cloud of toxic gas. Why had he bothered washing his hands if he was going to wipe them on his germ-infested Stubbies?

"Hey, Ben. Adam. What are you boys doing here?"

Ben reached to shake Dad's hand. "Hey, Mr Frazer."

Don't shake it. Don't shake it.

Their hands locked.

Aw, he touched it. I turned away to hide my unstoppable gag reflex.

"We're taking the boat out on the river tomorrow. Stewart, Bree, and Andy are coming too. We were wondering if it'd be okay if Will came along to keep Adam company?"

Adam and Will both clasped their hands under their chins and did their best impersonation of a begging puppy, complete with sound effects. I didn't know anyone who could say no to that. Except maybe Anna. But she wasn't here to see it, so ...

"I don't see why not, but I have to check with the boss first. Come in while I give her a call." Dad went to the living room.

I slipped off my shoes and dumped my bag at the door before going to the kitchen. "Do you guys want a drink?"

Leaving his bag under the breakfast bar, Ben nodded. "Sure. Do you mind if I use the bathroom?"

"You know where it is. Down the hall, first door on the right."

"Thanks."

I poured waters for all of us before handing the kids theirs.

"I hope Mum says yes." Will chewed on his thumbnail.

"She will. The pressure of you not missing out will get her." *I hope.*

Ben returned and I passed him his glass. "You didn't flush."

"I didn't need to. Thanks for the drink."

Oh. I smiled to myself. He'd gone to wash his hands. Bless his impeccable manners. He hadn't wanted to offend my dad. I bit my lip as I watched him drink.

"Good news." Dad came around the corner. "Anna said yes."

The boys gave each other a fist bump, their faces beaming.

"What time do you need him?" Dad rubbed a finger under his nose and I gagged again. I needed to remember to wipe the phone first if I ever needed to use it.

"We'll come and pick him up around seven-thirty, if that's all right?"

"Yep. That's fine. See you in the morning."

"Okay. Thanks, Mr Frazer."

"Thank Anna. When are we going to see you back in a Knights' jersey?"

Aw, shit. I pushed on Ben's back to get him moving—*he's like concrete*—and flashed my eyes at Adam to get his attention. "We gotta go, Dad. See you on Monday arvo. And maybe go change out of your sewer clothes."

"I was about to when your brother tried to knock down the door," he growled.

Maybe I'd been too harsh, but E. coli was no joke. "Okay. Good talk."

My eyes remained wide and I pasted on a smile, putting some distance between poo man and my chances of ever dating Ben.

Bree pivoted to face us as she walked backwards. "Your dad's kinda feral."

"I know." I grimaced.

"Nah, he's cool." Ben kicked a rock, sending it skidding down the footpath.

Adam chased it, booting it farther ahead. "I agree with Bree."

"He's cringetastic sometimes, but he's still my dad and I'm lucky to have him."

Ben's expression tightened. "Yeah, you are. He's one hundred percent on my dad."

Anger slammed into my gut, but it hadn't come from me. It sloughed off Ben like a peeling sunburn. Sympathy swelled in me to douse the burn. But I needed to share the remedy with him.

I stretched out to put my arm around Ben's shoulders, acting on instinct. He stopped moving. He didn't show it, but I could still feel his pain right in the centre of my chest. A cavernous abandonment that bored a tunnel from him to me. The drag of its teeth kept chewing and chewing, searching for something that would finally satisfy its hunger. It stole my breath.

I placed my other hand right on the middle of his chest and he angled himself towards me, putting his arms around me. Our pulses melded as one. Energy hummed between us, an osmosis of something more powerful than I could grasp. I knew it. Whatever this was, it wasn't going away.

I don't know how long we stood there. Long enough for the hungry beast to slow its scourge. Maybe there was something in me that could stop it altogether. Would I ever get a chance to try?

Ben let go first. I raised my head to search his eyes, but he'd turned away. Our siblings were nowhere to be seen. We weren't that far from home. I hoped they'd stayed together and were waiting at Mum's place.

"Sorry." His apology came out raw, delivered with his back to me.

"What for?"

"See you tomorrow." He jogged ahead, disappearing around the next corner.

The ache in my chest surged back to life, the teeth sharpening with each bite. It wasn't my beast to tame, but I'd take it on for him. If that was what he needed me to do, I'd do it, no question. Maybe that was what he'd been apologising for. He'd given me a piece of himself that he never wanted uncaged.

What he didn't know was that in my heart was a warrior. And it would slay whatever misery plagued him, just to see him smile.

Chapter
7

Andrea

Rockhampton, Australia
23rd June, 2006, 7:07 p.m.

"Five, six, seven, eight." Janice faced the wall of mirrors. The class lined up behind her, following her lead. "Scissor, two, three, four. And drop, roll, plank, twist." She fired her instructions, not a hint of fatigue in her voice.

Sweat poured down my face despite the fans spinning above us. We'd been going through this routine for nearly an hour. I'd lost count of how many times we'd repeated the same movements. Pauline had it perfect. Janice needed to employ her to help because seriously, she was amazing. If she didn't pursue a professional dance career, I'd be stunned to silence.

Like I had been only a couple of hours ago.

My thoughts went straight to Ben and the way he'd taught me a lesson in communication. I messed up the next dance move and stumbled sideways into Jess.

"Stop, stop, stop." Janice grabbed the remote and cut off the music. "Andrea, what was that?"

"I lost my balance, sorry."

"Where's your head tonight? You and Jess are way off your game."

Jess and I locked eyes in the mirror. She bit her lip, her forehead crumpling before she dropped her gaze.

"Okay, maybe that's enough. I'll see you all on Tuesday. Have a good weekend."

We all beelined for our bags before grabbing towels and drink bottles to mop up the sweat and replenish our fluids.

Jess threw the strap of her bag over her shoulder. "You okay?"

The bottle made a sucking sound as I took it out of my mouth before swallowing. "Yeah. My head was elsewhere. How about you?"

"Same."

"I'm pretty sure I know where Andy's head was." Kate cocked a brow, giving me a knowing look.

"Oh, Ben. You're so ripped. Let me feel your muscles." Pauline put on a breathy voice, like she was channelling Marilyn Munroe.

I guess I'd been obvious because I hadn't said a word to anyone. Except Will. Damn it. Why couldn't I keep my feelings hidden? I normally wouldn't care. But this seemed way more precious than anything I'd ever longed for. I'd wanted to keep it to myself until I knew if my feelings were reciprocated.

Too late for that now. "He let me feel them today. It was better than I imagined." I wiggled my eyebrows up and down.

"I hate to be the bearer of bad news, but I think he's dating that Kelly chick in year eleven." Jess looked apologetic as she wielded the words like a meat tenderiser aimed at my chest. "Sorry."

Kelly? The leggy wannabe WAG from McDonald's. "Yeah, I saw them together at Macca's several weeks ago." Ugh, I wanted to be sick.

Sitting on the floor, I pretended to fix my shoelaces. My nostrils flared as I dragged in air. He'd felt what I felt. Hadn't he? *God, maybe it's all in my head.*

Pauline broke into my reverie. "Dad's here. Do you still need a lift, Kate?"

"Yeah."

We said our goodbyes before they took off.

Jess slid down the wall to sit beside me. "You really like him, don't you?"

More than I can admit. "Nah. He's friends with Spew. There's something seriously wrong with him if he likes my brother." I smiled through the crushing pain surging inside. I was supposed to be checking up on Jess anyway. Not lamenting the loss of someone I'd never had, and probably never would. "Can I ask you a question?"

"Shoot."

"What's going on with you? You're extra quiet and you avoid direct eye contact like the plague. You don't have to tell me all the gory details, but I know something's up. Tell me to piss off if you don't want to talk, but I'm here if you need me."

Her brows pinched, eyes dropping to her hands as she steepled her fingers.

"Mum has a new boyfriend. He thinks my blonde curls are *pretty*." She added a sarcastic twist of her lip on that last statement.

Creeper. What the hell was her mother thinking? I engulfed her in a hug.

It was rough—the initial shock of your parents separating, and the massive adjustment that came afterward. She was probably blaming herself. We all did it. Every kid I'd known whose family was torn apart had blamed themselves at one point.

It had taken many therapy sessions for me to realise it had nothing to do with me. We learn patterns of behaviour from our parents and develop coping strategies to deal with the shit they put on us. Then as we grow, we figure out the crap we have to *unlearn* to function as normal human beings. Some of us never get there. I was still a work-in-progress. Jess ... Jess was in the coping stage.

"Has he done anything?"

"No. It's just—the way he looks at me is *ugh*." She shuddered.

"Have you said anything to your mum?"

"She won't listen."

My eyes narrowed to slits and my nostrils flared. I'd make her listen and my mother would help. "Do you want to sleep at mine tonight?"

"I don't have any stuff."

"You can borrow my PJs. We always have spare toothbrushes. I'll ask Mum if we can stop at the shops on the way home. She should be here soon."

"I can't, Andy. Thanks, though."

"Are you sure?"

"Yeah." She looked out the windows. "That's his car. I've gotta go."

"*He's* picking you up? How long have they been together?"

"A month." She struggled to her feet. "He's very helpful. He even does the washing."

Creeper was probably sniffing Jess's knickers. I screwed up my nose.

I stood to give her a hug. "Take care of yourself. Barricade your door and window if you have to."

"I already thought of that. Thanks, Andy. I might see you over the holidays. Call me when you want to catch up."

"How about we meet at the shopping centre on Monday morning? Main entrance."

"What time?"

"Nine a.m. We'll make a day of it."

"Okay. Sounds good."

I followed Jess through the door, spotting my mum's white Camry in the car park. Creeper was parked three spaces away in a beat up orange Datsun. There weren't too many of those around anymore. He'd be easy for the police to find. *God, why had that horrible thought entered my brain?* I prayed that it wouldn't come to that. Every step she took towards that car felt like she was stomping on my stomach. The tingle was back. It raced down my spine and lodged behind my belly button. If my navel was a mouth, it would've opened wide in a scream.

"Jess."

She looked over her shoulder, holding the passenger door open.

"Just ask if you can sleep over."

Her attention was pulled into the car before she turned back to me. Her head moved slowly side to side like the twist of a boot on top of a bug. "We're going out to dinner. I can't."

"Oomph." The tingle flared to a searing pain, folding me forward. "I—" Gritting my teeth, I pushed my plea out. "I really think you should stay over."

Please, please, please.

"I'll see you Monday." She disappeared into the car.

The snap of the door shutting was the final crushing stomp. I let out a cry of despair. "I hope so."

Shuffling over to Mum's car, I threw my bag in the back seat before tossing myself in the front.

"Hey. Everything okay?"

Shaking my head, I had to bite my lip as tears swelled in my eyes.

"What happened? Are you hurt?"

I shook my head faster.

"What's going on, sweetheart?"

My hands flailed as I fought to open the glove box and pull out a tissue. I sucked in a breath before blowing it out in a gush. "I've got a bad feeling about Jess. Her mum is dating a sleaze who thinks Jess's hair is pretty."

"I met him last week at the butcher. He seems like a nice guy. Leona is happy with him."

I raised my brows. "Mum! I have a *bad* feeling."

"Oh."

"Yeah, *oh*."

She frowned and started the car before backing out. "What did Jess say? Has he done anything?"

"He's just making creepy comments and watching her with his slimy eyes."

"I don't know what to tell you, honey. We can't steal her away. Unless there's proof that she's in danger, we don't have a reason to act."

"That's bullshit."

Her eyes shot to mine before fixing back on the road. "I know." We stopped at a red light. "I could broach the subject with Leona, but I wouldn't know where to start."

"Ask her if Jess likes him. If she says yes, she's lying."

"Let's give Jess a call tomorrow after our outing. Maybe she'd like to sleep over."

"I tried to get her to stay tonight, but she couldn't."

"We'll ask tomorrow."

"Okay."

I only hoped tomorrow wouldn't be too late.

Chapter
8

Andrea

Rockhampton, Australia
24th June, 2006, 8:37 a.m.

I couldn't stop staring. Kelly with the legs and the WAG ambitions had draped herself across Ben's bare torso as they lay on a picnic rug. She'd brought her friends along, the same ones who had been hanging around the tables at Macca's. A blonde, a brunette, and a redhead. What a neat combo. Kelly was the blonde. At least now I knew he liked blondes. *Way to think of the positives. Go me!*

"Did you know they were coming?" I asked Letitia.

"Yes. The boys organised this whole thing because they wanted them to come."

Of course they did.

"Why are *we* here?"

"Ben's mum insisted it be a family day out."

Just as I'd thought.

The brunette gave Spew the eye like she had a twitch or something. Poor Lee was attempting to start a conversation with the redhead, but she was watching Ben and Kelly with a green tinge behind her gaze.

I probably looked the same.

Forcing my head to turn away, mist cooled my face as the boat zoomed past, the tube carrying Adam, Will, and a trail of screams dragging in its wake. Behind them, the Fitzroy River Barrage divided the waterway into salty and fresh, all eighteen of its gates raised. Mount Archer hefted and warped the horizon in the distance.

I caught a glimpse of Mr Hooper behind the wheel. Ben's stepdad had the widest grin plastered on his face.

Not all stepdads are horrible. Sheree didn't have to worry about any daughters, but sons were just as vulnerable. Ben was way bigger than his stepdad now, but back when he'd come on the scene, Ben would've only been seven. A year younger than Will and Adam.

God, I hope Jess is okay.

I was having fun. I honestly was. But I could not shake the sick feeling in my gut and the scratching at the back of my neck.

"Can we go next?" Bree skipped over to me, taking a seat on my towel.

"I don't know. It's up to Mr Hooper."

"Who are you riding with?" I asked Letitia.

"Lee told me he'd go with me." She hugged her knees, rocking back to balance her weight on her tailbone.

That boy had a heart of solid gold. The redhead was stupid for not seeing how great he was. She obviously had no sense of humour. Letitia was lucky to have him as a big brother.

Spewart flirted with the brunette. Whatever he was saying, she thought it was so hilarious she had to fall back on the rug in fits of laughter. I needed to give Spewart more credit based on his choice of friends alone. Maybe I wasn't seeing something in my brother that they did. He genuinely didn't mean any harm. But why did he have to be such a dick towards me?

"What's it like, having an older brother who actually cares about you?"

Tish placed her feet back on the towel before crossing her legs. "What do you mean? You have Stewart."

Bree snorted. "Exactly."

Tish looked at her, puzzled. "Lee said Stewart ripped into a couple of year-nine idiots who were saying stuff about you."

"Who? And what did they say?"

"One's name started with a T. Maybe Troy?"

"Terry and Dean." It had to be those tools.

"Yeah, that's them."

I lifted a brow. "What were they saying?" I could only imagine.

"Lee didn't tell me. I guess he didn't want to repeat it."

"Is one of them really tall with black hair?" Bree added.

"Yeah, that's Dean." How did Bree know anything about this?

She wiggled her toes. "I went out to pick up a pizza with Dad and Stewart a couple of months ago, and Stew went to talk to a couple of kids who were hanging around. It got a bit heated. They took off on their bikes, looking scared."

That was why they'd backed off? Those two jerks had been teasing me since grade one. Mostly about my lack of height. But in grade nine they'd graduated to a new subject—my small boobs.

Until recently.

Thanks, Stewart.

Maybe it was time to call a truce?

The boat slowed to a stop, and the tube drifted to shore.

"Aw, I wanna go again." Adam bobbed around as Will struggled to get off.

"Nah, let someone else have a turn. Do you girls wanna go next?" Ben sat up, peering past Kelly to her friends.

"No, let the little kids go first." Kelly sent a smile my way, her eyes calculating. The way she looked at me had blood rushing to my limbs, getting me ready to run. Or fight.

Little kids. I was two years younger. Two.

"Emmeline, you and Bree are up next."

My gaze shot to Ben. He stared right back. What had he just called me?

His face morphed until his eyes were a deep brown, his hair longer and shaggy, and his skin not quite as tanned. I pushed the heels of my hands into my eye sockets. When I checked again, he was back to normal.

What. The. Fuck?

"Come on, Andy." Bree waved me over to the life vests stacked near the picnic rug.

I hadn't slept well, but that wasn't normal. Then again, this was me. I wasn't normal. Feeling other people's emotions—that wasn't normal. Having a gut instinct so strong it felt like the plunge of a knife—that wasn't normal.

And now faces warping and hearing things. That face had been so familiar. And Emmeline ... that name was like a key to some lock that protected buried treasure. Or imprisoned buried nightmares. My insides churned when I heard it.

"Andy?" Bree called from the water's edge as she snapped herself into Adam's life vest.

"Yep. Coming."

Ben held out a vest for me. "That should fit."

"Thanks."

My gaze collided with Kelly's. Her hand covered Ben's abs as she smiled sweetly. "Have fun."

"I will." I bared my teeth before heading to where Bree was waiting. I secured my floatation device and waded in, grabbing the side of the tube. "How did you get in?"

"Back up and plonk your butt down."

I gave it a go, but the tube shot backwards and I landed arse-first in the water.

And the crowd went wild. Yeah, that's it. Everybody laugh. One of them sounded like a donkey. I stood, following the sound. It was the redhead. Lee edged away from her, wiping his fingers across his brow.

"Nice wedgie, sis. The glare is unreal. Lucky we're wearing sunnies."

Truce, truce, truce.

I reached back to pull my bikini bottoms from between my snow-white cheeks as Bree paddled closer to shore. So much for not flashing my behind.

"You might need to jump like I did. We're the same height."

Yes, I was the size of an eleven-year-old, and so was my nine-year-old sister. *Thank you for the reminder.*

Performing a spin and jump, I managed to land perfectly the second time around. Bree bounced, clutching the handle to stay on.

"Sorry. Think of it as payback for calling me short."

"You ready?" Mr Hooper called out.

We both gave him the thumbs up before the rope went taut and our heads jerked backwards with the force of the take-off.

The wind whipped the hair off our faces. Water spray peppered us. I had to hang on. Every time we skimmed through the wake, our bodies would become airborne in the roughest trampoline ride ever. As we came closer to the barrage, Mr Hooper turned in a wide circle and the tube skimmed way off to the side. Our ride smoothed out for a few seconds until we straightened up and were pulled back across the waves.

"This is awesome!" I screamed as we passed the onlookers. Bree laughed hysterically. I checked her face to make sure there was no trace of panic and witnessed pure joy instead.

The roar of the boat's engine changed to the rumble of hooves as I was sucked into the memory of another exhilarating experience. Riding a horse galloping at full-speed down tree-lined pathways and through wildflower-covered fields. I could smell the horse, feel the prickle of its hair under my palm. My white-knuckled grip tried to slow it down. Only it didn't. Because I wasn't on a horse. I was riding a giant, inflatable, plastic doughnut.

I had never ridden a horse in my life.

Okay, I was officially freaked out.

What the fuck was happening to me?

———

Rockhampton, Australia
26th June, 2006, 9:27 a.m.

My knee jiggled up and down as I bit my thumbnail. I sat near the main entrance of the shopping centre, surveying every person who walked through the doors. *Where is she?* Jess was never late. Wrapping my hands around the nape of my neck, I squeezed to try and ease the sting.

Gone.

The word stamped into my frontal lobe with the fall of a gavel.

Gone? What did it mean, gone? And what the hell was *it*, anyway?

I flipped open a magazine that had been abandoned on the bench seat, staring through the pages until the print became blurred, scribbled blotches. It was like my mess of thoughts had tumbled onto the paper in a haphazard chaotic porridge.

Gone. Gone. Gone.

I should've made her stay.

Dead.

With a gasp, I tossed the magazine away, not bothering to hang around. I jumped on my bike, unlocking it before racing home.

"Mum!" Bursting through the door, I skidded to a halt finding Ben, Kelly, Stewart, and the brunette in the lounge, taking turns on the PlayStation.

"She's in the kitchen." Ben glanced my way before fixing his eyes back on the game.

Kelly didn't smile. She edged closer to Ben and watched me until I'd left the room.

Whatever, honey. If you want him, you've got him. I didn't give a shit anymore. There were way more important things to worry about than who the fuck was dating who.

"Mum!"

"Yes, what is it?" She spun around from her position at the sink.

"Jess. I think she's gone."

"Gone where?"

"Gone. Gooone. Dead. He killed her. She's—" My breath sawed in and out, stealing the words from my mouth.

"Sweetheart, slow down. What are you talking about?" The gloves landed on the sink with a slap as Mum pulled them off.

"Can you ring her house?"

"Of course."

She picked up the receiver and punched in the number I gave her.

"It's engaged."

"It was engaged yesterday and Saturday, too." I shook my head, eyes as wide as a scream. Tears blurred my vision.

I jumped as the phone started to ring.

Mum answered. "Hello." Her forehead creased as her eyes fell to mine. "What news?" Hand tightening on the phone, her lids dropped closed and a tear slowly seeped out.

I leaned my back against the counter for support, the strength draining from my muscles.

"When?" She opened her sorrowful eyes. "Saturday afternoon. Are they continuing the search?"

Oh, God. They haven't found her yet.

"No, she's right here. I'll let her know. Thanks." Her mouth curled in a weak smile. "I love you too. Don't forget to pick up Bree at three. See you later." She placed the handset down and cleared her throat.

I held my breath.

"That was Peter. He saw Jess's mum in town. Jess stormed off on Saturday afternoon and hasn't been seen since. They don't know where she is."

I do.

Not her body. But I knew where her spirit was. If there even was a heaven.

"I need to tell the police what she told me about the creeper."

"His name is Cameron." Her tone held disapproval.

I didn't care. He'd made Jess uncomfortable. That was enough for me to put a big goddamn spotlight in his face and handcuffs on his wrists.

"Leona told Peter they'd spent the morning in Yeppoon and had only been home for an hour when they had an argument and Jess left. She said she wouldn't be back. Apparently, she's done this before. They've been driving around looking for her. He hasn't left Leona's side, honey."

"That's her story."

Mum tilted her head, her bottom lip puffing out before pulling me in for a hug. "Leona is a mess. Do you really think she'd cover up for someone if she knew they'd hurt her baby? Not a chance. Honey, let the police do their jobs. Hopefully they'll find her quickly. She may even come back on her own."

No, she won't.

She can't.

God, I was so confused and frustrated. If he didn't do it, who did?

Rage boiled behind my skull. I needed answers. I needed someone to pay. I needed my friend to be okay.

It didn't look like any of those needs would be fulfilled.

Jess was gone. And no one could get her back no matter how long they searched.

A ringing took over my hearing like the receiver in my head had switched channels. The floor wavered under my feet. I was thankful Mum was holding me or I might've fallen in a heap.

"Hey, what's going on?" Stewart crossed to the fridge.

Mum lifted her head. "I think it'd be best if your friends went home for now, Stew."

"Why?" He stuck his head in the door, cold air curling at his feet in a mist.

"Because something bad has happened and your sister needs quiet." Mum raised her voice.

"What happened?" His head popped up.

"Stewart, just do as I ask or I'll kick them out myself."

"Okay, damn." He lowered his head again, reaching in for the milk.

"Stewart!"

"I'm doing it. Just let me have a drink first."

She let go of me and marched to the lounge. Stewart dumped the milk carton on the bench and chased after her.

I spun and held onto the bench, trying to decide what to do with myself. Jess was dead. I wanted to deny it. I couldn't.

Decision made, I retreated to my room. I didn't want to see Stewart or his friends.

We were all under the illusion that we had any control over our lives. We could try and force things, engineer opportunities to get us what we wanted. But if it wasn't meant to be, it would be taken from us regardless.

There was a greater force in charge than any weak human attempt we made.

And sometimes that force was an unjust bastard.

Chapter
9

Andrea

Brisbane, Australia
26th December, 2016, 1:22 a.m.

Oh, my God. This hurts like a bitch.

I cried out as the muscles in my abdomen clamped with a force I'd never believed was possible. Sweat dripped down my neck as the breath sawed from my lungs. I curled around my concrete uterus, under siege until the pain subsided, before collapsing back against the mattress. My arms and legs lay limp beside me in a strange, detached limbo as I tried to decide if I had the energy to move them.

My uterus was in control. I wasn't.

Flopping my head to the side, I speared Ben with an accusatory look. He gazed back, blue eyes filled with pleading apology. Emotions broiled inside me with the ebb and flow of each contraction. So many that I couldn't grasp them. I'd been at the mercy of my uterus for thirty-one hours and counting.

"You bastard—*aargh.*"

Shoulders seizing, I tipped my head toward my chest in protest at the excruciating agony surging through me once more. "It's ... your ... bloody fault." The words squeezed through gritted teeth, and between pants.

The midwife patted my leg, each tap shooting pins into my flesh, making me flinch. "You're doing really well, Andrea." She didn't meet my eyes, and her voice caught on my name as she watched the monitor beside the bed. I shook my head and pressed my eyes shut in denial. The knowing came anyway. *Something is wrong.*

The pain eased off again, leaving only a little relief in its wake. I figured I only had a minute's breathing space before it would return with even more force. Tears formed in the corners of my eyes before Ben's callused fingers brushed my cheek, wiping them away. Flopping my head back, I lifted my eyes to the ceiling and prayed. *Help me.*

"Shh. You can do this, Andy."

"I can't bloody do this. You've implanted me with a monster!"

Wincing as the words slipped out, I wanted to grab them and smoosh them back into my mouth. Dropping my head, I rubbed my belly. *I didn't mean it, baby. You're a blessing.*

Gripped in a vice of crushing pressure, I could do little but twist my head to the side and cry as I rode out the agony.

I can't do this. Something is wrong.

Tears came in a torrent now as the last of my energy reserves drained away. I was vaguely aware of the obstetrician at the foot of the bed, poking and prodding at my girly bits. I didn't care. I'd left my dignity at the door before I checked in two days ago. His voice came in clipped tones, nipping at the heels of the nurses. My attention piqued when I caught one of the words.

Caesarean.

"Andrea." The doctor leaned over me, his brow scrunched so tightly that all the lines seemed to merge into a mountain range of concern.

I blinked. That was as much as I could manage as another contraction surged through me.

"We're taking you to theatre to do a Caesararean. The baby is stuck in the birth canal. He's a big one, and we're concerned that his heart rate keeps dropping. Okay?"

My heartbeat thumped harder as if it could make up for the deficit in my child. The gloom of my emotions darkened. *My baby is in trouble.*

I nodded in agreement. Ben's warm hand gripped my fingers tighter and he leaned over, brushing a kiss against my sweaty forehead. Even set in grim lines and covered in scruff, his face was beautiful to me. I searched every feature, scared that this would be the last time I'd get to see him. Somehow I knew that my life, and the life of our baby, hung in the balance. The thought was so solid in its presence that it couldn't be denied as it sat on my chest. I fought it, the meaning so abhorrent that I could barely comprehend the repercussions.

My fingers flexed in Ben's grip. After all we'd been through, it couldn't end this soon.

The next contraction inflicted a pain so intense it felt like I'd been ripped in half. Eyes rolling back, I wanted to scream, but couldn't find the strength. Wetness gushed between my legs and my heart stuttered in my chest.

"Why is there so much blood?" Ben's frantic voice broke through the buzzing in my ears.

The bed started to move and the scuffle of shoes on linoleum grew louder with the shouts of the medical staff. Fluorescent light flicked across my closed eyelids and a shiver ran through me as the cold hospital air rushed past the bed, seeping its way into my skin.

The knowledge continued to sit heavy and melancholy on my chest, slowing my heart.

It couldn't end this soon. Could it?

The chill seeped deeper.

Ben's palm slipped out of mine.

Yes ... it could.

———

Andrea

Rockhampton, Australia

2nd of July, 2006, 4:38 p.m.

Propped on my bed, I stared at my feet, the TV screen flashing a moving backdrop behind them. There was still no sign of Jess. I'd seen footage of Jess's mum and her boyfriend, Cameron, sitting behind a table in a press conference. They'd appealed to the public for any information on her missing daughter. Leona had been a total mess, red eyes, quivering bottom lip, leaning on the guy I suspected had done her the most grievous of injustices. I'd watched him through narrowed eyes, looking for any hint that he was a liar. He'd kept his arm around Leona's shoulders, appearing suitably sullen.

Jess's face flashed across the screen with every news update throughout the day. Her disappearance was the top story along with a fire at Mount Archer National Park, a fatal shooting during a jewellery store robbery, and Michael Schumacher winning the US Formula One Grand Prix for the fifth time. I knew this because I hadn't left my room or turned off the television for a whole week. I kept it on mute, only turning the sound up when the news came on.

Bree would curl up at my side a couple of times a day and I would stroke her hair and cry. Even Will had come to visit. I think I freaked him out by bursting into tears and he hasn't been back since.

Mum and Peter were letting me wallow, but I could tell they were growing tired of my personality one-eighty. Every time she'd collect the food tray left at my door she'd sigh, taking in the cold, soggy plateful left behind. I might've picked at bits here and there, but they sat in my stomach like pebbles irritating my twisted gut.

My emotions had me swinging on their vines. Disbelief, anger, denial, depression. If I let go, I feared I would fall into a bottomless pit.

How could Jess be gone? If only she'd stayed over, maybe she'd still be alive.

Cameron. What did the news say his last name was? Thwaite? I sat up, throwing my legs over the edge before standing. Bursting through my door, I followed a path to the computer in the living room.

"Andy!" Mum squeaked.

"Yeah?"

"You're up."

"I am." I booted up the computer.

"What are you doing?"

"Just gotta check something."

"Okay." Her voice cracked.

I raised my eyes from the screen and caught sight of a tear running down her cheek. Pushing my chair back, I ran over to her and wrapped my arms around her waist. "I'm sorry I've been out of it. Don't worry about me. I'll be okay."

She bobbed her head, swallowing. "Are you hungry? Can I get you anything?"

"I can get something later."

"I made pancakes. Would you like some?"

It would make her feel better if I ate. "Sure, that'd be great. Thank you."

She went to the kitchen and I opened the web browser before typing in Cameron Thwaite. Opening another tab, I typed in *things to do in Rockhampton,* just in case Mum came back. I stared through the screen, thinking of what I could search rather than reading about the town I'd grown up in. *Things to do in Rockhampton—go to Yeppoon.*

Waiting until she'd put the plate next to me and left the room, I switched tabs. *Cameron Thwaite.* He had a profile on Facebook. I clicked on it. His face appeared. I clicked in the about section. He was fifty-four. In a relationship with Leona Barrett. Works as a manager at Bulldust Bar 'n' Grill. Jesus, it was scary what you could find out about a person online.

I absently picked up a pancake and stuffed it in my mouth. *Mm.* Damn, I was starving. Flicking through his photos, I stopped at one with him, Leona, and Jess. He sat between them, with his arms around their shoulders. Leona and Cameron were smiling. Jess looked as though her cheeks were made from plasticine. Had the police even treated him as a possible suspect? So what if his alibi was solid? Maybe he had someone working for him and they'd grabbed Jess, holding her until Cameron could do whatever evil he'd planned while Leona slept.

I dropped the rest of the pancake on the plate, the masticated food in my mouth travelling down my oesophagus at the speed of a traffic jam. I screwed up my nose and waited for the discomfort to ease.

Abandoning the idea of food, I clicked through a photo album until I found one of him with another young girl. They had their temples together, locked in a side-hug.

Who is she?

He hadn't tagged her, but there were several more photos of them together. I stopped when I found one with a comment.

'Happy birthday to the love of my life, Bella. I still remember the day you were born.'

He had a daughter.

"Please tell me she's alive and well," I mumbled to myself.

I searched for a Bella Thwaite, but came up blank.

"Hey, Mum?" I closed Facebook and went back to my search on Rockhampton.

She came rushing into the room. "Yes, honey. What is it?"

Guilt had me slumping in the chair. She looked so eager to please, I hated using her like this, but she wouldn't agree with what I was doing. "Can we go to Bulldust Bar 'n' Grill for dinner? I feel like a steak."

"Oh, that would be lovely. I'll call Peter and tell him."

And I'll pack a notebook in my handbag. I was going to need it.

———

Rockhampton, Australia
2nd of July, 2006, 6:39 p.m.

Bulldust Bar 'n' Grill had a prime position overlooking the Fitzroy River and plenty of glass windows to take advantage of the view. I wouldn't call it classy. It was comfortable and neat. Jeans and an Akubra weren't out of place at all. Neither was a longneck beer, judging by the patrons lined up at the bar.

"I'm going to grab us some more water." I stood and was gone before they could tell me the water bottle was already full. So it was full. I didn't care.

I sidled up to one end of the bar where a young woman was putting away glasses. "Hi. Do you mind if I ask you something?"

"How can I help?"

"My name's Andy. I'm thinking of applying for a job here and was just wondering what the manager is like."

"Cam? He's great."

"Really?"

Really?

"Yes. He gives me all the public holidays and lets me have a Friday night off once a month so I can have a life. Know what I'm sayin'?" Her grin was cheeky.

No, I'm fourteen. I spend Friday nights on the couch.

"So he's okay with young women? You know how creepy some bosses can be."

"Oh, you don't have to worry about that with Cam. He's like an old woman—very protective of his staff."

"Right."

"Would you like an application?"

"No, I'll think about it some more. Thanks for your help."

"No worries. Enjoy your meal."

"I will." *Not.*

I passed the water station and swiped a fresh bottle before making my way back to the table. Sitting in my seat was none other than the man himself. I waited just behind him as he recounted how distraught Leona was and how her mother was staying with her to help her through this difficult time. My senses didn't prick. The hair didn't rise on my arms. I didn't get a pain shooting down my neck.

It wasn't him. He didn't do it.

I was both relieved and stricken at the same time, the conflicting feeling warring in my stomach.

Thank God it wasn't him. How would Leona ever forgive herself for bringing a monster into her daughter's life, if that had been the case? But now I was at a dead end. Literally.

Who the hell had killed Jessica Barrett?

———

Call me John Doe

Rockhampton, Australia
24th of June, 2006, 6:16 p.m.

I drove along the quiet suburban streets, the window cracked just enough to invite the smell of cut grass. I hated the smell of freshly mowed lawn. It was a Saturday staple, just like the sound of a football siren during the season, or the growl of a motor boat on the Fitzroy River. Fucking straight-laced suburbia. What about the squealing of tyres as someone burned rubber to make their mark on the main drag? Nah, it wasn't allowed. The fucking cops would nab you and your car.

That was why I'd taught myself how to boost cars. I sneered at the Mercedes symbol in front of me. Scouring the streets for something to do, my gloved hands flexed and released on the unfamiliar steering wheel. Mr Businessman shouldn't have left his car parked on the street.

I cracked my neck, trying to release the tension. It wasn't gonna do the job. I'd been hard up for some action for too long. The urge to reach out and take what I wanted was too strong. I didn't want to fight it anymore. I wanted to give in to my animal.

"Whoa, there she is."

It was the doe I'd picked out right there on the side of the street, wearing tight jean shorts and a baggy T-shirt. The shorts would be a problem. Skirts were better. Skirts were no barrier at all. Dealing with a button and zipper, that was a problem. And denim was hard to rip. I'd tried it before. I had to knock the girl out to get her jeans off. It wasn't as much fun that way. I preferred them kicking, screaming, and begging for mercy.

She wore her blonde hair in a ponytail. Ponytails were the perfect handle. I could lead a girl around by her hair and she'd have no choice but to follow.

Slowing the car, I turned the corner. This street was lined with rundown shops, half of them out of business. It could not have been more fucking perfect if I'd planned it. It was like God was saying, *take what you want—mi casa es su casa.*

I parked on the wrong side of the street, needing the driver's side to face the curb. If anyone was looking it'd be harder to see anything. Tugging down my cap, I took the bottle of chloroform from the glove box. I did a quick check of the side mirror. No sign of her yet. Pulling a wadded rag from the centre console, I got ready to douse it in the chemical. Another check of the mirror showed me she'd be passing the car in half a minute.

My cock swelled, my pulse thumping against the side of my throat. I upended the liquid, holding my breath. Recapping the bottle, I tossed it in the glove box before opening my door. She pulled up two steps from me, alarm peeling her lids back. I moved quickly, making it look like I was hugging her, but holding her face to my chest with the rag smothering her cries. I didn't have to wait long for her to go limp in my arms.

Embracing her, I smoothed a palm down her ponytail. "We're gonna have some fun, you and me."

I opened the rear door and slid her shoes along the ground until I got her seated and belted. "Get used to being strapped in, doe."

I got back in and drove off with my reward, the beast inside me salivating for a feast.

Chapter
10

Andr–

Somewhere. Everywhere. There.

Swirling ... spinning ... floating ...

I couldn't get a grasp on where I was, or what I was doing. Even who I was. I tried to recall my name, but it was like the word was a smudge of graphite in the top corner of a blank exam paper. Whatever this test was, there wouldn't be a score, or even a question. It just was.

I'd been shunted from what had been my existence. I had no form. No flesh. No blood. No atoms. I was less than dust scattered on the wind. All that remained was *me*. *Me* without a body. *Me* without a name.

I AM because I'm aware I AM.

It became clearer that there *had been* more. There *had been* flesh. There *had been* graphite scrawled on a page to form a name. Before the nothingness had swallowed everything but *me*.

What was *me*?

I couldn't ponder this further as my awareness thickened, slowly becoming heavier, particle by particle. A landscape stretched out before me—rolling green hills, dotted with lakes and dissected by fences and dirt lanes. I remembered that I'd been a part of the land before. The land was a part of me. We were one. Before the parting. Before the nothingness.

Drifting by a grand manor, I found my way to a building of stone and wood, much smaller by comparison. It was larger than many of the other buildings settled in the surrounding hills. I reached for the handle to enter, but I was not yet flesh. I was still formless. There was nothing to reach with. Similarly, the material plane was no barrier for *me*. I could go anywhere I pleased.

Immediately, I found myself hovering over a girl as she hid inside one of the empty stalls. Her body was barely visible under the glow of red, orange, and yellow hues encompassing her. She was the reason I'd been drawn here. She and I were one.

In a flash, my awareness merged with hers.

My name is Emmeline. Emmeline is *me*.

———

Emmeline

Hampshire, England
15th of September, 1858

I spread my fingers out, looking at them in wonder as they buzzed with energy. What just happened? I swallowed as footsteps crunched along the debris of dirt and straw, coming to a halt outside my hiding place.

Enraptured, I flattened myself against the side of the stall, ensuring my view of the stable master's son as he entered the stall. Fingers pinching my nose to guard against the smell of soiled straw, I held in a lungful of air. He had been clever to don a handkerchief, tied around his neck and covering his mouth. Upon his head, he wore a brown railroad cap, dark tendrils of hair curling about the edges. I could barely gain a glimpse of his eyes from my position to his flank. But there was an issue far more pressing. The need for air. Keeping one hand firmly on my nose, I raised the fabric of my pinafore to cover my mouth before sucking in a breath.

He spun, pulling the cloth from his face. "What are you doing here, miss?"

Drat. Creeping out of my hiding place, I brushed the straw off my skirts and straightened my clothing, giving myself a moment of composure. "I was simply inspecting the stall to make sure you had done your job correctly. Father says not to trust the servants, after all."

Although his face was barely visible under the smears of dirt, I caught the boy's scowl without question. "My father taught me right. I know how to muck out the stalls, and I do a fine job. Enough to make him proud. You would not do any better."

Flattening my mouth as I tugged on my dark plaits, I refrained from stomping my foot. "I doubt it is hard. Whatever you can do, I can do. And I will do it better."

"Is that a fact?" Reaching for his pitchfork, he stared me down with eyes as black as a crow's feathers.

My arms fell to my sides as the blood drained to my feet. "Ye-s." Unable to stop the quiver in my voice, I swallowed, wishing I could retract the challenge.

"Well, let's see you go to work then. I have five more stalls to do. And you best get them finished before my father returns from his supper."

The boy was only an inch or two taller than me. He could not have been more than ten years' of age. Maybe an anniversary or two ahead of me. But he looked at me with a surety that I was inferior. If anything got me riled up, it was that. The boy was a stable hand. *How dare he!*

Pinching my mouth tight, I swiped the fork from his hand before charging towards the next stall. Plunging the tool into the hay with a grimace on my face, I held my breath against the stench. With the fork full, I turned, glaring at him as he leaned against the door, arms crossed.

"Well, where do I put it?"

"I thought you already knew?"

Huffing in annoyance, I pushed past him, searching for a barrel, or perhaps a cart.

I found a cart a few stalls down and dropped my offering into it before adding the fork and wheeling it over beside the boy. With a sweet smile on my face, I retrieved the tool and began loading more soiled hay, ready for disposal. I laboured steadily without complaint, proud of myself for matching his challenge, though it was the hardest thing I had done.

My arms burned. I squirmed, needing to peel my sweat-soaked clothing from my skin. Out of puff, I eyed the boy past the mountain of hay overflowing the cart and squared my shoulders before grasping the handles. With a great heave, I prayed for the load to move.

It did not.

"What troubles you, miss?" Glee sparkling in his eye, he feigned concern.

I pulled in a breath through my nostrils, narrowing my eyes. "Nothing at all, young man. I am perfectly fine."

Another heave, and to my delight, this time it budged. Gripping the handles until my knuckles were white, I pushed with my legs. The cart moved a few inches before the top-heavy weight began to topple sideways. I screamed, jumping back in despair as all my hard work spilled across the brick floor.

"Oh, more is the pity. You need to work faster if you are going to catch up."

My lip quivered, eyes stinging as I clenched my fists. Another scream caught in my throat, this time from frustration and hatred for this infuriating boy. I held onto it, not wanting to give in to his childish game, but the tears came. I could not stop the wretched things from wetting my cheeks, and all at once I collapsed in defeat.

"Now, hold your tears." He crouched in front of me, dipping his chin. "You asked for this, remember?"

I would have thought he was basking in his victory if it was not for the panic on his face. The scoundrel had been toying with my good intentions. He wiped the sweat from his brow and sank his teeth into his bottom lip. It suddenly occurred to me that I had a distinct advantage. His game had turned against him.

Sniffing and wiping my face with my pinafore, I set him in my sights. "If you wish to avoid my father becoming aware of your deception, whereby you will surely lose your position, you will help me clean this up."

"Oh, no. You said you could do the job better than me. You made the mess; now it needs fixing." He pushed the fork in my direction with an infernal tilt to his lips.

I got to my feet, crossing my arms. "I do not have to do anything, but I am willing to finish what I started ... with your help." It was of great importance to me—the following through of one's promises. I was aware that his intention was for me to scuttle away with my tail tucked under my skirts, never to return, but I was inclined to prove him wrong.

There was an added incentive. To have to endure my presence and assist me in completing the task with which he had been charged—at half the pace to which he was accustomed—would surely drive him mad.

He scrambled up, his mouth twisted, eyes merely slits.

I should have walked away. He had taken advantage of my naïveté, but I had managed to turn things around.

I had him.

Triumph.

Still, I wanted to prove to myself that I could do the job, even if it was with a little help.

He scoffed. "Fine. But you will do as I say without protest."

"I shall try."

"And I do not want to see you back in the stables."

"No. This is my property. You cannot deny me access."

The boy rolled his eyes as he put the cart back on its wheels. "I know you're not supposed to be here. I shall report you to the steward."

"And I shall tell him that you are but a weak little boy, incapable of fulfilling your employ."

He made a choking sound as he gaped at me. I held my lips steady, though they wished to curve in delight.

"Stop talking. A girl your size should not be talking like a grown woman. You are too cunning for anyone's good." He shoved the fork into my hand, and stomped off before bringing back another.

The boy huffed and puffed, scowled and murmured under his breath almost the entire time we worked. Once we had reached the last stall, his protests had turned to song. He pursed his lips, whistling a tune I had not heard before. And quite possibly would never forget. Hours of gruelling labour. Bloodied, torn palms. Aches in every part of my body. It had all been worth it.

My mouth stretched wide in a smile that could not be dismissed.

If I was not mistaken, I may have found a friend.

Chapter
11

Ben

Rockhampton, Australia
7th October, 2008

I took my boots off in the garage, stuffing my sweaty socks inside before entering the kitchen. Tumbleweed bounced over the deep crevices and crusty tastebuds on the surface of my tongue. The fridge looked like an oasis. I aimed for it, almost ripping the door off in my desperation to quench my thirst. *Orange juice. Awesome.* Grabbing the carton, I downed the contents in less than ten seconds.

Being a chippie was thirsty work. We'd put up most of the frame of a house today. One of the windows had been in the wrong spot and I'd had to dismantle the frame and reconfigure it. But other than that, it had been a standard day on the job. I couldn't wait until the day the roof went on. It was fucking hot working under the sun. It didn't seem to matter how much I drank, I always came home with a tongue like a galah's. It was even worse for Lee. Being a redhead, half his day was spent applying sunscreen. The both of us had landed apprenticeships at the same firm after school. We planned on studying our architecture degrees together. *Later.*

After dumping the carton in the recycling, I took off my shirt. About a pound of sawdust dislodged and fell to the floor. *Ah, shit.* I should've stripped everything in the garage. I wiped my mouth on the bunched up fabric before fossicking under the sink for the dustpan and brush. As I swept my mess, I registered a conversation coming from the back of the house. Adam must have a friend over. Lucky I hadn't stripped. I'd have to pass them on the way to the bathroom. Hopefully they wouldn't smell me.

"Whatever you do to the top, you do the same to the bottom."

The voice sounded like Andy's, but that couldn't be right. I hadn't seen her in more than two years. The last time I'd set eyes on her was just before the news of her friend's disappearance. What would she be doing here?

Padding through the living area, I glanced through the doors to the lounge and froze in my tracks. I tried to swallow but choked instead. *Jesus Christ, it's her. All grown up.*

"Hey, you're home," Adam chirped.

I strategically placed my wadded up shirt in front of my crotch and got a little closer, but not close enough that my odour would waft over. "Hey, buddy. How was school?"

Don't look at her tits. Don't look at her tits. My eyes dropped. *They're fucking huge.* I held my shirt with both hands, pressing down, telling my body to quit reacting to my friend's little sister. It *had* been six months since I'd had sex. My body was eager to get back in the game.

"Boring as usual." My head swivelled to my little brother as he tapped a pencil on his notebook, resting his head on his palm.

"Are you doing some homework?" I glanced at Andy as I asked the question, catching her eyes sliding down my body. The mutiny in my pants escalated.

"Yeah, Mum roped Andy into helping me."

"Did she?" I'd have to thank her later.

"Hey, Ben." She sent me an unaffected smile.

She's playing it cool. I can do that too. "Hey, Andy. How've you been?"

"Great."

"Great." I slowly nodded. "Well, I'm gonna go hand—have ... I'm gonna *have* a shower." And give myself a hand because this thing wasn't going to go away by itself.

"Have fun with that." She winked before getting Adam's attention.

She winked.

Fuck me.

I turned around and hobbled off before I made a total fool of myself.

Stewart's little sister is all grown up.

Shit.

———

Emmeline

Hampshire, England
2nd of April, 1863

I skipped up the grassy hill, pausing every now and then to pluck a cheerful yellow daffodil from its mooring. The spring afternoon sunshine had the ground firming after the soggy melt of winter snow. I breathed in the smell of fresh blooms and country air. Reaching the top of the hill, I caught sight of the river that ran through my father's property and continued all the way into town. The whinny of a horse caught on the tail of the breeze, making my smile even wider. If I wasn't mistaken, the sound had come from Admiral Caine. In my opinion, the prized Friesian stallion was a brute, but I loved him all the same. The horses were the best part of my world. The only animals that seemed to understand or tolerate me in the least. And visiting them was the one part of my day where I could fill my lungs to capacity away from the stifling walls where etiquette and expectations ruled.

Admiral seemed to favour Sebastian—the stable hand—a fact that ached like a stinger embedded under my skin. At first I had thought it to be a preference for the male gender, but that was before I had spotted the black horse landing a kick to Sebastian's father as he attempted to secure a saddle on the stallion. Mr Brennan had walked with a limp ever since.

I made my way along the river's edge until I caught sight of Sebastian astride Admiral's back, taking the horse for a swim. The pale skin of his back gleamed in the morning light. A pair of drawers seemed to be the only garment he was wearing. Soaked through, as they were, they appeared translucent. Moral fortitude would have had me avert my gaze, but somehow I was unable to locate mine. I stared unabashedly, studying his young male form.

I had witnessed the maids bathing their young using the washtubs in the scullery. Never had I seen a male of the same age unclothed before. His limbs were slim, but bore the mark of physical labour in a musculature developed beyond his years. Through some probing, I had recently discovered that although he was a head taller, he had been born a mere six months prior to me. There was an injustice in that I had yet to unburden myself of.

Beside the riverbank, his clothing lay scattered, patches of brown and cream against the burgeoning green blanket of grass. I hatched a plan sure to ruffle the young rooster's feathers. Lifting my skirts, I scurried down the slope to the water's edge and gathered his belongings. I checked over my shoulder to see if he had noticed my presence. Admiral tossed his head, but continued to move across the current to the opposite bank. Hurrying back up the hill, I reached the crest and spun around to lie flat on my stomach and observe my foe from behind a screen of bluebells.

Leaning forward, Sebastian gripped the reins and kicked his heels into the horse's flanks. Admiral took his cue, galloping forward.

My head popped above the cover, fearful that I would witness a tragedy at any minute.

Fool! What was he thinking, racing without a saddle?

He failed to slow down. They vanished over the next hill.

Keeping my eyes fixed on the same spot, I listened for them. The sound of their retreat soon faded, overtaken by the trickle of water along the riverbed and the trees spilling their song.

I flopped onto my back, plucking a bluebell and adding it to my posy of daffodils. I would wait for his return. If he had not reappeared by the time the sun crouched near the horizon, I would simply take a horse and find him.

A nearby cedar tree invited me over with its outstretched limbs offering protection from the sun. Clearing away some discarded cones, I curled against the trunk. His clothes provided an adequate pillow. The smell of cedar wood filled my lungs. Letting my eyelids fall as the breeze kissed my face, I hummed the tune Sebastian had whistled the day we'd met.

His face entered my thoughts. It had changed in the last five years—elongating and losing the fleshy padding that children had in their cheeks. I took a daffodil from the bunch and feathered it across my cheek. I had yet to lose the extra flesh. Of course, this had more to do with the offerings in the drawing and dining rooms than with my youth. I possessed a traitorous sweet tooth that was often the cause of my undoing. Father frequently scolded me for reaching for the desserts a second time. Nevertheless, I continued. Sugar was somewhat of a balm for a life of boredom and discontent.

A yawn stretched my mouth in an unladylike display. Fortunately, the only creatures to bear witness were the bees searching for pollen and the birds twittering above. I sighed, hoping Sebastian was still intact. It would be altogether ghastly if I had to search for him and found him broken. *Perish the thought.* I preferred to have faith that he would return just as I knew him to be. Infuriating, loyal, hard-working, impatient.

My stomach quivered the more I held him in mind. I found myself in the unenviable position of having grown attached to a boy who, at best, found me tolerable. It was my own fault, I supposed. I'd presented him with a challenge at every available opportunity. Such as now. I adjusted my head on my 'pillow', smiling a devious smile.

He secretly thrived on our exchanges. Surely he did. The fraction of a second between seeing me and his controlled responses, his eyes always sparked. That fraction of a second was what I held in my heart. I hoped that it would one day provide enough warmth to foster a true friendship.

My eyes flew open, thoughts scattering as droplets of water sprayed across my cheeks. I sprang up on my elbows, screaming, "Sebastian!"

Standing over me, he maintained his dignity by cupping his palms over his crotch. His drawers were alarmingly transparent at this distance. "Give me my clothes."

"They didn't appear to be a requirement."

"Emmeline." His ears were red. I could be certain he was angry when his ears flamed, and he addressed me by my given name rather than the preferred honorific of Miss.

My eyes dropped to his hands. I feared it was the devil whispering in my ear for the next thing to come out of my mouth was questionable indeed. "Uncover yourself and I shall return your garments."

"Pardon?" Pink infused his cheeks.

My eyes rose to his face. "Remove your hands. Please? I want to see."

Keeping covered, he squatted before resting on his knees. "It is hardly fair if you get to see me, but I do not get to see you."

A kaleidoscope of butterflies took flight in my stomach. I was fairly certain my cheeks were the same shade his ears had been. "My drawers are not see-through, as yours are." They were, however, quite open in the middle, if one were to part the two halves.

Admiral whinnied in the background, as if warning me not to cross the precipice I was standing on.

"It matters none." Sebastian shrugged.

It mattered quite a bit. Nonetheless, I was inherently unable to stand down from a challenge. As I slowly stood, he mirrored my movements. I started to lift my skirts, but he shook his head.

"Take off the dress."

His demand unhinged my jaw.

"I stand here in only my drawers. You will do the same."

"No."

He stepped toward me, looking at the clothes still under the tree.

"Wait. I'll give you your shirt."

"Fine." He nodded.

Spinning around, I pulled the shirt from the wad before handing it to him. He stepped close, eyes on mine. Snatching it with one hand, he turned away before slipping it on.

I admired his buttocks the entire time.

Facing me, he placed his hands on his hips, securing his shirt out of the way. This time, I stepped closer. The outline of his appendage was clearly visible. It was quite a bit bigger than what I had seen of the little boys in the scullery, appearing to have a ridge near the tip. *What on earth was that for?* And it did not flop down as theirs had. Instead, appearing somewhat rigid. Surrounding the base was a slight darkened area. *Was that hair?*

"Your turn, Emmeline." I peeled my gaze away to find Sebastian watching me with hooded eyes.

I breathed in before swallowing past a tightened throat. My fists clenched handfuls of fabric, inching it up. My chest rose and fell in rapid succession. I reached under the layers of petticoats to find my chemise and hefted the weight to my waist. My legs shook. I was in grave danger of falling, so I sat instead, before reclining back on his trousers.

Sebastian fell to his knees, taking me in with great concentration. I know not of what possessed me, but I let my knees fall to the sides. He had shown me himself through the flimsiest of shields; it was only fair that I exposed as much of myself as he. My only regret was not asking him to remove the barrier.

His hand flexed as he stared. His appendage seemed to strain at the fabric.

"Is that not uncomfortable?" I made a point of looking at his predicament to ensure he knew of what I spoke.

"Yes, it is."

"What do you require to ease the discomfort?"

He groaned. Shaking his head, he covered his crotch with his palm. "I'll need to go for another swim."

"Oh." I sat, pulling down my skirts. "Are you feverish?"

He made a choking sound. "You might say that."

"Have I made you unwell?"

"In all the right ways, Emmeline. May I have my trousers, please?"

I twisted to collect my captives before handing them to their rightful owner. I released a gasp. To my shock and delight he had dropped his drawers, slipping his trousers on without an undergarment.

He grinned as he fixed his suspenders. "It's only fair."

My heart swelled as my face broke into a smile. I was so pleased I had escaped the drudgery of the afternoon—watching Sebastian had been infinitely more enjoyable.

I waited until he was dressed before I leaned forward and pecked him on the cheek. "Thank you."

His movements slowed. He ensnared me in his gaze. The spark I'd caught fleeting glimpses of was now a simmering ember. It burned me to my core. Reflexively, I pressed my thighs together. With unmistakable intent, he held me by my forearms and placed his lips on mine.

Overcome by a rush of euphoria, I fell into him, circling him with my arms. He was still rigid. It pushed against my stomach. My body responded with an ache between my legs. I broke away from the kiss, needing to share my epiphany. "Oh, now I know what you meant by feverish. I feel a discomfort down there. Is it the same as what you experience?"

He blew out a breath, resting his forehead on mine before laughing. "I suppose it is." He kissed me again.

I held him tightly, never wanting to let go. "I wanted to touch it," I whispered.

He growled. "Stop."

"Did you not want to touch me?"

"You will be the death of me, Emmeline. Mark my words."

Grasping my hand in his, he marched me down to the riverbed to collect his shoes and the Admiral. We walked ever so slowly until the chimney stacks of the manor came into view. He loosened his grip on my hand, pulling it up to his mouth for one last kiss before leaving me behind.

The servant and the daughter of the manor would never be acceptable company.

Chapter
12

Ben

Rockhampton, Australia
7th of November 2008, 8:52 p.m.

"We're stealing his balls," Stewart slurred before chugging back the rest of his beer.

The backyard of our mate's semi-rural home had been converted into an outdoor pub, complete with a nineties cover band in the back corner. The music vibrated my whole body with every beat. A corrugated iron and wood bar sat snug against the rear kitchen entry, and a pool table invited players into the shed. Someone had strung party lights in the trees and set up tables and chairs across the lawn. Down the side of the house, lining the driveway, were his-and-hers Portaloos. Nobody was allowed inside the house. I wouldn't have let this lot in my house either.

I squinted at Stew. "You wanna what?"

He grabbed me by the back of the neck and yanked me close to his face. Just as the song finished, he yelled, "I want that set of balls."

Cheers and whistles came from the crowd. Some guy yelled, "Go get 'em, son."

"Ehhhh!" Stew raised his bottle, a grin splitting his face.

Several more blokes unleashed filthy comments. Stewart just kept on smiling before lifting his middle finger at the intolerant assholes. "Fucking homophobes."

Whatever their comebacks were, the next song drowned them out. One of the little weasels stepped up to Stew, who was too busy head-banging to notice. I crossed my arms, giving the guy a hard stare. He got the message and took off with his mate.

"Stewart! Benny!" I grunted as a hand smacked me on the back. "Thanks for comin' to my party, man." He said it twice. Once to me and once to Stewart.

"Happy birthday, Johnno."

"I'm finally legal." He raised a pointer finger to the sky, tipping back a bottle of Jim Beam. His eyeball rolled to the corner as he watched a tiny chick with black hair dance past. Lowering the bourbon, he trailed after her with the amber spirit dribbling down his chin.

"What, no goodbye?" I laughed.

"He's too busy chasing tail." Stewart hooked me around the neck again. "Where's Lee Major?"

"Stop fucking doing that." I threw his arm off. "He's over at Larissa's."

"What the fuck? Why isn't he out getting pissed with his mates?"

"He'd rather have sex than a hangover."

"Why can't he have both?"

"She didn't wanna come."

"Where's the fun in that?" He guffawed at his own joke before asking, "Why the fuck not?"

"Because of you."

"Is she still pissed about the beach incident? That was six months ago."

"You untied her bikini top and she flashed everyone."

"I didn't untie it. I might've accidentally pulled the string when I went for the ball. It was a freak accident. I told her that."

"Jesus, you're so clueless."

"Yeah, well, I've had more pussy than you."

"I prefer quality over quantity."

"Is that why you dumped Kelly?"

"You must be maggoted if you're asking me about my love life." *No fucking way am I telling you shit about my sex life. Or lack of.*

"Fuck. Yeah, you're right. I don't give a shit." He put the beer to his lips before realising it was empty and dumping it on a nearby trestle table. "I want the bull's balls."

Here we go with another half-cocked Stewart special. I loved the guy, but *Jesus*, he needed to grow up. "Which bull?"

"The Welcome to Rockhampton-motherfuckers-kiss-my-arse-Brahman."

"Is this some ploy to impress a girl? I can tell you now, they don't give a rat's arse about your trophy collection."

"Why are you tryna kill my joy? Seriously, how long has it been? You're as uptight as a nun in a brothel."

Maybe because I can't stop thinking about your sixteen-year-old sister.

Every Tuesday and Thursday afternoon, I'd get home from work and she'd be sitting at the dining room table, helping Adam with his assignments. She was so good with him, too. The way she explained things using pictures or objects—he just got it. Once, she'd cooked a chocolate cake and they'd sliced it up into fractions. She made things fun. She cared.

I narrowed my eyes, shaking my head. I needed to stop thinking about her. I needed to stop complicating my life with females. And parties. They weren't as much fun without alcohol. I sounded like a dick just thinking that. Alcohol was not a requirement for having a good time. Neither was sex. I pictured giving myself a black eye for getting on the hamster wheel of internal dialogue I had going. Why the fuck was I even here? I'd been up since five a.m., working my arse off all day. I just wanted to veg in front of the idiot box. Johnno was more Stewart's friend than mine anyway.

Fuck me for volunteering to be the designated driver.

"I'm done for the night. If you want a lift home, we're leaving. If not, suit yourself." I walked off towards the side gate.

"Benny, Benny, Benny." He almost went arse over tit as he ran in front of me, turning to put his hand against my chest.

I grabbed his wrist and removed it.

"Are you leaving already?" I twisted around, finding Andy behind me.

She was wearing tight jeans and a tank top. Her hair was loose. I dunno what she'd done to her face, but her eyes looked twice the size they normally did. Some weird shit was happening in my chest, like my ribcage had shrunk and couldn't contain what was inside it anymore. "What are you doing here?" *And what the fuck are you doing with a beer in your hand?*

"I was invited."

My brows dropped. "By who?"

"Johnno's sister. What is this? Twenty Questions?"

Stewart leaned his shoulder into mine. "Didn't you see her when we walked in? She was talking to that twat from school." He tried to click his fingers, but failed. "What's his name?" Swinging a finger at Andy, he blurted, "Michael, right?"

I was not prepared for the force of the kick to my gut. My hands formed tight fists at my sides.

Michael.

What's his address?

His phone number?

Where does he work?

What's his IQ?

What kind of car does he drive?

What's the number plate?

... What the fuck am I doing?

"Yes. And he's not a twat," she volleyed.

"Is too," Stewart slurred.

Mouth flattening, Andy's lids slowly dropped. Her chest rose with a slow breath in. I averted my eyes to avoid being a creep, but damn, her tits were hard not to notice.

Eyes popping open, she gave us a smile. "Were you guys leaving?"

She needed to stop smiling like that. She was too gorgeous. "No. Stewart just needed to take a pi—" I coughed. "A leak."

"Actually, I do." He stumbled off to the Portaloo before banging on the door and yelling at whoever was in there to hurry up.

I shoved my hands in the pockets of my jeans. "Where have you been hiding all night?"

"In the kitchen. There's a game of spin the bottle going on."

"And you were playing with Mikey?" I bit the words out.

Why the fuck was I so pissy? Maybe I did need to get laid. I'd broken up with Kelly five months ago. She'd been more interested in portraying an image than actually into me. She liked my muscles. She liked that I played union, not league. She liked that I earned my own money. She liked that I had a career as an architect planned out and that meant more money. She didn't know my favourite colour, or my favourite food. Or why I didn't want to move out of home yet. She didn't even know that I played guitar.

I hadn't given a shit that she didn't know those things. But the clincher for me was the fact that she could never remember Adam's name. Who the fuck dates someone for two years and can't remember the name of their brother?

Andy remembered Adam's name.

"Yeah. And a bunch of other people. What's your problem?"

"Nothing. I guess I'm having a hard time with the fact that you're sixteen and standing here drinking a beer at an eighteenth birthday."

"I've grown up since you last saw me."

I huffed a laugh. "Yeah." Hell yes, she had. "Which one is Johnno's sister?"

"Kate. You met her outside the primary school a couple of years back. We danced together."

"Right. Was that the tall one?"

"No. The redhead."

I remembered that day. She'd been with two friends. One of them had been Jess, the girl who'd disappeared the next day and still hasn't been seen. She'd just up and ghosted. The word around school was that she didn't want to be found. People liked to make up all sorts of bullshit stories to explain the inexplicable. Maybe she *had run* away. It would be easier to accept that than the possibility that she'd been murdered. It didn't look like we'd ever find out the truth.

I stared at her, crossing my arms. "She was with Jess. I'm sorry about your friend." What else could I say? Losing a friend like that was fucked up. "Do you think they'll ever find her?"

She dropped her chin and mirrored my stance. "Not alive."

"You don't reckon she took off?"

"I know she's dead."

"How? The cops don't even know that."

"I just know stuff. Thoughts pop in my head from nowhere and they're always right."

"So, a thought popped into your head telling you that she'd died?"

"Yes. I heard the word *dead*."

Whoa.

I didn't want to detract from the magnitude of what she was telling me, but at the same time, I couldn't deal with talking about her murdered friend. I focused on the revelation of her abilities instead.

"That's a pretty formidable gift you've got."

"I suppose it is."

"What else do you know?" Did she know how Jess died? Or who'd killed her?

"It's not like I can pluck information from the air whenever I want it. Answers come to me when they're supposed to come. I can't control it."

"If you could control it, the government would either have you committed, or they'd employ you."

"Probably."

"What other talents do you have besides dancing and knowing stuff?"

"I kick arse at spin the bottle."

I didn't want to think of her playing that game with Michael and every other horny teenage boy at this party. "What else?"

"I can touch my nose with my tongue." She demonstrated, poking her pink tongue out and curling it up.

I blinked at the sight, my groin tightening. *Damn, put that weapon away.*

"What can you do besides build houses, and play rugby—both codes?"

"I can speak Spanish."

"Really?"

"No, that's a lie."

She punched me on the arm, drawing a smirk to my face.

She wanted to know about *me*. I'd willingly tell her everything. Even my faults; and there were plenty. "I can play guitar and sing."

"Seriously?" Her face lit up with excitement. "Go on then."

"What? Here?"

"Yes! I wanna hear."

"Nah."

"Why not? If you've got it, flaunt it, right? Isn't that why you take your shirt off when you get home from work?"

I almost snorted. Had she just complimented my body and called me a show-off in one sentence? "I take it off because I'm always filthy and Mum doesn't want sawdust in the house."

"That's very considerate. I'm a little disappointed that you don't strip purely for my benefit, but I'll live. Can you sing now? Please?"

And now she wants me to strip for her. *Fuck.* I blew air through my nose and thought about my grandmother's bunions. "I don't have my guitar here."

"Borrow one from the band." She shrugged.

Grabbing my hand before I could say no, she led me through the crowd to the stage. We waited off to the side for the song to finish. Her warm hand stayed in mine, not letting go. I didn't want her to let go. Ever. At that moment she wasn't my friend's little sister, or Michael's friend. She was ... what? My friend? Nah, friends didn't mess with my insides like she was doing. She was mine. I *wanted* her to be mine.

The song cut off and she stepped up onto the side of the stage, beckoning the lead guitarist. "Hey. You guys sound awesome. Thanks for entertaining us. Do you mind if Ben plays some guitar and sings for us? Just one song?"

"Is he any good?"

"Of course. He's brilliant."

I dropped my gaze to the crown of her head. She had no idea what she was talking about. Nor could she possibly know how much her faith in me meant. I stretched my neck before pulling my shoulders back. I'd played in front of a crowd before. The revellers here probably wouldn't give a crap if I was good or bad because most of them were off their faces.

"What do you wanna play?" The guy handed me a Fender.

"'Use Somebody' by Kings of Leon."

"Great song. C major, right?"

I nodded.

"This is Jack on drums, Nick on bass, and Stevie on the keyboards." He pointed to each member as he introduced them. "I'm Caleb."

"Ben. Thanks for this, mate." I shook hands all 'round before hooking the guitar strap over my head. Strumming a chord, I checked that the guitar was in an open C. *Perfect*. I turned to the drummer. "Count us in?"

He smacked his sticks together, counting *one, two, three, four* before the music roared through the speakers. His drumsticks flew and I nodded to the beat as I played the intro. Spinning around for the first verse, I leaned into the mic and opened my mouth. My eyes found Andy as I sang about wanting someone like her. She was lit up like a neon sign that said, *'Here she is, ya dope. What took you so long?'*

It was getting easier to forget how we'd met each other. This Andy, the grown-up flirty version, she pulled at me to dig under the surface and get to know her on every level. The huge smile she aimed at me was a dare to walk a forbidden path.

She was only sixteen ...

She was my mate's sister ...

She is mine.

―――

Andrea

Rockhampton, Australia

7th of November 2008, 10:32 p.m.

After his performance, Ben and I dragged a couple of camping chairs into a quiet corner. I nursed a pretty decent buzz from having two beers and watching my crush rock out on stage. My heart was still thumping, but that could also have been because there we were, hiding in a dark corner, basically alone. I'd known he'd be good. And that song, sung in his deep, gritty voice, had me heating up at my core.

My instincts had told me to get him onstage. I always listened to my instincts. They'd also told me to get him alone in this corner. He didn't seem to mind. He seemed to love it, actually. Slumping down, we tipped our heads back to watch the galaxy roll on by.

"I have another talent," I muttered to the sky.

"What is it?"

"I'm a space nut. Ask me something."

His teeth flashed in the dim light. "Which one is our closest star?"

"Alpha Centauri. Hang on, where's the Southern Cross?" I scanned the sky, pointing when I'd found it. "There. So Alpha Centauri and Beta Centauri are the bright stars to the left of it. They're both triple star systems, actually."

"Really? Which one is the brightest star?"

"Sirius. J.K. Rowling should have named Sirius Black, Sirius Bright, but that would've ruined the surprise.

And anyway, our neighbouring planets usually look brighter than the stars."

"Is that right?"

"Yeah. When I was a kid, I used to make a wish on the first star I saw at dusk. I didn't realise until later that I was probably wishing on Venus."

"The goddess of love. That's not so bad."

"Oh, that's perfect. I didn't think of that."

"What did you wish for?" He twisted his head to take me in.

I met his stare. "I can't tell you that."

"Why not?"

I refocused on the cosmos. "Because I'm still waiting for it to come true."

"Hm." Heaving himself up, he slid his bottom back in the seat and rested his elbows on his knees. "Can I ask you about something? Tell me to mind my own business if it's too personal."

Uh-oh. "Shoot."

"Why did you ghost for two years? Where were you?"

Huh. He noticed. "I was processing."

"Processing?"

It was hard for me to bring up those memories. I'd gone from bright and bubbly to emo in the space of a few days. At the time, I'd let my anger over Jess's death consume me. I'd stopped dancing. I'd stopped going to watch Stewart play. And, yeah, watching Kelly paw at Ben had tipped me over. I wasn't going to tell him that I had been ridding myself of my addiction to him as well.

Jealousy was a sign of insecurity. There was never a reason to be jealous of anyone. I understood that now. I was born the way I was for a reason. I would never be someone else and no one could ever be me. The right partner would see sunbeams shooting from my arse, so I didn't need to worry. If something was meant for me, it would come when the timing was spot on and not a second sooner.

What I'd had to do was let go of my expectations. Expectations were sneaky fuckers that could ruin a perfectly good twist of fate.

I slapped at the back of my neck as pain sank its stinger into my flesh. This was no insect bite. I only experienced this when my senses pinged, warning me of bad juju. It was the same feeling I'd had just before Jess disappeared. My eyes scanned the crowd. There were still as least sixty people milling around. Many of them familiar to me from school and rugby.

Was her killer at the party?

Did I know him? Or her?

Him.

The pain receded almost as fast as it came. I had no way of searching for the possible killer without my sense as a guide. *Fuck.*

"Andy?" Ben's question yanked my attention away.

I would have to let it go for now. It could have been a warning about something else.

What were we talking about? Oh, right. "Yes. Processing losing my friend. But I had some growing up to do, too."

"I think you succeeded." He snared me in his gaze for the longest moment.

Any dark thoughts instantly cleared under his scrutiny. My breath caught in my throat. "Thank you." Heat rushed to my cheeks and it wasn't from the alcohol. "You've done all right in that department, too." Hadn't he ever. He was bigger now. The manual labour was doing all the right things for his body. But more importantly, he seemed to have his shit together. He was putting in the effort to get what he wanted out of life and that was fucking sexy. "Congrats on getting the apprenticeship."

"Thanks."

"Do you enjoy it?"

"It's hard work, but yeah, I do. I like working with my hands. I'm gaining insight into considerations when designing a structure."

"When do you plan on starting uni?"

"Maybe in a few years. It means a move to Brisbane and I'm not ready to leave Adam yet. I want to watch my little brother grow up."

A mix of emotions washed through me. He was leaving. I'd figured he would need to, but hearing confirmation took a chunk out of my heart. I wanted him to succeed and follow his dreams. If that meant we had to part, so be it. I adored that he was putting his degree on hold to get some experience in the industry, and to strengthen his bond with his little brother.

"He's hilarious. Love that kid."

A grin spread across Ben's face. "He's the best."

You're the best.

"What about you?"

"I want to be an early childhood teacher."

"I can see you doing that."

"Thanks." If I wanted to say anything more, I couldn't because my mouth was hijacked by a yawn.

"You're tired." He pulled out his phone, the screen casting a blue light over his features. "It's eleven-seventeen. Do you want a lift home? I'm taking Stew anyway."

Would I like to ride shotgun with you in your car? Um, yes. For life.

Settle, petal. He's not offering. And expectations, remember? "Yeah, sure. Thanks. I'm at Mum's, though. Stewart is going to Dad's. Is that okay?"

"Whatever. I'll drop you wherever you've gotta go."

"Okay. I'll go say goodbye. Give me five minutes. Maybe ten."

———

Ben

Rockhampton, Australia
7th of November 2008, 11:22 p.m.

I found Stewart asleep in a deck chair near the stage. The band had clocked off about an hour ago and Johnno's mum had cranked up the stereo on the back patio as their replacement. I shook his shoulder. "Stew. Wake up, mate. It's time to go." His head lolled to the other side and he let out a snore. He was out cold. *Damn.* Lifting his arm, I pulled his weight forward and bent him over my shoulder in a fireman's lift. "Don't vomit down my back." I passed Johnno on the way out. "Thanks for having us. Stew says bye."

"No worries. Catch ya later."

After unlocking the ute, I opened the back before strapping on his seat belt. "If you spew in my car, I will make you clean it out with a toothbrush." I got nothing but a snore in response. "Okay, then." I slammed the door shut and took a seat behind the wheel. Fiddling with the stereo, I tried to find a decent song before giving up and putting in a Foo Fighters CD.

The passenger side opened and Andy slid inside. "Hey. Thanks for waiting."

The moment she shut the door, the confined space seemed half the size. Or maybe it was that I felt twice as full—I didn't know. Being around her was opening my eyes to something that needed to be explored. Her scent filled the car with a sweet floral honey. *Lickable.* Damn.

"Not a problem." I shifted in the seat before turning the key in the ignition.

I drove under the speed limit just so I could take her in for as long as possible. She didn't speak. She didn't need to. I caught the rise and fall of every laboured breath in my peripheral vision. The way she wedged her hands between her thighs. The nervous jiggle of her knee that was out of time with the tempo of the music. Did she notice my white-knuckled grip on the steering wheel and the strain of tendons in my neck? I would've loved to reach across, put my palm on her thigh in those tight jeans. I thought about pulling over, kicking her brother out, sliding her across the centre console and sitting her on my lap. My jeans were way too fucking tight.

Fucking concentrate on the road. Jesus.

From Scrubby Creek, we headed north on the Bruce Highway to make our way home. Which meant we had to pass through the roundabout where the Brahman bull statue welcomed people to Rocky. And there he was. I never understood why they faced his back end towards the outskirts of town. Nobody I knew ever said welcome with their back turned.

"Pull over!" Stewart barked from the back.

"No." *Fucking way.*

Andy twisted in her seat, wide-eyed. "Are you gonna spew?"

"Shit." I chucked the gear box down to second, skidding to a stop on the grass.

He fumbled with his seat belt before yanking the door open. Falling out onto the grass, he blew chunks over the nature strip.

She blinked at me, her mouth set in a grimace. "At least he gave you some warning. I hope he didn't get it on the car."

"I already warned him he'd be cleaning it if he did."

"Stewart? Cleaning? You've seen his room, right?"

"We generally stick to the lounge when I visit."

She raised her brows. "Solid plan."

A minute later, some rattling came from the tray of the Hilux. "What is he doing?"

The rear-view mirror showed Stewart wandering off with what appeared to be my bolt cutters in his hand. "No fucking way."

"What?"

"He's going for the balls."

"I'm sorry?" She twisted to look out the back window.

I undid my seat belt. "The bull's balls. He's taking them."

"Oh, shit. Are there any cameras around here?"

"Dunno. But if there are, they've got my number plate and tyre tracks."

"Stupid bloody tosser." She opened her door.

"You said it, not me."

We both hopped out and followed him down the road.

"Stewart, don't be an idiot," I bit out.

"If you know Stewart at all, you know that's an impossibility." Andy rolled her eyes.

"I can hear you," he threw over his shoulder.

"I know," she sang back.

I'd missed this. The love bombs coated in insults flying between them. None of their ammo was ever intended to inflict any damage. I could kick back with some popcorn and watch for hours. I hadn't known what my life had been lacking until she'd shown up again. And weirdly, this was a part of it.

"Andy, you cover the spotlight." He let out a ripper of a burp, taking a second before the rest of his instructions tumbled from his mouth. "Ben, help me out with the cutters. My arms aren't workin' right."

"Gee, I wonder why?" Andy returned.

His legs seemed to tangle as he crossed the road to get to the middle of the roundabout.

"Jesus, we might be scraping him off the bitumen if a car comes screaming around the bend." I shook my head, grabbed Andy's hand, and dashed after him. Luckily the road was pretty deserted at this time of night.

Finding him hunched over with his head between the bull's back legs, he worked the bolt cutter on the chain that attached the balls to the statue.

Andy propped her hands on her hips. "I thought they were putting steel rods through all the boy's bits?"

"They are. This one hasn't been done yet." I scanned the area, looking for a camera. Maybe they were hidden. If I copped a fine, Stewart was going to be the one paying it.

"Lucky me!" Stewart chimed as he finally broke through the metal and held up his prize.

"Congratulations, Stewart. You finally have a set of balls," Andy said in the driest tone.

"Oi." Stewart held the concrete set to his chest

I snorted, a smile splitting my face. *This girl.*

"Let's go." Andy took off back to the car.

"You guys are killjoys." Stewart tripped over his own feet, just catching himself before he fell.

I spun my keys on my finger as we crossed the road. "Feel free to walk home, Stew."

"Nah, I'm good."

His sister coughed. "Biggest lie I've heard in a while."

We got to the car. "Don't step in the vomit, Spew," his sister reminded him.

Love bomb.

"Ah, shit. Too late."

Fuck.

"Sit your arse on the seat and take your shoes off." I tossed a plastic bag onto his lap.

"I got it, I got it."

"He got spew on his shoe, is what he got." Andy giggled. "Stew got spew on his shoe." She put a hand over her face, pressing her temples. "Ah, I crack myself up."

"All good." Stewart dropped the bag on the floor and shut his door before pointing at the road ahead. "Home, James."

I dropped Stewart at his dad's, personally depositing him face down on his mattress. Making my way back to the ute, I swiped my sweaty palms on my jeans. Andy was changing the CD when I shut us inside with a snap.

It was just me and Andy, and a palpable tension so thick it needed its own name. Visions of slick palms pressed against fogged windows entered my mind and I had to adjust my jeans to give myself more room. The way the seat belt cut across her chest accentuated her assets even more. Cranking the engine, I dialled up the air conditioning and pointed the vents right at my face.

I cleared my throat, turning down the music as we drove to her mum's. "I had a good time tonight. Thanks to you."

"Me too, thanks to me. You had absolutely nothing to do with it." She smiled at her interlaced fingers in her lap.

"Harsh."

"Okay, you might've had a little bit to do with it."

"My performance alone should warrant a higher rating than that."

"You want a score out of five stars?" She raised her brows, a smirk on her face.

"Hit me."

"Four and a half."

Hm, not bad. But ... "Where'd the half a star go?"

She giggled, the sound revving me up even more. "The universe doesn't allow perfection."

"That depends on your idea of perfect."

"What's your idea of perfect?"

You. "I like things a little unpredictable. I like a bit of colour mixed in with my black and white. I like aiming for left of centre. That odd bit of something special thrown in to set me off balance—that's my perfect."

I waited for the comeback.

She was quiet. Too quiet.

I glanced over and caught her looking at me with hooded eyes, her chest rising and falling rapidly. My cock twitched. My lungs cramped. Clenching the steering wheel, I focused back on the road to avoid crashing the car.

Kelly had never made me react like this. Never.

I had been so fucking blind.

The timing hadn't been right before. Maybe now

...

Pulling up to the curb in front of her house, I turned off the engine.

"Here we are."

"Home sweet home." She smiled.

"Can we—" My throat closed off the sentence without warning. I swallowed, twisting towards her. "I'd like to start over. Take you on a date. Maybe a movie?"

Her smile spread slowly. Beautifully. "That depends. What are we watching?"

Elation hit me like a Mack truck. Was that a yes? "Whatever you want to watch—I don't care." My eyes would no doubt be straying to the girl sitting beside me. She could tell me she wanted to watch *My Little Pony* and I'd agree.

"*Quantum of Solace?*"

My grin was instant.

And her taste in movies is badass.

Perfect.

Chapter
13

Emmeline

Hampshire, England
16th of August, 1866

I lifted my shoulders, deliberately pushing my stomach out as Marybeth tightened the ties of my corset. Touching my braided chignon, I ensured that the pins had not fallen free. Light poured in through the lace curtains, bathing me in its reflected glow in the mirror. I leaned forward, noticing a few extra freckles across my nose, a blessing from the sun. My feet itched to be out in its direct glory.

In the last few years, I had taken to enjoying outings to satisfy my craving for something more than a luncheon of sandwiches and an afternoon of embroidery. Although he was pleased that my sweet tooth had gained some control, my father would be most displeased if he were to uncover the truth behind my afternoon jaunts.

Marybeth, my chambermaid, was quite happy to provide cover so she could carry on an illicit affair with my uncle, Tobias. He was betrothed to another—a rather arduous ordeal for both parties if one was to read their body language correctly when poor Lady Margaret endured weekly visits to the estate for luncheon of a Friday afternoon.

Tobias and Marybeth thought their rendezvous were discreet. Perhaps anywhere other than the glasshouse would have been a more suitable choice where the pitiful greenery and the calcified ghosts of raindrops on glass provided minimal cover.

Sometimes I'd entertained myself by spying on them through the panes, listening to Marybeth's high-pitched squeals as the flash of pale, white buttocks clenched and thrusted atop her body. Uncle Tobias grunted like a boar, while the maid's vocalisations resembled that of a piglet. It was all quite incestuous. And ... amusing.

Tobias always returned to the house first, leaving his mistress to wait an hour or so in the humid, loamy air. Without fail, his coat and the knees of his trousers sported patches of dirt, making a mockery of his cries of innocence when confronted by his sister, my mother. He purported to be extremely fond of gardening.

He did rather enjoy planting his seed, as it were.

If it was a wife's duty to be rutted upon by a boar, I wanted no part of marriage.

I had finally grown tired of the show and taken to borrowing a horse. Give me the open fields and the wind in my hair, and I was most content. And if the opportunity arose for me to cross paths with Sebastian, my contentment brimmed over into joy.

If my father were to find out, it would surely mean an end to my afternoon rides, and an end to Tobias's affair. Hence, it was advantageous for all involved if tongues were kept caged behind tight lips. I'd been sure to point this out to my chambermaid, who'd agreed, albeit peevishly.

"I shall be taking my leave earlier this morn."

"No, miss. Your mother requires your presence in the drawing room."

I tutted, pulling on a corset cover. "What the devil does she want now?"

Marybeth's eyes flitted to the mirror, but did not raise to the level of mine. "She has an urgent matter to discuss." She reached for the crinoline.

"I refuse to wear that ghastly contraption of torture. Let us try layers of ruffled petticoats." I added a smile to soften my delivery. I would simply remove several of the layers before embarking on my outing.

She bowed her head, fetching the muslin.

"Mother's urgency is usually another's trivial passing thought."

"She was quite insistent, miss."

But of course. That was Mother's nature. Should I choose to ignore her request and satisfy my own urgent need, I would surely expose both my own and Marybeth's deceit.

She brought over a pretty, blue silk dress with white ribbon trim.

It would not do. Not in the least. "Where is my Garibaldi shirt and the dark blue skirt?"

"Your mother has requested that you wear this."

That could only mean one thing. She was expecting a visitor. Releasing a sigh, I bowed my head for the maid to lower the dress over my head.

It would do. For now.

Moments later, I found myself perched on the edge of the French settee in the drawing room, sipping tea with my mother and Lady Victoria of Pembrokeshire. A severe-looking woman, she wore a deep brown silk dress with the barest lace ruffle at her throat. Her greying hair was pulled back in the style Queen Victoria herself favoured.

Puffy pale grey eyes held me in their piercing stare. "She's quite the beauty, Lady Olivia. What is her age?"

"I have just turned sixteen years this July." Why she would not address her question directly to me, I had no clue. I sipped a little too loudly, drawing a disapproving look from Mother.

She cleared her throat. "As you can see, Emmeline is quite mature for her age and equally headstrong." She flashed her eyes at me in warning.

"Headstrong is not a quality a woman should possess. My Reginald will beat it out of her."

I lowered my cup, clinking it on the saucer. "May I ask of whom you are speaking?"

Her shoulders rose as she lifted her chin. "My son, Reginald Fortescue the Third, Earl of Pembroke."

The Third? How alarming. "Why exactly would he feel the need to beat me?"

"As your husband, he will have the right to treat you as he sees fit."

"Indeed." I pursed my lips together, my eyes trained on the ornate rug at my feet. I begged them not to water. "When might I be expecting the nuptials?"

"In your seventeenth year, my dear. The earl is currently on a sojourn in India. Upon his return, he shall make you his wife."

I would prefer a sudden painful death.

"Indeed." I swallowed against the rising tide of bile threatening to spill. "If you'll excuse me, I must retire to my rooms. I feel quite unwell. Please enjoy your visit, Lady Victoria." *For you shall surely burn in hell when the devil sees fit.*

I gave a curtsey to each of them before taking my leave, hurrying to the rear courtyard. A nearby garden bed provided a place for my stomach to empty of its contents.

My throat burned. I ducked through the scullery and into the kitchen, in search of a pitcher of water and a cup.

"Everything all right, miss?" The maids hurried around, completing their chores.

My visits to the servants' quarters had been frequent when I was younger. I'd become aware of the inner workings of the household and the hours of labour it took to keep our home functioning. However, in recent years my visits had declined. The steward frowned upon my association with the staff.

"Yes, quite. Please disregard my presence."

I found what I was looking for, washing down the bitter taste and taking an apple to cleanse my mouth.

I inspected the pale pristine silk I wore. A dress chosen by my mother. Pretty, delicate, feminine. Hardly me at all. And the man she'd chosen to be my husband—a beast by his mother's account. Neither of Mother's choices were particularly palatable.

If I had no say regarding to whom I would be tethered for life, I could certainly decide never to wear this dress again. What, then, would it matter if I were to ruin the silk by taking a horse and riding as far as I could go?

———

Andrea

Rockhampton, Australia
21st of November 2008

The Monday after Johnno's party, Ben surprised me by waiting outside the school gates to give me and our siblings a lift home. It sure beat walking in the sweltering heat. He'd come back every afternoon for two weeks. I guessed there was one advantage to the early starts the tradies endured. They generally clocked off early, too. It had been two hours since he'd dropped us home, and two weeks since he'd asked me out on a date. He'd be back to pick me up in two minutes.

Pulling the lounge room curtains aside, I surveyed the street for the blue Hilux.

"Looking out the window isn't gonna make him arrive any sooner." Bree laughed.

"I know. I'm just checking."

I walked to the mirror in the entry, searching for lipstick smudges on my teeth and discovered that I had sweat patches under my boobs.

"Oh, my God. I've got boob-sweat! Why didn't you tell me?!" I dashed to my room, ripping off my tank top before snatching a bunch of tissues from the box. Flinging the sweaty bra across the room, I yanked open my lingerie drawer.

Crap, crap, crap. Where are my goddamn bras?

I wedged tissues under my breasts and twisted the fan switch until the conditions in my room became cyclonic. *Bloody tropical bullshit.* Spotting my washing basket overflowing in the corner of the room, I dug through it until I came across a bra. Hot pink lace. *It'll do.* I really needed to fold my washing. And now I had to change my whole outfit. The pink showed through everything but dark colours. Coat hangers scraped along the metal rail in my wardrobe as I sorted through possible candidates. Guys didn't have to worry about shit like this. They wore T-shirts and shorts. Unless they were wearing white shorts. Then they had to worry. I'd seen a guy in the line at the grocery store once, wearing red undies under white shorts. It wasn't a good look.

Focus, focus, focus.

"Andy!" Bree gave me a shout.

"I'll be out in a minute." *Fuck, fuck, fuck.*

I found a black tank dress and tossed it over my head before realising that I hadn't put the bra on yet. After fixing the problem, I sprayed more deodorant and went out to greet him.

Oh, he's delicious. "Hi," I breathed, the sight of him stealing my voice.

His T-shirt fit him snug across the chest and biceps, and cargo shorts gave me a glimpse of powerful legs. The shorts were khaki green. What colour undies was he wearing?

"You ready to go?"

Since I met you, yes.

His lips tilted in a crooked smile as he muffled a laugh.

"I said that out loud, didn't I?"

"Yep," Bree answered for him.

Jesus.

"I'll see you later." I widened my eyes at Bree before calling out to the parents. "Bye, Mum. Bye, Peter."

Mum poked her head around the corner. "Bye, kids. Have fun."

"Don't be late," Pete yelled from the living room.

"Oh, Peter," Mum scoffed. "It's fine. I know Ben will look after you."

I gave her a hug and skipped out the door.

"Wait up." Ben jogged ahead, opening the door for me.

Did guys still do that in this day and age? I guessed they did. I kinda liked it.

He closed us in, clipping on his seat belt before leaning towards me. My lungs nearly collapsed at his close proximity. His hooded stare was unnerving in all the right ways. And then he spoke.

"You have a tissue stuck under your armpit."

Oh, my fucking God. My stomach sank through the floor. I fished the offending item from said pit before blurting, "I had boob sweat."

Jesus H. Christ.

"Left of centre," he murmured, a smirk on his face. "Don't sweat it, Andy." He bit his lip, obviously fighting a smile. "I guess you already did though, huh?" Bursting into laughter, he started the car.

I had to laugh. It was stupidly hilarious. But I sincerely hoped it wasn't a story he'd be telling our grandchildren.

"Your mum and Peter seemed okay with me taking you out."

"Yeah. They're cool."

"I'm looking forward to spending time with you without Stewart being around."

"Oh, God. Me too."

"Did you tell him we were going out?" He concentrated on the road, appearing relaxed, but I sensed a waver in his tone. Was he having doubts?

"No. Did you?"

"Nope."

"He'll find out eventually. Do you find it weird, dating your friend's younger sister?"

He reached over and interlaced our hands, resting them on my thigh. "No. Stewart no longer comes to mind when I see your face."

That was a relief.

I dropped my eyes to our hands. The warmth spread through my dress and sent tingles up my thigh. I chewed on my lips and dragged in some air. Reaching over to the vent, I pointed it at my breasts, and discreetly turned up the fan speed. *No boob sweat.*

Ten minutes later, we made it to the ticket counter before purchasing some snacks to take in. Turning around,

I spotted Lee with his girlfriend, Larissa. She was tall and so thin she might snap if she sneezed. Her eyes roamed the crowd, running up and down the female competition with disapproval.

"Hey." I waved and caught Lee's eye.

He pulled her towards us to say hello. "Andy. And Benny. Together. This is a surpr—actually, no, it's not. Not at all. I saw this coming a mile away. So, do we call you Bendy now, or what?"

"I wouldn't, if I were you," Ben warned.

"How are you, Lee Lee?" I gave him a hug.

"Yeah, good. What movie are you going to see?"

"Double-oh-seven. What about you guys?"

He hesitated, giving Larissa cause to cut in. "*Twilight.*"

"Oh, good. That should be ... interesting." I ordered my cheeks to pull the corners of my mouth up.

Glancing at Ben, I found him chewing on the corner of his lip, his eyes crinkling at the corners. "How've you been, Larissa?"

"Good." Looking anywhere but at us, she tugged on Lee's hand.

My eyes widened before I controlled them. Was this chick for real? I schooled my features and addressed Lee. "How is Letitia? I haven't seen her in ages."

"She's doing great. The school holds a robotics club one afternoon a week, so she's learning all about the programming and mechanics of that. Dad passed her his engineering genes."

"You got them too, though."

"Maybe. We just found out Mum and Dad are planning a second honeymoon to Daydream Island next winter so it'll just be me and Tish for a week. She's not impressed that I'll be in charge."

The room blurred in and out of focus. Ice trickled into my veins. The back of my neck burst into a bonfire. The word *dead* popped into my head. "No."

Lee's head reared back. "No, what?"

"Don't let them go."

Plane crash. Dead. Plane crash. Dead.

The warning played on a loop as Lee looked at me strangely.

"Of course I'm gonna let them go. As if I can stop them. Have you been smoking the wacky weed?"

"Don't let them get on that plane," I begged, grabbing onto his arm before Larissa pushed me off.

"What are you doing, freak? Bradlee, we're going."

"Yeah, okay. I'll see you guys later. Enjoy that movie." He was still frowning at me as he let her lead him away.

"What was that about?" Ben reached for my hand.

I bit my lip, tears welling in my eyes as our stares locked.

No more death. Please, please, please.

"I—" Blowing out a slow breath, I frantically rubbed at the nape of my neck. "There's something—" I growled, frustrated with myself. "Do you remember me telling you how I know stuff?"

"Yeah."

"I think something bad is going to happen to Bradlee's parents."

"For real?"

"Yeah. I felt it even stronger than I felt what was around Jess."

Ben tucked me under his arm and steered me to a quieter spot. "We don't have to see the movie. I can take you home if you need."

I shook my head. "No. I'll be fine. I just need to get my mind off it. I could be wrong, right?"

"I hope you are. No offense."

"None taken." I reached up and locked my hand with his. "Let's go in. It's about to start."

We lifted the armrest between our seats so I could cuddle into his side. He fed me popcorn as I watched the movie playing in my mind rather than the one on the screen. Jess's face. The news reports on her disappearance. Her mother pleading for her return. Brad and Tish sharing a tube ride. His parents on the sideline at his rugby game, cheering him on. All it took was one bad decision, or one ill-timed move, and everything could come crashing down.

Ben held me through the whole movie and all the way to the car. He clasped my hand on the ride home. He hugged me on my doorstep and gave me a kiss on the forehead before saying goodnight. "Try to get some sleep."

If I had one reason to have sweet dreams that night, it was that man.

———

Emmeline

Hampshire, England
16th of August, 1866

Sunlight flickered over my eyelids, its rays blocked and revealed in flashes by the canopy zipping overhead. The horse's hooves thundered along the ground as my long plaits whipped my back, urging me to go faster.

My grin stretched wide. I relished the taste of freedom in an otherwise cloistered life.

"Miss Emmeline! Slow down!"

The rumble along the ground doubled as another four hooves joined in chase. *Sebastian.*

I leaned forward, squeezing my thighs, a frown pulling on my mouth. My horse responded with a great surge of power on sure legs. Holding the reins in an iron grip, I was thankful I had ignored the protocol of riding side-saddle and wished I could also rip off my skirts in favour of the buckskins worn by the men.

"I said, slow down! I know you can hear me."

"Why do you not speed up?" I yelled, ducking under a low branch.

"Are you suggesting a race, miss?" His voice was louder, having gained several feet. Admiral had plenty of vim today.

"Is that not what we are already engaged in?" *Come on, Miss Modesty.* I raised off the saddle, gripping the reins against her neck.

"The Admiral always gets his female." Sebastian zoomed past in a show of superiority, laughing hysterically.

I had never been this far out before. The river appeared much wider, and the forest thicker on this part of the property. Such beauty. And I would no longer get to enjoy it.

We came to a clearing. Sebastian circled back around as Miss Modesty slowed, not waiting for his stallion to come to a complete halt before dismounting. Holding my chestnut mare steady by the reins, he offered his hand in assistance.

"Thank you." I struggled with my skirts, finally managing to get my legs over to one side.

Sebastian gripped me by my waist, pulling me down. He held me against him for an interminable minute, our eyes locked in a dance we'd started years before. My heart bled for the loss of something that would never be mine. How could I tell him?

I hate to say goodbye to you.

I have no choice.

I blinked as his beard grew before my eyes. His hair shortened as if clipped by magic. And his eyes. Did they change to blue? It lasted but a moment before my Sebastian returned.

What the devil?

We broke apart as Admiral nickered, pacing back and forth with his ears pricked. His top lip curled and his nostrils flared. The mare grew agitated, her tail flicking. I scrubbed my hand through her black mane before patting her neck. She tossed her head, grunting in response. I backed away.

Sebastian worked hastily to remove their saddles.

The stallion wasted not a moment before mounting the Hanoverian mare. She accepted him, growing more calm as Admiral Caine performed his task.

Indeed. Miss Modesty had not quite lived up to her name. I suspected she'd lost the race deliberately to satisfy her urge for some male attention.

I stared, fascinated. Admiral was vastly more majestic with his powerful thrusts than Uncle Tobias had been. "I was under the impression that breeding season had ended."

"Not entirely, as you can see. He has been itching to get at Miss Modesty. We were going to free her from her stall this morning and pen them in together. My father was not happy to discover she was missing. But if this results in a foal, all may be forgiven."

"Oh. I was unaware. I do apologise." I tilted my head to take him in as he stood beside me. He was taller than my father and still had years of growth to come. What would he look like as a fully grown man? Would he have a beard, a moustache? Or would he shave?

I pulled at my lace collar, heat consuming me. I suspected it was not due to the fact I no longer had the wind whipping my face. Was it being here with him, or witnessing the mating ritual between two magnificent beasts? "I cannot say I blame them. It is rather hot and the day is splendid. I think I may need a swim to cool off." I unfastened the brooch at my neck before unbuttoning the bodice of my dress.

"What are you doing?" Sebastian's eyes could not have been any wider.

Saying goodbye. "I do believe I already informed you of my intentions." Removing my arms from the bodice, I shimmied the fabric over my head before starting on the removal of my petticoats. "Would you mind untying my corset?"

He made a sound as though he were choking.

"Sebastian?" Standing in only my corset, chemise, and drawers, I turned my back.

I smiled as he tugged on the laces, and I worked on freeing my braids. Within a minute, the stiff garment fell forward, catching on my arms. I whipped it off, discarding it onto the grass. Pulling my chemise over my head before untying my drawers, I finally freed myself of my restraints, symbols of the life I fully intended to leave behind.

Spinning around, I smiled. "Are you not swimming with me?"

He answered by reaching for the buttons of his vest. His head bobbed up and down as he took me in.

Leaving him to undress, I made my way down to the river and dipped my toe in the chilly water. Goosebumps broke out all over my skin. I hugged my arms around my waist and stepped in up to my knees. Unable to stop the shiver, I questioned my judgement.

"It is much easier if you jump in quickly." Sebastian demonstrated his theory by barrelling past me and flopping backwards into the water. The splash had my shivers intensifying and a squeak of shock catching in my throat.

His head popped out of the water and he flicked his hair to the side, sending another spray my way. "The longer you stand there with wet skin, the longer you will suffer. Though, I am enjoying the view."

I walked until the surface reached the tops of my thighs. Filling my lungs before pinching my nose, I closed my eyes and dove in. In a rush, I expelled my lungful under the water. The cold was like thousands of tiny needles piercing my muscles. Sebastian's hands found me and pulled me to the surface. I immediately dragged in as much air as I could. How had he been doing this all these years? And in spring and autumn when it would surely be much colder.

"Breathe. Your body will adjust."

"I think I may have failed to mention that I have never been swimming before." I panted, trying to calm my besieged system.

His eyebrows climbed towards the heavens. "You cannot swim?"

I shook my head, still shivering and out of breath.

He barked a laugh before pulling me close, overcome with hilarity. "You ludicrous girl. I love you."

Nobody had ever uttered those words to me before. His declaration should have filled me with immense joy. And it did. But the preceding events marred its affect. I could not imagine anything I wanted to hear more than those three words coming from Sebastian's mouth. Unless it was my mother telling me that she had made a grave mistake, and I no longer had to marry Reginald Fortescue the Third.

I pulled back to look at Sebastian, raising my hands to his face. Under my palms, the prickle of his regrowth scratched at my skin. My shivers waned. I became acutely aware of the press of my breasts against his chest and the rigid protrusion now tucked between my thighs. Gently squeezing my legs together, I tilted my head and found his lips with mine.

I love you. More than anything in this world.

He folded me into the cocoon of his strong arms. Where our mouths touched, a delicious sensation spread. Then Sebastian's lips parted mine. Shocked, I broke the kiss to peer in his eyes. He watched me with a lascivious stare before leaning down to take my mouth once more. I opened, hesitantly at first, but when his tongue caressed mine he had me begging for more. He took me to a place where impossibilities became reality.

I had imagined this moment ever since I'd watched him take Admiral for a swim. At the age of thirteen, he had awoken a need in me of which I had no comprehension until Marybeth and Uncle Tobias had enlightened me.

And in all honesty, three years ago, I had not been ready for it. I still was not completely certain. But if this was the only chance I would have to explore the physicality of my love for him, I would take it.

Lowering until he was pressed against the juncture of my thighs, I hooked my arms around his neck and planted a kiss to his breastbone.

His ribcage surged and he moved his hands until they gripped my hips, holding me still. "What are we doing, Emmeline?"

Bending one leg, I curled it around his waist. My pulse quickened, suddenly completely unsure if he would accept my offering. Again, I planted a kiss to his chest, waiting for his approval.

"Why?" he questioned.

Rejection gripped me by the throat. I let my leg slip, but he pulled it back up, bringing the other side around to settle me in place. His hard length caressed my folds.

"Why did you race off on Miss Modesty? And why did you come so far?"

He pushed my hips back and forth, slick flesh dragging against slick flesh. My centre tightened in response while my head fell back. Sebastian dragged his lips down my neck.

"Why?" He spoke against my breast.

"Why are you talking?" I cupped my hands around his ears to bring him closer.

He laughed, kissing my nipple. "I fear that you raced off because you were out of sorts. I worry that you have not yet recovered and perhaps might be trying to distract yourself with me."

"It is true that you are a distraction. However, I find that in this moment I have extraordinary focus and it is entirely on every place where your body touches mine. Nevertheless, I do wish you would employ your mouth in a more productive pursuit than conversation."

"As you wish." His tongue circled my nipple before he enclosed it with his lips and sucked.

"Ah," I cried.

He repeated the move on the other side. I instinctively dug my heels into his buttocks; the friction between us was delightfully addictive. I didn't stop. Each drag seemed to cause my belly to clench. My legs, my buttocks, my body followed suit.

"Are you certain you want to give me this honour?" His gaze probed somewhere deeper than the surface.

"Yes."

Reaching between us, he positioned the tip of his penis at my opening. As he pushed forward, he covered my mouth with his. He used gentle thrusts at first, stretching me slowly. I tried not to tense against the pressure. It hurt for only a few seconds before the pleasure started to build. The river flowed around us, adding even more sensation and gifting us with buoyancy to ease the strain on our muscles. It gave me the feeling that I was floating higher and higher and higher until I might disappear into the clouds.

Quite suddenly, a great wave of ecstasy crashed over my body. I could not refrain from crying out in repeated whimpers until the tide finally ebbed.

"Oh, goodness." I struggled to catch my breath.

"That was incredible." His eyes roamed my face, awestruck. "I've heard the men talking about it late at night. Now I have seen what it looks like and it is truly beautiful. You are beautiful."

"Did you feel the same?"

He shook his head, smiling.

My face fell. "Did I do something wrong?"

"No, Emmeline."

"Then why?"

"I think I need to get out of this cold water."

"Oh." I started to unwrap myself, but he held me still, shaking his head.

His legs moved us to the shore, hands cupped around my behind as he lifted us out of the water. Once we reached the grass, he kneeled. Finding his shirt, he placed it over my shoulders to ward off the chill of the breeze on my damp skin. We remained connected as he rested on his knees with me straddling him, holding him in an embrace.

He put his lips to my ear and whispered, "Ride."

My body flared to life again. I knew how to ride. Planting my feet flat on the ground, I gripped the nape of his neck in both hands and let my thighs do the work.

He said *I* was beautiful.

He was utterly resplendent.

How could I ever have imagined leaving him?

Now that I had unlocked the gates to pleasure beyond anything I had dreamed, I found the idea of shutting them again inconceivable. His hands roamed my skin, his lips following the trail. I shivered at the tingles he evoked. Our gazes held each other, silently communicating the love building between us.

Beneath me, he stiffened. He dug his fingers into my hips and yanked me up until I stood.

What is he doing?

His eyes squeezed so tightly. Teeth bared, jaw clenched, he groaned before bowing his head. Spasms wracked his body, a creamy substance spurting from his penis.

Oh. How fascinating.

His fingers flexed on my buttocks before loosening and slipping to the backs of my thighs, his arms relaxing. Air rushed in and out of his lungs and across my legs. My fingers dove into his hair as he rested his head on my thighs.

Raising his head, he blinked several times, his pupils two large pools of ink. He craned his neck to place a kiss at the juncture of my thighs. Pulling back, he licked his lips as he looked at me. Hunger overtook his gaze and he lowered his attention to my centre once again. "I have heard the men speak of something else. Would you mind ... if I tasted you?" Sliding one hand around to the front, he swiped his thumb over my most sensitive parts. I jerked, sucking in a breath.

Could I allow him to do such a forbidden thing?

Yes. Yes, I absolutely could. I nodded once, watching intently as his eyes lit up. I swayed on my feet. "However, I do have but one request."

Uncertainty dampened his delight. "Anything you wish."

"May I lie down? I am feeling rather weak all of a sudden."

His arms scooped me into his embrace and reclined me until his face pressed between my breasts. Placing a kiss to each side, he carefully lowered my shoulders and head onto the green carpet of grass. My legs wrapped around his waist, back resting on his thighs. His palms caressed from my neck, over my breasts, down, down, down, until his thumbs parted my flesh, opening me to his gaze. He rubbed the pad over my swollen parts.

My mouth levered wide as he grabbed handfuls of my buttocks, lifting me to his mouth before licking through my folds. "Oh, that is—" I could not finish my sentence.

My head thrashed from side to side as he became more vigorous in his pursuit. I closed my eyes. All I could do was feel the throbbing through my body, warming me to a simmer. The pulsations came in quick succession, growing and growing until my centre sent shockwaves to consume me whole. I jerked and clenched, babbling cries rendering me incomprehensible.

Flopping my limbs to the sides, I was unable to move.

He blew his hot breath over my folds before bestowing one last kiss. "I could do that forever. Could we stay like this?"

You have no idea how much I wish for that to be the case.

Miss Modesty whinnied somewhere off in the distance. *The horses!*

"Gah! I failed to secure the horses." He scooted out from under me and jumped to his feet.

"I shall assist."

We ran off, following the equine sounds. They had not roamed far, both enjoying the longer grass that grew near the tree-line. Sebastian took Admiral Caine's reins first before leading him over to the mare. We walked them back to the river and tethered them to a tree.

"I think I shall go for another dip."

"Brilliant idea."

I waded in to my thighs, bracing myself against the cold before dipping under the surface. Sebastian ran into the water and dove under. We stayed long enough to wash down before finding our way back to the grass.

Lying on my back, I hummed, enjoying the feeling of complete bliss and satisfaction. The way the sun kissed my skin. The breeze washing over my nakedness. His body covering mine.

"I have a confession to make," he mumbled into my neck. "I took care of myself by hand after I caught a flash of you through the windows this morning. I have been unable to stop thinking about making love with you since the day you asked me to uncover myself, and gifted me with a glimpse of you. When I saw you charging off on Miss Modesty, I waited a little while before I followed, questioning whether it was the right thing to do. I sensed that you needed space. I also hoped that you might need me. Not in this way, but simply as a comfort."

Yes, Sebastian. I always need you.

"I remember telling you I wanted to touch it that day."

"You were so surprising."

"May I touch it now?" I tiptoed my fingers down his back and pinched his behind.

"Ow." He laughed, rolling to my left before resting flat.

I propped myself up on my elbow and reached out my hand to stroke his length. "Your skin feels soft, like velvet." I circled my fingers around his penis. "It grows rigid when you are aroused."

"It was quite happy and relaxed until you started to play."

Dragging my fingernails through the surrounding curls, I moved my hand between his legs to cup the sack that hung beneath. He bent his left knee. The stroke of his gaze on my face, an encouragement.

"I love your curiosity."

"I love you." *I said it. For the first time. Out loud.*

He surged upwards, clamping his mouth onto mine. I placed my hands on his chest to steady myself against his enthusiasm. He kissed me like he wished to merge us together as one. It had the potential to be overwhelming, but in my heart it expressed the ultimate freedom. There was nothing I would not give him. Nothing I would not do.

My hand found its way to his arousal. "I want to kiss it."

He cleared his throat, mouth opening and closing but expelling no reply.

Sitting, I placed my hand on his thigh and took him in my other palm. Lowering my head and raising him to my lips, I placed a kiss on the end. Under my elbow, his stomach tightened. His clenched fist came to rest on his left hip.

"Do you think it feels the same for you as it does for me?" I held him against my mouth as I spoke and he shuddered.

"I ha-ve no idea."

"I think it is similar, but nevertheless different. We are built differently, after all."

Indeed. I tightened my grip with a gentle pressure, unsure quite what to do next. Should I use my tongue, as he had? Why not try? I ran it from the tip to the base, taking in his taste. He blew out a breath as his hand relaxed and clenched. Retracing my path, I stopped to place another kiss on the end. His hand enclosed mine, showing me how to work up and down his shaft.

"Emmeline. Would you ..." His other hand caressed the back of my head. "Would you kiss it again. Please." He kept his hand over mine until I secured a rhythm.

I bit my lip, nodding before lowering my mouth to him. I kissed and licked. He pushed gently on my head to encourage me further. I opened my mouth, taking him inside.

His hands disappeared and I heard them slap on the ground. "Holy Mary, mother of Jesus. Do not stop."

I did not. Not until he pushed me away, curling forward as ecstasy gripped him in its hold. The evidence of his release covered his belly and legs. Before he could discourage me, I dipped my finger into a drop and touched it to my tongue. He tasted salty, and earthy.

His ribcage surged, eyelids peeled as he witnessed my taste test.

"I swear you will be the death of me." He barked a laugh before flopping onto his back.

The declaration hit me in the chest. I closed my eyes, captured by something that did not want to release me until it had delivered its message. A vision of a woman giving birth entered my head. The man holding her hand had short dark hair and blue eyes. He wore a simple shirt without buttons and a ring on his finger. They were in a strange setting with contraptions I had never seen beside the bed. I was drawn to the pair. Like I knew who they were at their core. Unlike that of a friendship, it ran much deeper.

I witnessed a gush of blood coming from between her legs before Sebastian broke the spell. "We must be getting back."

I opened my eyes, drawing in a lungful of air. *What was that?* I found myself clutching my belly as though it had been me in the throes of labour. *Calm yourself. It was just a passing thought. An unwanted one, at that.*

Raising my face to the sky, I took in the shapes created by the wispy clouds above. I wanted to stay here—with Sebastian. The fate that lay ahead for me was too wretched to bear.

Reluctantly, I gathered my chemise and drawers and began to dress. We had a little time together before the earl's arrival. I would focus on that. And when the dreaded moment was upon us, I would leave. With or without Sebastian. "Would you mind?" I hooked the corset over my arms and held out the cord.

He took it, moving behind me. "I completely forgot. Marybeth came looking for you."

My head snapped to the side, fixing him in my peripheral vision. "Has something happened?" Dread sank into my veins. Had she and Tobias been discovered? Had she let loose her tongue in an act of betrayal against me?

"She said your mother wished to check on you. She managed to divert her, but for how long, she was not certain."

No doubt Mother would be showering me with more attention now that she had a vested interest in marrying me off. I was curious to know if there had been an exchange of money, or perhaps property in their endeavours. Did my father have an association with the East Indian Trading Company? I had heard him speak of them in passing as he'd read the newspaper. Was that how my fate had come to cross with Reginald Fortescue's?

My mother and father had no business deciding my future. What an archaic idea it was. I was entirely capable of planning a life of my own choosing.

I would simply have to engineer it so that I never had to see the earl's face. For to do so, would surely be the makings of a nightmare.

Chapter
14

Ben

Rockhampton, Australia
6th of December, 2008

Stewart showed me through to his bedroom at his mum's place. He'd decided to move all his stuff to his dad's house. He didn't want to split his life between two homes anymore and today was the day. I couldn't blame him. I guessed that was one good thing about having a dead-shit father—I'd never had to do the switch.

His room looked like a laundromat, a sports locker, and a takeaway all threw up in there. It smelled of stale socks and week-old burger. Stewart let one rip, cocking his leg for theatrical effect. Or maybe spreading his cheeks helped the gas escape.

I added methane to the list of odours I could smell, curling my lip. "Could you not have done that outside? Or at least given me a warning?"

"You're in my space now; enter at your own risk."

I waved a hand in front of my face, but it made it worse. "Do you want me to help you or not? If you keep gassing me out, I'm gone."

"I'll warn you next time." He turned the fan on. "I can't hold it in or I'll explode."

How had this guy managed to get any women?

I searched for packing boxes. All I saw was a messy bedroom. Nothing was put away, or packed up. "What are we moving?"

"Everything but the furniture and the curtains."

"You haven't packed?"

"Nuh."

"Why not? How are we supposed to move all your shit if it's spread everywhere?"

"I thought you were gonna help me pack."

"I said I'd help you move. You've gotta meet me halfway, mate."

"I packed one box." He pointed to a cardboard carton shoved in the corner next to his bed.

A shiny, gold trophy poked out the top. "You packed your trophies?"

"Chick magnets. The most important things go first."

Right. I bet the next things he'd packed were condoms, his thongs, and maybe a stubby cooler.

"I've got the boxes under the bed." Getting on his knees, he dove under the mattress to retrieve a stack of flattened cardboard cartons.

Right. Well, that was a start. "Got a Sharpie?"

"What for?"

"To write on the boxes so you know what's in them. Haven't you done this before?"

"Not on my own. That's why you're here."

"Please tell me you've got tape."

"Uh ..."

For fuck's sake. I turned tail and went looking for a sensible person who would know where to find what we needed. Any other member of this household would've fit that description, but there was one in particular who I wanted to see.

Her room was across the hall so I didn't have to go far. I rapped my knuckles on the wood.

"Come in," she called out.

Stretched out on the bed with a book in her hand and the stereo playing in the background, she stole my breath. "Hi." She sat up, crossing her legs, yoga style.

There was a lot of leg showing. A lot of smooth, pale skin exposed by loose cotton shorts. And when she crossed her legs like that, I got a peek at pale pink knickers.

I emptied my lungs and thought of her brother. It was the quickest way to deflate my rising erection. "Hi. Can I ask you something?"

"Mm-hmm."

"Why is your brother so clueless?"

She snorted. "Because he's had women running around after him his whole life. If we hadn't done anything to compensate for his lack of initiative, he might actually be a capable human being."

"I doubt it."

"Oh, me too."

"We need some packing tape and a permanent marker. You wouldn't happen to know where we could find those, would you?"

"Yes. Follow me." She jumped up, pulling her shorts down at the back before padding off through the house.

She could pull the fabric down all she liked; they'd never cover much more than just below the crease of her cheek. If she bent over, I'd be able to spy the fleshy part of her bum. *Damn.* My mouth watered, thinking of what it would be like to bend her over. The sway of her hips put me in a trance until we reached the kitchen and she looked over her shoulder. I snapped out of it, raising my eyes and catching her amused grin.

"The junk drawer." She pulled it open. "It's like a treasure trove. I found scissors in here when I was a kid and gave myself a God-awful haircut. They took all the sharp things out after that, but we should be able to find tape and a marker."

"Did they take photos?"

"Yep. And I found them when I was twelve and tore them up. I never did find the negatives though."

I bet she was still cute.

I stepped up behind her, reaching over her shoulder to retrieve a roll of tape. Her body would fit mine just right. I could tuck her under my chin and cocoon her in my arms. Being this close had my body humming and my mind singularly focused on her.

Andy leaned into me, closing the small space between us with a sigh. Grabbing a thick, black marker, she read the label, "Whiteboard marker," before tossing it back. After a minute of rifling through the assortment, she found what she wanted. "Here ya go. Anything else you need?" Her question hitched a ride on thin breath.

I dropped a kiss in her hair and hooked an arm around her waist. "Time alone with you."

"When?" she whispered, eyeing me over her shoulder.

"Tonight?"

"Yes."

My hand retreated, sliding across her belly to grip her hip. "I'll pick you up at six." I imagined my fingers roaming to the hem of her shorts, but it was too soon for that. We'd only just started dating. But damn, in my brain I'd had her in ten different ways already. I needed her to know it wasn't just a physical attraction for me. This was so much more.

"Okay." She did a little hop on the balls of her feet, her face beaming.

"Okay." I spun the roll of tape on my finger, my lip quirked. "Have you got a gas mask hiding somewhere? I could use one of those, too."

"Sorry, no."

"Damn. I'll just have to hold my breath." Reluctantly, I stepped away, giving her room to move. "I gotta go help trumpet bum, but I'll see you later."

"Yep."

I winked and took the items back to Stewart's room. He'd piled his clothes onto the bed and was rummaging around in his cupboard for something.

"Looking for a suitcase?"

"A suitcase. Good idea. Why didn't I think of that?"

"Because it's a *good* idea." I raised my brows, flaring my eyes. "I got tape and a marker pen." I put the items on his tallboy and grabbed one of the flattened boxes. After folding it into its 3D shape, I ripped off a bit of tape and stuck the bottom together.

"Found it." He pulled out a bong from the back of the top shelf. "This is going in with the trophies."

I forgot about the bong. Condoms, thongs, stubbie cooler, trophies—AKA chick magnets—and a bong. "What about your stick mag collection? Found that yet?"

"I've got them stashed in my car, all ready to go."

"Are the bull's balls in with your trophies?"

He scoffed. "Of course." Yanking a suitcase from the bottom shelf, he unzipped it and started tossing in his clothes.

My eye twitched at his idea of packing. I turned away and went to clear off his desk.

"I heard you took my sister to a movie." He threw a pair of shorts at me.

Here we go. "Yeah." I chucked them back.

"What the hell took you so long? You've been making eyes at each other for years."

"I didn't realise you'd noticed."

"Mate, we all noticed."

Is that right? I hadn't noticed—how had they? "And you're okay with it?"

"I never want to hear the details of your sex life." He shook his head, cringing. "You never dished any details on Kelly anyway, so no loss there. If I hear you spilling private info on my sister to anyone else, I will thump you."

I would thump myself. "Can we talk about something else?"

"I'm serious, mate. Don't fuck her over."

"Stewart, I respect her too much to play her like that. I don't do games. You know I don't. Maybe you should thump yourself because the way you treat women is like you've forgotten that they're somebody's daughter or sister. Think about that, huh?"

He looked stunned. His throat jumped as he swallowed. "Don't screw with my head like that."

"You need to pull your head in."

He groaned. "Always with the lectures. I would've asked Lee to help me, but he's too busy being pussy-whipped."

I couldn't argue with that. Larissa had him on a leash. "He has his own shit to deal with. Are we done with the big brother talk now?"

"Yeah, we're done."

"Good."

"Thanks for helping me today."

"You're welcome."

One good thing about Stewart was—he didn't dwell. If he had an issue with you, he aired it and then it was done. And he loved his sister, despite all the insults he plied her with. That alone made him okay in my book.

———

We took two hours to pack and did a couple of trips back and forth before he was finally all moved in at his dad's. Almost all moved in. After his earlier trumpeting, he'd forgotten the box of trophies stashed in the corner. I offered to get it. Any excuse for another glimpse at his sister.

I knocked on the door and Stewart's mum answered. "You're early."

"Early?"

"For your date." Her eyes dropped to my sweaty shirt and baggy shorts.

"Um, no. Stewart forgot a box."

"I'm not surprised. Come on in."

"Thanks, Mrs Furnville." I stepped over the threshold.

"Call me Mary."

I didn't think I could. I'd been calling her Mrs Furnville for years. "Okay."

Walking to Stewart's room, I went in search of the 'chick magnets'. I found the box. The fucking bong sat on top. How was I going to walk out of here with that in full view? The box didn't have a lid.

After shooting across the hallway, I tapped on Andy's door. "Andy."

I caught sight of her head wrapped in a towel through the narrow crack as she answered my knock. "You're early."

"No, I came to get the last box, but I have a problem."

The barrier swung open as she let me in before shutting it again. I spun to face her and froze. She was fresh out of the shower, standing in her underwear. My jaw dropped. *Holy fuck.*

"What? You've seen me in my togs. This is basically the same."

"It's not even close. And I haven't seen you in togs for over two years. You look a lot different now."

"Not that much."

A fuck-load, actually. Her tits were even bigger than I'd thought. My cock sprang to attention. There was no stopping it. "Could you get dressed?" My pulse punched out a backbeat to our exchange.

"Am I making you uncomfortable?" She sounded like she'd just downed a shot of whiskey.

"I think that's pretty obvious." I dropped my eyes to my tented shorts before peering at her through my lashes.

Her gaze fixed on my crotch as she bit the corner of her lip. Arms, once hanging loose, were now reaching for me.

I hopped back. "What are you doing?"

She snapped them back, folding them across her middle. "I—sorry." Her wounded expression had me wanting to punch myself.

"What were you going to do?"

"I wasn't thinking. Sorry." Her arms tightened as she turned her head away.

I reached for her, unfolding her limbs. Opening her defences. "What were you going to do," I said again softly. "Were you going to touch ... me?"

"Yes."

My cock got painfully hard and I groaned. I pulled her hands up and placed them flat on my stomach. "Do what you want, babe. But only if you're doing it for you. I'm yours."

She blinked at me, sucking in that plump bottom lip before lowering her eyes. Her fingers flexed on the spot, not moving just yet. I could almost see the dirty thoughts flooding her mind. I bet her knickers were wet. Her chest heaved as she balanced on the edge of good girl versus naughty girl. I'd take both versions. Whichever side she chose, she needed to be kissed.

I bowed my head, hovering my lips over hers, waiting for her silent consent. She angled her head and captured my mouth with hers. Her minty breath mixed with mine. Her kiss lit a network of fuses throughout my body, tiny bonfires flaming to life. I fought to keep my fists clenched by my sides. I wasn't going to push her too far. She hadn't asked me to paw her. She wanted to paw me. But I had to keep control. I hadn't forgotten that her mother was just down the hallway, expecting me to leave any second. And Andy and I were still new. Maybe this was too much too soon.

Her palms moved south and I jolted at the contact. Dragging in some air through my nose, I parted my mouth, my tongue searching for hers. She eagerly welcomed me in, tangling her flesh with mine. Leaning forward, she aligned our bodies, her hands wrapping around my wrists and pulling my arms behind her. With a surge, I lifted her off her toes, holding her flush against me. My arousal pressed into the juncture between her thighs. I hadn't intended it, but once I was there, she pushed against me in what I understood was a silent request for more. Our kiss went deeper than I'd known kisses could go. With Andy it was different. Because she meant more to me than any other girl. I couldn't think about the reason behind that just yet. I could barely think at all. She'd turned me into a slave to my senses.

Andy broke the kiss, chest surging as she seemingly fought for breath. I let her feet slide to the floor while I tried to calm my hyped system. Undoing me further, she ran her fingers along my hard bulge. "It's harder than I thought it would be."

I laughed and it jerked under her touch. "He's not fully there yet. I'm kinda restricted here." She looked at me with a glint in her eye. "No, I'm not taking him out. Jesus, Andy. I came in here to borrow a towel. What are you doing to me?"

She untwisted the towel from her hair, the wet strands falling down around her slim shoulders. "Here."

Christ, she could've been a commercial for soft drink. The ones where the chick walks out of the water and holds the cold can against her chest to cool herself before quenching her thirst.

Think about Stewart and his bong.

Think about killer bees.

Think about politics and corruption.

"Thanks."

She smiled at me and everything else wiped from my brain.

Fuck. "I gotta go. I've got a hot date to prepare for."

"Oh? Who is she?"

"She's the best person I know." It was the truth.

Her eyes went soft and the hollow at the base of her throat deepened as she held her breath.

"I'll see you soon." I pecked her on the lips and dragged myself away. It was the last thing I wanted to do, but knowing I'd be spending time with her tonight made it easier.

Did I deserve her at all? She was the perfect girl.

And I was far from being able to match that.

Chapter
15

Emmeline

Hampshire, England
12th July, 1867

The window seat in the library was my favourite place to sit. The view captured the grounds of my father's estate, spreading out for miles. A colourfully decorated canvas of nature's doing providing endless wonderment for my soul. Additionally, the window framed the stables where I could see Sebastian at work with the horses during the day. All the more reason to burrow in to the soft cushions and pretend to read one of the prescribed books on etiquette for girls of my age. Should Father discover that I had successfully procured a copy of *Adam Bede* by George Eliot, I would surely be banned from reading altogether.

Just this morning, he'd proclaimed the women's suffrage movement as "the end to rationalism in society." A mild use of terms given the female presence in the room. His language would certainly have been far more severe and descriptive in the company of his male counterparts.

Mother had continued to sip her tea between savouring bites of dry toast and peaches. I had foolishly hoped my mother had sequestered the petition with the intention of signing it before Father saw fit to destroy it. But of course, what hope was there that she believed women had an equal right to the vote? My mother found no fault with the idea of marrying her only daughter off to a man known to beat women.

I had heard talk of Reginald Fortescue the Third following the Sunday sermon. Word of our upcoming nuptials had spread. The Welsh earl was quite infamous in the area. Apparently he had been trialling the fruits of many women with great hubris prior to his departure to India. He was due to return within the week, according to a telegram we had received from Lady Victoria. The staff were preparing for his visit as I sat here with my nose pressed against the glass, counting down to the end of my life as I knew it.

Sebastian entered the pen where Miss Modesty lay resting. Her tryst with Admiral Caine almost a year ago had indeed resulted in a pregnancy. She was due to foal at any moment. I had observed her taking more rest periods than was customary in recent days. My wish was to be present for the birth. My worry was that the earl would arrive before the foal and I would have to leave without witnessing the miracle. It would break my heart just that little bit more.

This man that I had never met would take away everything that I knew and loved. I hated him with a passion that equalled the level to which I loved Sebastian. They both consumed me whole. One with fire, one with ice. Either way there would be nothing of me left. But with Sebastian, I was reborn from the ashes. With the earl, I would be frozen—a memory easily forgotten as time left me behind.

There was only one thing to do. Closing my book, I took one last look at my love before dashing to the armoire. If I didn't hurry, I would lose my bravado, for the plan I had formulated was as good as an axe to the heart.

I recovered a satchel and tossed it upon the bed. Ignoring the silk and taffeta hanging from the rail, I searched the shelves for a more sensible offering. Drawers were essential. As was a chemise. I threw two of each over my shoulder, unaware as to their landing place. If need be, I would retrieve them from the floor in due time. The only other items of any use were my nightgowns, a pair of boots, and stockings. What the devil should a female pack when planning to escape on horseback? Certainly not the cumbersome gowns, as was the fashion. I moaned in despair, slapping my palms on my skirts. 'Twas hopeless.

My mind drew on memories of visiting the scullery. "Hope restored." My lips tilted in a sly smile.

I hid my book under the mattress and shoved the clothes in the bag, making sure to stash it behind the dresser before making my way downstairs.

"Morning, miss." The butler dipped his chin in greeting.

"Morning."

I slowed my pace until he had disappeared from sight before resuming my chase. The maids would have done the washing and pegged it out to dry. My timing could not have been more perfect.

Casually, I skirted through the utility areas, greeting the staff as I went. I received some curious looks. I supposed it had been a while since I had graced them with my presence. Not through my own discretion. The bowels of the house were more a home to me than the grandiose upper levels. Thanks to my adventures as a young girl, I could map these rooms by memory.

I exited the scullery and went directly to the line. My heart leapt at what I found. Everything I could need was there for the taking. It was as if I had planned it. Or at least received a helping hand from those unaware of my scheme.

Heart pounding, I checked my surroundings for witnesses, finding none. After retrieving a couple of shirts and buckskins, I made quick work of tying my petticoats into a pouch of sorts and securing the items undercover.

I straightened and clasped my hands in front before strolling my way to the courtyard. Eyes darting around for any threat of discovery, I refrained from wiping the sweat trailing down my neck as I made my retreat. This time, I used an alternate entrance before travelling to my quarters.

I closed myself in, leaning against the door as I took in a deep breath. "I did it."

I could have smiled, but my small victory was superseded by the tragedy of it all. I should not have had to perform that mission at all.

After adding my acquisitions to the satchel, I stuffed it back in its hiding spot before returning to the window seat. Sebastian wheeled a cart stacked with straw on a path to the stables.

"All I ask for is one more chance to show him the magnitude of my love before I go." I sent the prayer, hoping it would be fulfilled.

Wishing I could ask for forever.

'Twas not to be.

I would take the bag with me when attending the foaling.

And then I would leave.

———

Ben

Brisbane, Australia
26th of December, 2016, 7:22 p.m.

He was so perfect. How could something so tiny and so perfect be the cause of so much agony?

How could the most beautiful moment of my life also be the most tragic?

Why?

I fitted the tip of my finger into Seb's little palm and bowed my head, squeezing my eyes shut as hard as I could. Was I trying to keep the memory of my wife's death out, or was I trying to keep the picture of my newborn son at the forefront of my brain? I couldn't separate the two.

The tug of war between joy and pain, wonder and denial—it pulled apart my insides. A giant fissure dividing me into mourner and father. Pressing a kiss to the top of his soft, fuzzy head, I leashed my grief. He needed me to show him love. To prove to him I could be strong for him.

He smells divine. Andrea would love his smell.

They'd revived her. Three times.

She was upstairs, plugged into God knew how many machines, pumps, and bags of fluid draining life back into her veins. It all seemed a hopeless waste to me. My wife was no longer in that body. I couldn't *feel* her. And still, I couldn't let her go. How long would it be until they suggested I pull the plug? I'd never be capable of making that decision.

Once he was strong enough, they'd laid Seb on her chest as the machine inflated and deflated her lungs in a calculated sequence. His little body had squirmed with life while hers only moved under artificial instruction.

It had broken my heart.

I'd had to bring him back down to the nursery, leaving half the fleshy beating organ in my chest behind. The last thing I'd wanted to do was leave her side, but Seb needed a parent.

I needed her to stitch me together again.

This was all my fault and I couldn't fix it. Couldn't fix her.

Seb made a little squeaky noise as he stretched his arm and flopped his head to the other side. The remaining half of my heart hiccupped.

"Ben."

I lifted my head. "Mum." My mouth shaped the name without any sound.

Her knuckles strained where she gripped the straps of her handbag. Her pained gaze dropped to the bundle I held against my chest, shoulders rising as she took in a breath. She stepped into the room, nodding to the nurse who sat at the desk in the corner.

The only other occupant was a tiny baby with a shock of black hair. There were several empty cradles pushed together in the space to the rear. They had little use for this room now that babies stayed with their mothers. The only reason a baby would be in here was if the mother needed a break for a little while. Or if she was unable to care for the baby.

I couldn't get my head around the fact that I'd soon be bringing Seb home without Andy.

After pulling a chair over, Mum took a seat across from me and placed her palms on my knees. "How is she doing?"

I shook my head, unable to speak through the firm clamp my emotions formed around my throat.

She reached out and gently touched Seb's head. "He's beautiful."

I nodded, pressing my lips shut.

Cradling him in my palms, I leaned forward and passed him to her. She took him against her chest, tears forming in her eyes. "He looks just like his daddy."

I tapped a finger near my eye and shook my head. He had his mother's eyes. I needed to point that out. Needed to include Andy in the equation. Seb had as much of her in him as he did me. She wasn't gone yet. I had to believe she was still fighting.

I stood, motioning a drinking action with my hand before going to the bubbler in the hallway. Maybe if I forced a cup of water down my throat it might open. I might be able to fill my lungs to capacity for the first time since Andy's waters had broken.

I held the plastic in my hand, staring at the bubbles rising in the dispenser of water. It looked about the same size as her stomach had been. All that fluid had come gushing out. Had I caused any damage, giving her all those orgasms?

My hand crushed the cup, spilling the drink over the sides. "Shit."

Hmph. Got my voice back. I chugged the rest of the liquid and threw out the cup before going into the nursery to find paper towels.

After cleaning up, I took my seat next to Mum. "Thanks for coming."

She smiled, resting her cheek on Seb's head. "Do they know what happened?"

"Placental ab-something. The placenta was detaching from the wall of the uterus. There was so much blood." I leaned forward on my knees, holding the weight of my head in my hands. "They think some of the amniotic fluid got into her bloodstream causing a bad reaction." I dropped my arms and faced my mother. "They did a hysterectomy."

She gasped, causing the baby to stir. "Shh, sh, sh. It's okay, bubba. Nanna's here." The rhythmic sound of her hand patting his nappy mimicked the ticking of a clock.

Were we counting down my wife's final hours or were we adding up the minutes of my son's life?

Push, pull. Give, take.

"Have they said anything more?"

"She's going to be on life support for a little while. Her oxygen levels dropped and she lost a lot of blood. We don't know what damage was done yet."

"Oh, God."

Yeah. Oh, God.

Where the fuck was he when we needed him?

Chapter
16

Andrea

Rockhampton, Australia
16th of May, 2009

I pulled out my new lingerie. I'd bought the bra and knickers set with the money I'd earned helping Peter at his office over the Christmas holidays. It was pink. It was see-through organza with lace decals placed in strategic positions. It would drive Ben wild. If he would let me show him. Six months we'd been dating and his hands hadn't ventured underneath my clothes once.

They'd explored outside. Many times. His stoicism was not a virtue. Jesus, I was ready to rip his clothes off every time he walked in to my room. Tonight,

I wanted to be ready. Just in case. I didn't want to expect anything, but my God, I was horny.

I slipped the straps up my arms and leaned forward to jiggle my girls into place. Stepping into the G-string, I smoothed the elastic over my hips. If I looked in the mirror, I might lose my nerve. The reflection might speak of a girl on the verge of seventeen rather than a woman needing to be loved by her man. I'd been through enough that I'd grown beyond my years. I needed him. I wanted him. And if it should happen, it would be the final passage into womanhood.

I put on my comfy shorts and a tank top. He had a thing for the shorts. He could never stop staring at my legs when I wore them. Looking at the box on my bed, I smiled. The final weapon in my arsenal. His celibacy and my virginity were toast. Ah. Expectations were such a bitch. Or maybe it was hormones.

I trotted to the kitchen where I enlisted Bree's help to make dinner.

"Should we save some for Ben?" She took the cutlery from the drawer.

"He didn't say he wasn't coming. He would've told me if that was the case." I served the steaming lasagne onto our plates and put the leftovers back in the oven to keep warm.

We ate it in front of the TV, watching some reality garbage. My leg jiggled as I checked the time. Seven-thirty. *He's usually here by now.* I'd hoped tonight would be pivotal for me. Maybe he'd forgotten to let me know he was busy? Doubt tried to sneak in to dim my shine. I glanced at the front door too many times to count.

Relax.

He's coming.

"Yes!" *Thank you for the confirmation.*

"Huh?" Bree turned to me, confusion evident in the bunch of her brow.

I needed to learn to keep my thoughts to myself. "Time to clean up. Come and help me?"

"You're way too excited about the dishes."

So excited. "Life's short. You've gotta find the joy in everything."

I hit the volume on the remote control and shook my butt to Flo Rider. Gloved hands dipping into the suds, I scrubbed another pot while Bree dried the dishes.

"Is Ben still coming over?" She shook out the tea towel.

We both turned at the knock on the door. I flashed my teeth, took off the gloves, and ran to let him in.

"Hey. Sorry I'm late. Adam and I were having some bro time." His scent hit me—that mix of sawdust and soap that had me melting on the inside.

His eyes wandered over my body before he leaned in for a kiss. "Are you having a party?"

"Girls' night in."

"Oh, where's Peter?"

"Mum and Peter are in Hervey Bay, having a dirty weekend."

He made a noise in his throat, smirking. "I'm sure that's exactly how they described it."

"I know how to read between the lines."

"So it's just you and Bree?"

"Not anymore. You're here."

"Should I go?" he joked.

I grabbed his arm and dragged him into the kitchen. "Don't be silly. We've been expecting you."

"Hi, Ben," Bree chirped, putting a plate away.

"Hello. Did I miss dinner?"

"We saved some for you." She opened the oven. "It's lasagne."

"My favourite."

I know. If only I was old enough to buy beer.

He ate with a smile on his face while we finished doing the dishes. Bree used the whisk as a microphone while I drummed a bit of Black Eyed Peas against the bottom of a pot.

"Hey, Bree, can you go and get the box off my bed, please?"

"Yep."

She scooted off as I took a seat in Ben's lap. "How was your day, dear?"

His hands came around my back. "Superb. How was yours?"

"Wonderful." I placed one arm around his shoulders and the other on his chest, slipping my fingers under his collar.

"Is Stewart going to come over and check on you?"

"What for? We're capable of looking after ourselves."

"I know. But if you were my sisters, I'd be here."

And that was one of the things I loved about him—his protective instinct. "You're here now."

"I won't want to leave tonight."

I fell into his crystal blue stare. "So don't."

"What about Bree?"

"She sleeps like a log."

He opened his mouth to reply, but I cut him off by laying one on him. His fingers gripped me tighter as he tilted his head and leaned into the kiss.

"Here—" She stopped as she caught sight of us. "Are you guys gonna be like this all night? Because I don't want any lifelong scars.

I hopped up and held my hands out for the box. "Thanks. Are you ready to play?"

"Can I spin the wheel?"

Perfect. "Yep. Let's see how flexible Ben is." I twisted my head and gave him a wicked smile.

"Is that Twister?"

"Yes indeedy."

"I haven't played that since I was eight." I couldn't tell if he was looking at it with amusement or distaste. His mouth was twisted to the side, eyes unsure.

My smile dropped. *Oh, God.* I'd let my teaching aspirations bleed into my relationship. He was a man, not a child.

"Maybe you can spin the wheel and Bree and I can play?"

"No, I'll have a go." He rose to his feet.

"Okay." I opened the box and spread out the plastic sheet covered in coloured spots before handing the spinner to Bree.

"Left foot, yellow," she called out.

Ben and I stood on opposite sides of the mat, mirroring our moves and our grins.

"Left hand, red."

We both bent, me to the left, him to the right.

"Right hand, blue."

I bent forward, arms spread wide, and my left leg bent to the side. He had to cross his arms to reach his target. I took in the way his shoulders and back stretched to accommodate the move. The guy was built like a tank. I fucking loved it. His gaze targeted my cleavage. It was pretty clear by the glow in his eyes that he liked what he saw.

Several moves later, his arm was across my back, and my leg stretched between his. I hadn't thought this through. It was tempting to wriggle my butt against him, but Bree was watching. This was getting weird. His breath brushed my ear. Hair-raising tingles spread along the backs of my thighs as his jeans rubbed against me. My mind went straight to the gutter, picturing this position, but naked and without a witness. I couldn't take it. I collapsed, laughing at myself. How ridiculous. My seduction plan had backfired on me.

"Can we watch a movie now?" Bree grumbled.

"You don't want a turn?" I stood and pulled my shorts out of my bum.

She moved towards the TV. "Nah. I'm bored with it already."

I bent to grab the mat and his hand trailed up my thigh, landing on my arse cheek. I snapped upright, checking to see that Bree was concentrating on the DVD collection and not what Ben and I were doing. Music still filled the room with primal beats fit for a dance club. Angling my head, my nose pressed into his jaw as he placed his chin on my shoulder. His hand slid inside my shorts, a finger hooking into the back of my G-string. "I was wondering if you were wearing any undies at all." The words came out as a low rumble like distant thunder. A warning of an impending electrical storm.

"Now you know."

His other palm landed flat between my hip bones, holding me in place. He moved his hooked finger down, pulling my underwear away from my skin until his knuckle hit moist flesh. "You're wet. I thought so." Tugging the strip of fabric upwards, he made it rub against my sensitive opening. "Does that feel good?"

I sucked in some air through clenched teeth. *Fuck, yes.*

"Do you enjoy it when I torment you?"

I leaned against him, slipping my hand behind me to find his arousal hard. Giving him a gentle squeeze, I answered, "Yes."

"I've gotta go sit down before she sees my issue." He aimed for the big armchair at one end of the lounge, his hands working under his T-shirt to adjust his pants.

I dashed over to the stereo remote and shut off the music before grabbing the throw rug off the back of the couch. Offering it to him, he shook his head and patted his lap for me to sit. Carefully lowering myself across his thighs, I made sure to give him some room. The blanket provided cover over our laps. Bree pressed play before walking off in the direction of the kitchen.

"Are you getting drinks?" I called out.

"Yeah," she yelled back as the sound of the movie starting filled the room.

I turned to Ben "Are you still hard?" I whispered.

"Painfully."

"Undo your fly."

"I already did."

"Really?" I lifted his shirt and had a peek. Black jocks barely contained what he was packing. In fact, if I tugged on the waistband, I'd get to see. *Oh, my God. There's the head of his cock.* I raised my eyes, finding his smoking-hot stare aimed at my mouth.

Bree came back in the room and I quickly put the blanket back in place, feigning innocence. Sweat broke out along my top lip.

She placed three glasses and a bottle of lemonade on the coffee table before frowning at us. "Are you guys cold?"

Ben coughed. I half whimpered, half hummed.

"Do you want me to turn off the fan?"

"Nope," I yelped.

At the same time, Ben barked, "No."

"Okaaay." She raised her brows and twisted one corner of her mouth like she thought we'd gone cuckoo.

Turning off the light, she finally came back and lay on the couch, facing her feet away from us.

My gaze was trained on Ben as the flickering light from the screen played across his tight features. He returned my stare, the flare of his nostrils evident even in the dim room. I kissed the corner of his mouth. The poor guy. Two hours of this was going to be excruciating. I wasn't exactly comfortable myself.

I leaned forward, preparing to move seats, but his grip on my hips pulled me back. I shot him a questioning glance. He pressed his lips to my ear. "Don't move." My shoulder jerked towards my ear as his breath set off a cascade of tingles. My nipples tightened. He noticed, his hand reaching to pinch one through my tank. I bit my lip to keep from making a noise.

I was the worst babysitter in the world. *We* were the worst babysitters in the world.

His lips met my earlobe again. "Behave yourself."

I encircled his neck with my arms and placed my lips to his ear. "I can't if I'm sitting on your lap with your dick poking out of your undies."

He burst out laughing. Thank God it was perfectly timed with something funny in the movie and Bree laughed, too. On the screen, Jim Carrey made one of his rubber-faced expressions.

I hopped up before Ben could stop me, throwing the blanket back over him before going to the toilet.

When I'd finished, I filled the glasses with lemonade and handed Bree and Ben one each. Taking my own to the opposite side of the room, I settled into the spare armchair.

Ben narrowed his eyes at me over the rim. I volleyed a smirk. His brows rose. I winked. He mouthed, *"You are in big trouble."*

I certainly hoped so.

When the fuck would this movie ever finish?

———

Bree conked out about half an hour before the end of the flick. I had to shake her awake so she'd go to bed. After making sure she was settled, I shut her door and returned to the lounge room. Ben had turned the movie off and music played on low volume. I could only just hear Beyoncé singing about being single, but already my shoulders were bouncing.

"Dance for me."

"I am." I twisted my left hand back and forth near my face in Beyoncé's signature move, my other hand on my hip as I rocked from side to side. I spun around, shaking my booty in his face. He grabbed for me, but I danced out of his way, doing a lap of the coffee table.

Laughter tumbled from my mouth as I braced my hands on my hips and tried to catch a breath.

"I love watching you dance." He sat on the edge of his seat.

I smiled and shrugged as his compliment settled in my chest. "I stopped dancing a couple of years ago."

"Why?"

"After Jess died, it didn't feel right anymore." I didn't want to put a dampener on our night. But it was the truth. Partially. There was another reason. "But also, these happened." I grabbed my boobs. "They get in the way of everything."

Like a telephoto lens, he zoomed in on my rack. "I wouldn't mind them getting in my way."

"You like them a lot, don't you?"

"Stupid question." He looked down the hall. "Can we go to your room?"

"Yes." *Finally.*

In one swift move, he'd picked me up and tossed me over his shoulder. I cried out before slapping my hand over my mouth. *Shit. Stay asleep, Bree.* Luckily her bedroom was at the end of the hallway near Mum and Peter's bedroom. Mine was closer to the living area. There was a bathroom and laundry in between us.

He locked us in my room and put me on my feet.

"Those shorts drive me insane. Your boobs drive me mental. You make me crazy."

"The feeling is mutual. What are we gonna do about it?"

He lurched forward, locking his mouth to mine as big arms caught me in their embrace. He was my safe place. I couldn't have felt more secure. He was the one person I could unleash my true self upon, knowing he could take it. It was instinctual. Intrinsic. *Home.*

I slipped my hands under his shirt and into the back of his undies, rewarded with warm, smooth skin. His glutes clenched under my touch, and I pinched one in warning. Pulling up his shirt, he bent forward so I could rip it off. I didn't waste a second before my hands were spread across his chest, playing with the dusting of dark hair and the dips and valleys of his abs. God, I wanted to lick him everywhere. I did just that, starting at one nipple and travelling across to the other. He tugged at my tank, forcing me to step away so he could get rid of it. We'd already gone further than we'd ever been before.

A harsh breath rushed from his mouth as he tested the heavy weight of my breasts in his hands. "*Fuck.* You are beautiful." His words sank in to expand my heart and it responded by thumping with more veracity.

He kissed from my chin down my neck before lifting my boobs to his face and sucking wet kisses along the edge of sheer fabric. My palms caressed the bulges and striations of his back—the wide, winged trapezius muscle that made it impossible for his arms to sit flat against his sides.

I slid to the dip at his waist and the indents near his hipbones. My fingers worked the button and zipper and pushed the denim down his strong legs. There it was again. The head of his cock, poking out to say hello. My thumb found the tip, circling around. His hips jerked and a strangled noise muffled into my breasts. Without warning, my shorts landed in a pool at my feet and he retreated a step. "Turn."

My stomach clenched at his demand. I spun slowly. Large, sure palms halted my movement as they gripped the front of my thighs. Knees brushed at my ankles as he lowered himself to the floor. I didn't look behind me. I just closed my eyes and let my other senses take over. The calluses on his hands scratched against my skin, setting off sparks along my nerve endings. His stubble was rough against my backside as he kissed and bit his way along, getting to know this intimate part of me. His nose dug into one cheek as his teeth grabbed a hold of the flimsy fabric that ran along it, and he pulled it away before snapping it back in place. I jumped, laughing. *Playful Ben.* My body liked that side of him way too much, responding by soaking my G-string. I was so ready.

His hand slipped between my legs, his fingers playing along the front while his thumb probed beneath my underwear. He continued to plant kisses all over my cheeks as his free hand curled into the band of my lingerie and tugged it down my legs. The pads of his fingers played me like his guitar. I lifted one foot out of the scrap of lace and organza and widened my stance. He growled in response and bit my bum. My hips rolled as he kept swirling, rubbing, circling. I gasped for air as he consumed my body in flames. Rising to his feet without stopping, he unsnapped the clasp of my bra and pushed between my shoulders until I braced my hands on the edge of the bed, the straps acting as restraints around my wrists. Hips instinctively moving with sharp thrusts, I circled them on occasion. My nerves had me under their control and Ben was the messenger telling them what to do.

I opened my eyes, drawn to movement in my peripheral vision. The mirrored door of my wardrobe. He'd been watching us. My tits hung, brushing my elbows. His cock stood out straight as he bent over me. *Oh, my God.* His hooded blue stare was the most erotic thing I'd ever seen. He caught me looking and nipped at my shoulder as his fingers entered me. One. Two. His other hand reached around to continue playing my clit. I bowed my back, mouth wide in a soundless scream as an orgasm crashed my system.

I was still riding the crest of the wave when I heard the rustle of a wrapper before his dick slid along my opening, then forward and backwards through my slickness. "Fuck." His head lolled, as one palm urged my hips to press against him. He entered me slowly, fingers gently stroking my folds from the front. "Are you okay?"

"Yes," I whispered as my legs shook and my chest tightened in anticipation.

He inched his way in before pulling all the way out. With each slow thrust he got deeper and deeper. My orgasm was building again from his persistent playful fingers. Pressure swelled. It was more intense with him inside me. He pushed with a sharp jolt and something inside gave way. It stole my breath and my head bowed forward. He didn't retreat this time. Letting me get used to him, his fingers kept moving. I watched the flex of his hand and wrist as he drove me toward the precipice.

My hips began to circle. I writhed against him, my bum rubbing against his hips.

"Watch," he whispered, kissing behind my ear, his thumb nudging my chin towards the end of the bed.

Jesus. We were putting on our own porn show and I fucking loved it. His hands reached around to capture my tits, pinching at the nipples. They bounced every time we ground together. The muscles in Ben's neck strained as he clenched his teeth. Our action became frantic. The pulse between my legs strengthened, spreading over my whole body. Ben's hands squeezed harder as he bent his knees and pounded me from behind. I dropped to my elbows and his strokes went deeper.

"Fuck," he grunted. "Put your knees up on the bed and face the mirror."

I did as he said. He climbed behind me, pushing my knees wider with his. After grabbing my pillow, he placed it under my chest. My tits settled near my chin as I leaned on my elbows. Giving me a long kiss, he reached around and played with the soft flesh as his tongue tangled with mine.

Straightening, our reflections returned our rapt faces as he filled me again. I looked so small compared to his looming form behind me. His arms flexed as he worked my body. All I could smell was sex, sweat, and a hint of cologne. We both bit our bottom lips, the sounds of slick flesh slapping together turning me to liquid. My heart crashed around my ribcage as he reached around to press on my button. Quakes spread from my core, arresting my body into seizures of pleasure. Involuntarily, my eyes clenched shut, robbing me of the view of him falling off the cliff into pleasure. Hearing his grunts, I ordered my lids to open and caught his chin pressed towards his chest, his face screwed up in ecstasy. *Oh, wow.* He was divine. I smiled. His face relaxed and we kept our gazes on each other as our movements calmed.

He tugged me backwards to sit on him, keeping us connected, my knees resting outside of his. As he peppered the side of my face with kisses, his palms rubbed my nipples. "Are you sore?"

"A bit. But in a good way."

"Now that I've unwrapped you, I don't want to cover you up. If we lived together you'd have to walk around naked."

Ooh. I could imagine it all too well and my core clenched around him. Bending over to get the milk out of the fridge and him taking me from behind. Him sitting at the dinner table and me bouncing in his lap. Him coming home from work and me climbing on to welcome him. "Same rules would apply for you."

"Mm-hmm." He jiggled my girls in his hands, watching in the mirror.

"Pfft. You're a boob man."

"Yes, I am."

I climbed off and stood next to the bed, grabbing at the mattress as my legs wobbled.

"You okay?" He steadied my shoulder.

"Yeah. Sort of. I need to lie down."

He moved over and patted the bed. After ripping a tissue from the box on my nightstand, he took care of the condom before lying beside me. His arm was under my neck and around my shoulders. My arm was across his chest, leg rested on top of his. I kissed his stubbly chin. He kissed the tip of my nose.

We closed our eyes and went to sleep.

Chapter
17

Ben

Brisbane, Australia
30th of December, 2016

I took off Sebastian's nappy, exposing his scrawny little body. After grabbing a wipe, I cleaned his bum. His poos were finally becoming normal baby poos. That black tar shit that first came out was hard to get off his skin. The nurse said it was because in the womb they get their nutrients through the umbilical blood, so the waste is a different colour and consistency than when they're on milk. Andy would have known that already. She would've known how to swaddle him so that he would feel secure and settle quickly. She would've known how to give him a bath.

I was standing here, listening to the nurse talk me through the procedure for the second time. I couldn't fucking remember what she'd shown me before. Did I swaddle him and wash his hair first, or did I just hook my fingers under his arms and dip his body in?

Seb's little arms reached into thin air, shaking as he cried his newborn cry.

"Okay. He's not liking the cold air or the feeling of being exposed, so let's swaddle him first. Across one shoulder. Across the other. Fold up the bottom and tuck it behind. That's it." She made actions with her hands to guide me.

He quietened, blinking up at me with eyes like Andy's.

"Hold him like a football. You know how to do that."

That I could do.

"Wet the flannel and just trickle the warm water over his scalp. He'll love it."

His mouth formed an *O* as his eyes rolled closed. It almost sounded like he was purring.

"See?" the nurse chirped.

Yeah, I saw.

I chuckled. Man, this was amazing. Andy and I had done something incredible in making this miniscule human.

Guilt hit me a second later. How was I able to enjoy this experience when she was upstairs in the ICU fighting for her life because of our son's existence?

"Now you can unwrap him and hold him steady in the water like I showed you. But don't leave him exposed for too long."

I put him back in the plastic cradle before taking off the towel. His umbilical cord was still attached. A dried out, shrivelled up version of itself, the clip no longer holding on for any reason other than the fact that no one had taken it off. Andy would want to keep that. And the name-card on the cradle. His arm band. The hair from his first haircut. His first tooth. God, would she get to experience any of his milestones? She hadn't even set eyes on him.

"Get him in the water."

Right. *Shit*. The poor kid was stuck with me looking after him when I couldn't think straight.

I dipped his body beneath the water, holding him under the shoulders. He kicked his legs before going still and sporting that blissful expression he had before. The force of my love for this child was off the scale. He expanded my heart to the size of the universe. Endless. Ever-growing. Infinite. Timeless. It was so big it couldn't be contained by measures applied in this world.

I would love him with all I had.

I only hoped that would be enough for the both of us.

———

Emmeline

Hampshire, England
13th July, 1867, 12:21 a.m.

"Emmeline." I was awoken from my slumber by Sebastian's harsh whisper. I blinked groggily, unable to focus on his candlelit face. "It's time."

Oh. I pushed my elbow into the mattress and dragged my body upright. Dangling my stockinged feet off the edge of the bed, I waited for a minute until my faculties had restored their function. After pulling on a dressing gown, stockings, and boots, I held my hand out for his. "Oh, wait," I whispered, tiptoeing to the dresser to retrieve my bag.

I held my hand out again. He clasped it and led me quietly through the sleeping house. Had someone let him in? Did he have a key? It mattered none. He had come to get me just as he'd said he would.

"Is your father with her?"

"No. I have stable duty tonight. Father is sleeping in the servants' quarters."

I nodded as we crossed the courtyard and made our way down the hill to the stables. All seemed quiet. I had expected her to be making more noise. Sebastian blew out the candle and took a lantern from a hook, guiding us to the stall where Miss Modesty lay in the straw. It was the same stall where I had first set eyes on him. How fitting that our final moments together should be spent here.

The mare's breathing was only slightly laboured. She lifted her head to greet us before laying it down again. I put my hand on her belly. It surged beneath my touch. Sebastian positioned himself at her rear. Fluid trickled from between her legs. I stroked her coat, reassuring her in hushed tones. "All will be well, beautiful girl."

There was a gush before one hoof appeared, sheathed in a white membrane.

"Ooh, here it comes. Good girl. You are doing a fine job."

She grunted and nickered, taking a brief look behind.

A few minutes later, the second hoof and the tip of a nose appeared. Under my hand, her belly clenched and relaxed at decreasing intervals. The foal's head came out before sliding back in several times. "Should we help her?"

"No, she's managing."

The smell of manure wafted into the air. "Did she soil herself?"

"Yes. That is quite normal under the circumstances."

Oh.

The mare grunted again and her stomach clenched with a powerful force as the foal's head and shoulders finally made an appearance. Miss Modesty's legs jerked as if she were trying to stand, but she flopped back down. With the next contraction the rest of the foal came out. The membrane covered it from neck to hind legs. The mare sat, folding her front legs underneath her. She turned to sniff and lick at the baby as I marvelled at the majesty of it all.

"Simply amazing."

"It is."

"You did it, Miss Modesty. Well done."

The horse stood, positioning herself so she could attend to the foal, ridding it of the sac in which it had grown.

"Ah, she's a good mother. Her instincts are sound."

The foal lay, shaking in the straw. "Is it a boy or a girl?"

Sebastian lifted its tail. "It's a boy. He looks like his father. Admiral will be well pleased."

"I should think he would be pleased with whatever his blessing."

"True, Miss Emmeline. True." Sebastian's gaze locked onto mine, a sadness infusing the love I had grown to recognise in his eyes.

"What happens now?"

He backed out of the stall, finding his way to a cot in a room to the rear of the stables. "I'll check on them through the night." He dipped his hands in a bowl of water, rinsing off and indicating for me to do the same. "I would ask of you the same question."

I hesitated in the doorway. "Whatever do you mean?"

"I am referring to your packed satchel. I know of your parents' plans to marry you to the earl. The manor is abuzz with talk of him."

"Oh." *He knows. Of course he knows.* I crossed to the bowl and cleansed my skin. "I had hoped you would be spared of the knowledge."

"An impossibility."

"Indeed."

"What are you to do?"

"He arrives tomorrow. I must leave tonight."

His throat surged and he looked away. "Alone?"

"How could I ask you to abandon your father? Your responsibilities?"

"I would do it in a heartbeat." Sebastian tilted his chin, eyes flitting to the corner of the tiny room.

I followed his gaze and drew in a breath upon seeing that he had packed a bag of his own. "Sebastian." My voice was but a wisp of air. I shuffled into the room, taking a seat beside him on the cot. "You would do this for me?"

His fingers found their way into my hair, palm cupping my face as his eyes roamed my features. "How could you not understand I would do anything for you?"

I covered his hand with mine and leaned in to place my lips on his, unable to speak. Tears wet my cheeks. I blinked to clear my vision as I rested my forehead on his. His thumbs wiped away the wetness. My jaw loosened as he placed them in his mouth, sucking away my tears.

"I want all of you."

"You have it. You've had it from the beginning."

Our mouths met again, tongues tangling as I crawled into his lap, my arms wrapped around his back. My heart went from a steady beat to a riotous sprint. Nostrils flared, I fought for air. Sebastian's greedy hands roamed underneath the layers of my clothing. There was an urgency, an underlying need to join in union immediately. He pulled my robe along my arms before discarding it on the brick floor. I tugged on his shirt and flung it behind me. The air chilled my skin as he dragged my nightgown over my head. I stood, working on the buttons of his trousers before he slid them down his thighs.

Climbing atop his lap, I lowered myself onto his erect shaft. A moan escaped my lips as I revelled in the connection, the drag of his flesh on mine. Taking him into my body was so natural to me. It was like a welcoming home of my other half. The stubble on his chin scratched at my neck as his rough hands guided my rocking motion. My breasts rubbed against his chest, his mouth, his hands. He held me tightly as he stood, turned, and lay me on my back upon the narrow cot. He grunted as his hips thrust with passionate abandon, his breath harsh in my ear. I dug my fingers into his skin, holding on as my body broke apart beneath him. My cries drove him harder, faster, prolonging my ride on the crest of the wave. He followed me over with a long groan of release.

His body grew lax. I wrapped my arms and legs around him and let my eyes drift shut. Our respiration slowed. Our hearts settled into a gentle rhythm.

We fell into a blissful sleep together.

Chapter
18

Emmeline

Hampshire, England
13th July, 1867, 5:15 a.m.

It was Sebastian's cry of pain that abruptly woke me. My eyes sprang open a split second before the sound of a riding crop striking his flesh had my blood curdling and his body jerking atop mine. He was flung to the floor, uncovering my nakedness. I jolted up, pulling the blankets from the cot to cover myself as the horrific scene unfolded before me. A tall, thin man stood over Sebastian with murder in his eyes. He pulled his arm back, ready to land another blow to Sebastian's bloodied back. For too long, I sat frozen, trying to comprehend what was happening.

Who was this man?

Greying hair at his temples, finely tailored riding clothes, the devil in his sneer. I gasped. It had to be the earl. He had arrived early. How had he found us? Did he know who I was?

"Stop!" I cried.

"Silence, slattern," he bellowed.

My eyes narrowed and I sprang to my feet, searching the room for a weapon. I grabbed a lantern and swung it at his head just as he delivered another blow to Sebastian's battered body. The glass shattered, a shard biting into his temple. Oil trickled down his shirt. He paused briefly, snarling as he gritted his teeth and set me in his sights. He began to lurch towards me, but Sebastian wrenched to his feet. Charging at the man, he drove him into the wall. His head struck the brick with a crack. He fell to the floor, unconscious.

"We must hurry." Sebastian tossed my nightgown on the cot before yanking on his trousers.

I reached for my bag and pulled out my chosen outfit of riding pants and shirt that I had stolen from the scullery. I stuffed my nightclothes in the satchel before pulling on some boots.

"Are you ready?"

I nodded. "Yes."

We ran to Admiral's stall, Sebastian harnessing the saddle as I secured the bridle. I opened the stable doors, alarmed to see Marybeth, Sebastian's father, the steward, and my father running down the hill towards us.

"Get on!" Sebastian leaned down before pulling me onto the horse behind him.

I circled his waist with my arms. "They cannot catch us. Admiral is too fast."

We set off at a clip, leaving the shouts of our fathers behind us.

"Not as fast with two of us, but we should gain some distance before they follow."

I dug my fingers into his shirt. "What if they send a telegram to town?"

"We shall stay out of sight. Stick to the forest. They'll have a harder time finding us."

"Where will we go?"

He took his time to answer. "North. I have family in Scotland."

"Do you think they will search for us there?"

"It is a possibility." We ducked under a branch as Sebastian steered us through the trees. He circled around under the cover of thick greenery to head east towards New Forest. With any luck, they would search for us to the west, the direction in which we had set off.

Our first dilemma would be finding shelter, somewhere hidden and safe for Admiral Caine. The surrounding hills were largely exposed with the trees dispersed in sparse patches across the land. If we could safely retreat to the forest, we might have half a chance at freedom.

We came to a stream and followed along it for nearly half a mile to put them off our scent. If they were smart, they would call the dogs on us. Tripping up the shallow bank, we made it to an open field, a herd of deer scattering in our wake. Visible as only a speck upon the landscape, at the base of a valley I could see a township.

"We must skirt around it. The county police will likely be on alert."

"Agreed."

"Over there." I need not have pointed to the thicket of bushes as Sebastian had already guided our steed towards the cover.

He spoke over his shoulder. "We may be unable to penetrate the thick growth, but we shall stick to its edges. 'Tis better than being exposed."

"Indeed."

I worried for Admiral. We had ridden him hard for longer than was advised. He would be tiring by now and at risk of injury if we pushed him any further. "If it is safe, we should find a spot to rest the horse." No sooner had I voiced my concerns than the Admiral began to falter. His stride lost its seamless rhythm, a jagged canter taking its place.

"Okay, boy." Sebastian patted the horse's neck and pulled back on the reins.

We dismounted and walked for another couple of miles until we reached a second patch of forest. Following the sound of trickling water, we came upon a brook.

Sebastian led Admiral Caine to the water's edge, encouraging him to quench his thirst. He did so eagerly.

I kneeled on the moss-covered bank and leaned forward to scoop some water into my hands. Its cool medicine slid down my throat, a balm for my parched mouth and tired body. "Can we not rest for a spell?"

Sebastian wiped his face on his shirtsleeve, narrowing his eyes as he swivelled his head. Admiral's ears pricked and he whinnied, backing away from the brook. Sebastian sprang to his feet, grabbing Admiral's reins and brushing a hand down the horse's nose, murmuring to him.

"Do you hear that?" he asked.

I frowned, getting to my feet. Closing my eyes, I singled out the sounds reaching my ears. The water running over the rocks and tree roots. The wind rustling the leaves. Birds calling to each other. Creatures scurrying through the underbrush and matting of fallen leaves and twigs. My eyes sprang open. *Horses' hooves.*

"Yes."

"Quickly." He helped me onto Admiral before mounting at my front. I held on as Sebastian guided us away from the water and into the dense growth. We weaved through the trees until the canopy closed in, strangling any light-rays that attempted entry. And then we stopped. And waited.

Admiral Caine's tail swished, his nostrils flared. My shoulders kissed my ears. The noise of their approach grew louder before it seemed to fade. I hung my arms by my side, releasing a rush of air. Whomever they were, we had successfully avoided them.

Bang.

A gunshot rang out, startling the sleeping forest. Admiral squealed, rearing onto his hind legs. I snatched at Sebastian's shirt, but not fast enough to gain purchase. Tumbling off the saddle, I hit the ground with a thud, the wind stolen from my lungs.

"Emmeline!"

My mouth opened and closed in an attempt to draw air, but none came. I cradled my chest, grimacing, terrified of what I was seeing. Sebastian battled to hold on to his seat as he struggled to gain control of the horse. The muscles and tendons in his arms and neck strained, his face mirroring the fear carving a hole in my gut. Jumping free, he tumbled to the ground a few yards away. Admiral took flight, stealing any chance of our escape.

No. I dropped my chin. *No.*

Sebastian scrambled over to me before folding me into his embrace. "Breathe," he pleaded.

Once more I opened my mouth, finally with avail. I pulled my shoulder blades together as my lungs inflated.

Our heads jerked at the cracking of twigs under foot. I clutched at Sebastian, my mouth drying. They'd caught us.

"Over here!" The shout preceded the appearance of three police on horseback, truncheons drawn, cutlasses sheathed at their sides. Shiny brass buttons lined up on the front of their tunics. Their faces were set in grim lines under the shield of their helmets.

Behind them, another horse approached. *The earl.* His scowl was enough to curdle my blood and turn my stomach to dust.

"Seize the horse-thief. The girl is mine."

I screamed as two officers ripped Sebastian away. The earl pulled my arms behind the small of my back, locking them in his grasp. Snaking his other arm across my chest, he gripped my throat. "Hush now, my beloved. The constabulary have him in hand."

Beloved? A gross misrepresentation of his feelings for me in order to fool the authorities. Beloved was a sentiment that would never apply to our particular relationship. I stomped my heel on top of his boot and his hand tightened around my neck. "Careful, little fugitive. You are collecting more punishments than you can handle. I advise you to surrender before something nasty happens to your plaything." The cold hard press of steel into my back chilled my revolt.

He had pulled the trigger knowing it would spook the horse. And now he threatened to hurt Sebastian. I could not test his resolve.

"All right, sir?"

"Yes, officer. Everything is fine. Take him away. I shall see that my bride makes it home safely."

The officers tapped their hats in salute and rode off with Sebastian. He sat astride in front of one officer.

Wrists bound by rope, he mouthed a final, "*I love you,*" before disappearing. Would it be forever?

The darkness closed in and settled within every fibre of my being, winding me all over again. I fractured into pieces, releasing a wail so loud rabbits, squirrels, and deer scattered for shelter. The earl slapped his dirty hand over my mouth, but I didn't stop. Nothing would stem this release of anguish.

A moment later, the earl proved me wrong with the butt of his gun, a crack of pain registering a moment before everything went black.

Chapter
19

Andrea

Rockhampton, Australia
18th of May, 2009

I opened my eyes on Sunday morning to find myself alone. A knot immediately formed in my gut.

Gone.

The word sprang to mind—an answer to a question I hadn't asked, and the knot tightened. I reassured myself it was fine. He hadn't necessarily said he'd be staying the night. And Bree would have questions if he had anyway. It was the sensible thing to do. Then doubt put a tilt on things. Maybe he'd just gone to the loo, or to grab something from the kitchen?

Gone.

The knowledge was more forceful this time. It held more weight, more sorrow.

I pressed my lips together and swallowed the lump in my throat. I checked my phone. There were no new messages. Had he left a note somewhere? I looked on the night stand, on my sheets, on the floor, under the pillow. Nope. Not that I could see. I typed out a quick, '*Hey, where'd you go?*' text. Placing my mobile on the pillow where he'd slept beside me, I waited. It didn't vibrate, or light up. It lay there lifeless, inanimate, its silence mocking the rising panic inside me. Its quiet an echo of the void he'd left behind.

Maybe he was still asleep? *Oh, cut the crap.* Okay, so he'd gone. Expectations remember? But was it so wrong to expect your boyfriend to leave some form of goodbye, good morning, thank you for the great sex, let's do it again soon?

Stupid tears sprang to my eyes. A lack of expectations was no good if you didn't also have boundaries. The two seemed incongruous, but they worked hand in hand. I could love him and expect nothing in return. Love was a state of being. It didn't just stop when a person walked away. But if I gave myself intimately to someone, I deserved respect in return.

When I sat up, the vision of my well-fucked naked body greeted me in that mirror. That goddamn mirror.

Gone.

I pictured myself throwing the phone at the fucking mirror, smashing them both to pieces. It wouldn't matter. I'd still stare at the wardrobe door and see what we'd done. I could still feel him between my legs.

After dragging my stiff body from under the covers, I slipped into some pyjamas and tied my hair in a ponytail. I lurched for the door, eager to leave. But as I reached it, I paused. With my grip strangling the doorhandle, I arranged my face into some semblance of happy. On the other side of the wooden barrier, my sister would be lounging in front of the TV, probably eating cereal. It was her Sunday morning routine.

This is no routine Sunday.

The last person to walk out this door had been Ben. What had I done so wrong to make him run?

My brow scrunched as my tear ducts prepped for a deluge.

I gritted my teeth. *Don't you fucking dare.* I wasn't going to cry over a man. If he wasn't able to handle the magnitude of us then he didn't deserve my tears.

I waltzed out, determined to put on a show for Bree, and aimed for the kitchen.

"Hey," she mumbled through a mouthful of food.

"Morning. How'd you sleep?" I poured myself a glass of juice.

"Mm. Good." Her spoon clinked on the bowl. "What time did Ben go home?"

I stiffened at the sound of his name. Poising my drink at my lips, I prepared to douse the burn at the back of my throat. "Before midnight. He only just made it before he turned into a pumpkin." I tipped the juice, gulping it too fast as she laughed.

I choked, launching into a coughing fit. It was the perfect cover for the spring of tears. The bastards got past my guard.

"Are you okay?" She dumped her bowl on the coffee table and jogged over to me.

"Yep," I gasped. "Wrong tube." Slapping myself on the chest, I reached for the paper towel.

"What time are Mum and Dad getting back?"

I blew my nose and caught my breath before answering. "Around dinner time. Wanna help me cook a nice meal?"

"Sure."

"Great."

Let's soak everything in alcohol and flambé the shit out of it.

Maybe I could do that to my sheets?

And the mirror.

———

I'd called four times and left messages. He hadn't replied. Mum and Peter had come home that night and I'd had to pretend that there wasn't an empty space where my heart had been. He'd run off with it and dumped it somewhere on his way to ghosting me. At least he'd done the same with the used condom.

I'd been mechanical in my routine—eaten dinner, had a shower, gone to bed, gotten up, gotten dressed, eaten breakfast, gone to school.

Now here I was heading to fourth period. I pulled out my phone, checking for any messages. My face fell at the missing envelope icon at the top of the screen.

"Oh, shit. What's wrong with you?" Pauline approached me on the path leading to our class.

"Nothing."

"Okay. I believe you. *Not*."

"I don't think I can talk about it without bawling like a baby."

"I won't ask." She pursed her lips and peered at me through the corner of her eye.

"He ghosted me."

"Prick."

"I know I didn't do anything wrong. Things were going great." I threw up my hands. "He freaked. Things got real and he freaked."

"Sounds like it. Ben's the dependable type."

"Not so much. I don't know what to do."

"There's nothing you can do. The ball is in his court. If he needs space, give it to him. What's the first rule of dating?"

"Don't chase."

"Exactly. Guys are built for the hunt. If he wants you, he'll come and get you when he's ready. Then you decide if he's worthy."

"You're right."

"Just keep doing you, girl. Chase the goals, not the man."

She was so right. I sent up a prayer of thanks for having her in my life. "I love you, Pauline."

She hooked an arm over my shoulders. "Love you too, sweetie."

―――――

Emmeline

Hampshire, England
13th July, 1867, 2:56 p.m.

My father paced the floor of my bedroom as I lay curled on my bed. Left to right. Hands clasped behind him, eyes on his polished boots, he marched to the head of my bed and spun on his heel, before turning back the way he came. His nostrils flared as he pulled in air and forced it out again. We had been locked in this stand-off ever since he'd dragged me kicking and screaming to my room. Could it have been half an hour? An hour? I did not know.

His footsteps stopped and he twisted to face me. I stared at his belt buckle. Would he choose to use it as a punishment?

"I find it difficult to understand how my daughter—*my daughter*—could defy me in such a way."

I had not defied him. He had defied me. He had decided who I was to marry without consultation and without consideration of my heart's desires.

"Speak!"

"What would you have me say?"

He scoffed before landing a heavy blow across my cheek. I whimpered, soothing the sting with my palm as I pushed my face into the mattress.

"How long have you been consorting with the servant boy?"

If I answered truthfully, Marybeth would be in trouble and Uncle Tobias would be without his mistress. For the first time, I found myself empathising with a man I had previously considered self-serving, unctuous, and fickle. What if they were truly in love? What if my uncle had been forced to marry Lady Margaret to satisfy societal expectations when his heart yearned for another?

"Not long." *More than half our lives.*

"Who else is aware?"

"Nobody." I met his bloodshot stare.

"And it shall stay that way." He set off pacing again. "The earl is furious, as he is well within his rights to be. He has agreed to follow through with our arrangement. You are to be married in our chapel in the morn."

"The morning? The wedding was to be next month."

"Do not speak out of turn!" He delivered another slap to the cheek.

I hissed, stretching my mouth against the pain. It would come as no surprise if his discipline resulted in bruising.

"You are to remain in your room until you are sent for. Your chambermaid will be assisting you with preparations. Once you are married, you will be the earl's concern. He may choose how he deals with you. I pray that he has a merciful hand." He stomped from the room, slamming the door at his back.

Holding my cheek, I used my elbow to push myself up. Still wearing the shirt and buckskins, I shuffled around the bed and took a seat at the dresser. The sight that greeted me in the mirror was not unexpected: red eyes, cheek aflame with the outline of my father's hand. Hair in disarray. Tears streaking my face. I picked up a pitcher and poured some water into the washbowl it had been resting in. Taking the cloth Marybeth had set beside them, I wet it before placing it against my sore cheek. The cool provided little relief. I washed my face and brushed my hair before securing it into a braid. I let my hands fall to my lap as I considered the frame of my bed in the mirror. The four poster would certainly be sturdy enough to hold my weight as I hung from a noose. I could easily fashion one from the bed sheet. I was confident with all manner of knots thanks to my visits to the stables.

I spun around at a knock on the door.

Marybeth entered, keeping her eyes lowered as she approached. "I am to watch over you until your nuptials."

"Are you to sleep in here with me?"

"Yes, miss."

I placed my hands on my knees and bowed my head. My stomach lodged in my throat. I had successfully been stripped of all free will. I could not even choose how and when I was to die. For the remainder of my life, I was to be shackled to a detestable man for one reason only—I had been born a girl to parents of high social standing. If I were a maid, would I have a choice in whom was to be my groom?

I assessed Marybeth in the mirror. "Do you love Tobias?"

"I do." She dipped her chin.

"And yet you cannot be with him unless it is a clandestine arrangement. How is that fair?"

"'Tis an injustice of our times, miss."

"If you and he were of equal social standing, would you have the chance to be together?"

"I imagine so. My sisters have all chosen fine working men."

Hm. There was hope for this world. "What is it about my uncle that attracts you so?"

"He is a charming, honourable man, despite what anyone may think. He abides by his duties. I cannot resist him, no matter how hard I try. My heart chose for me. My mind had no say in the matter."

"Indeed." I pressed the heels of my palms to my cheeks, capturing the tears that fell. "You and I have much in common. Forbidden love is a torturous affair. Though a blind eye is turned to my uncle's indiscretions, mine are seen as unforgivable." I smiled a sad smile. "Love does not choose according to suitability of status, morality, or any rules of humanity." I reached for her hand and clasped it in mine. "Love—true love—is infinitely wiser than we." This time, my smile was genuine.

"I carry his child." Her chest rose and held in place as she bit her lip.

My eyes sprang wide. "Is he aware?"

"Yes." She slipped her hand from mine before locking her fingers together. "He intends to support us, but he cannot acknowledge the child as his own."

"How will you manage raising a child and attending to your duties?"

"We all band together to raise the babies, miss. We are fortunate that Mr Beauchamp allows us to have our families near."

How was it that my father could be extraordinarily accommodating with the staff, but deny his only daughter any happiness? My father believed a woman's primary role was to bear children. Perhaps this was his way of justifying keeping them in his employ.

"Then I am most happy for you, Marybeth."

If I could not attain any level of joy, I prayed that Marybeth would get my share.

Chapter
20

Ben

Rockhampton, Australia
24th of July, 2009

I'd fucked up big time and now I didn't know how to fix it. It was smoko break on a Friday, and like the sad fuck that I was, I sat alone in my ute listening to Beyoncé singing about angelic headgear. Fucking halos. Andy had one. I had devil horns. What kind of a bastard took his girlfriend's virginity and then fucked off without a word? I smacked my forehead on the steering wheel, spotting the red mark in the mirror when I straightened. Good. It was like an X-marks-the-spot of where my dick currently was—front and centre on my head. I growled at my reflection.

The passenger door opened and I punched at the stereo to shut off the sappy chick music, switching it to a rock station.

Brad took a seat, apple in hand, chewing as he eyed me sideways. "I think we've given you enough time to mope around. I'm surprised you haven't cut off a finger yet."

I nearly had about an hour ago while using the drop saw.

"It has been tough keeping Stewart from you. He's pissed, mate. Andy hasn't said anything, but despite appearances, Stewart isn't a dumb fuck. He's noticed your absence. What gives?"

I covered my mouth with a hand, pressing in my cheeks.

"Okay, let me guess. You cheated on her?" He took another bite of his apple, watching me. I didn't respond. "No? Okay. You ... found her screwing around?"

I let go of my face and gave him my best *you're the dumb-fuck* look.

"I didn't believe it either. Okay, um ... she dumped you because your dick is too small?"

My mouth flattened and I tapped my fingers on the steering wheel, turning my attention outside.

"You guys love each other. What the fuck happened?"

I shot him a glare. "My father fucked with my head. That's what happened."

"I'm pretty sure he's a serial liar, so why would you believe anything he said or did, ever?"

Lee had a point. My nineteen-year-old-self understood this. My seven-year-old-self had yet to learn.

I'd been over it a million times. There was no excuse for what I'd done. And the longer I let things go without talking to her, the further any chance of her taking me back got.

I'd watched her sleeping that night. Her blonde hair spread out on the pillow, lips puffed out and slack as she dreamt. Her naked body had pressed against me, and fuck me, I'd wanted her again. I'd wanted to be a selfish prick and wake her up with my tongue, but she'd needed sleep. She also deserved a guy who would've been gentle her first time. Someone who wouldn't put his hand in her pants while her sister was in the same room.

What the fuck was wrong with me? I was just like my dad. I'd taken her virginity on her narrow single bed while her sister slept down the hall. I'd wanted to make her feel special. Do the flowers and chocolates thing, and take her away for a weekend once she'd finished school. I'd only had to wait six more months, for fuck's sake.

"Hey."

My head cranked to the side to find Lee frowning at me, the masticated apple core pinched between his thumb and pointer finger.

"You're a mess. Get your deadbeat dad out of your head. He's ruined enough. Let him go now. You're not him."

He was right.

But after what I'd done, how could I convince Andy that I wasn't that guy?

———

Emmeline

Hampshire, England
14th July, 1867, in the wee hours

Jolted from a nightmare, I found my arms pulled above my head, my wrists locked under a tight grip. A heavy palm gripped my chin, muffling my screams—my nightmare come to life.

Reginald Fortescue's brandy-soaked breath poured over my face. "Do not scream."

He freed my mouth to reach for the hem of my gown before yanking it to my waist. I screamed before he smashed his mouth onto mine. He tasted bitter. I struggled in a futile effort to unchain myself from his restraints. His knees pushed my legs wider and he dropped his weight on top of me before reaching down to shove his length into my body. My cry of pain caught in my throat with nowhere to go. He pulled his lips from mine, replacing them with his hand. His skin smelled of brandy and vomit. I squeezed my eyes shut, not wanting the sight of him to etch into my memories.

"Open your eyes!" he spat. "I will be the last man who was inside you as you stand at the altar." He slurred his words, eyes boring into mine. His body drove into me with hard thrusts.

This was nothing like the love I'd made with Sebastian. This was dominance, control, power. This was the crushing of my soul into tiny irretrievable pieces. The movement of his body against mine was like sand in the eyes, grazed knees, sunburn. This was pain. And he was enjoying it.

He removed his hand to land a blow across my face. A burst of agony fanned out from my jaw before his palm smothered my cries. He did it again, landing a fist to the opposite side to even his score before cutting off my air. I tried to tilt my head to free my nose from the press of his hand, but he pushed my head farther into the pillow, rendering me immobile.

I stopped fighting against him. What was the point? It was already too late. He had taken from me, had violated my body and my spirit in irrevocable ways. My eyes rolled to the side.

Where was Marybeth?

Had she run? Had the earl threatened her, or worse, hurt her?

I prayed that she was safe. She needed to protect her baby. This would all be over soon.

For this occasion, if not forever.

If I survived, in a matter of hours, I would be his wife. He could do whatever he pleased with me. I would be kept among his many possessions, there to play with when the desire struck.

With a grunt, his movements became erratic before one final push. He collapsed on top of me, his grip on my wrists and my face falling free.

I gasped for air, waiting for him to move. He did not. His harsh breathing quickly transformed into soft snores. I pushed on his shoulders, sliding my top half out from under him. Digging my heels and hands into the bed, I scrambled away, leaving him asleep face down. I stood to the side, taking in the trail of blood left on the sheets. The evidence of his deed ran down my thighs. I dashed to the washbowl, needing to clean myself immediately. I wanted him off me. Sobbing, I scrubbed with the cloth until the water in the bowl was red and my thighs were raw. Using clean water from the pitcher, I rinsed down my legs before patting my skin dry.

I stood on the towel as it soaked up my mess, assessing my reflection. No amount of washing would ever clean me of his mark. It was there in the hollows under my eyes, and the pallor of my skin. It was there in the haunted look, setting in for the duration. Bruises bloomed on each side of my face. They would fade. His mark of violation would not. Turning away, I dressed in clean drawers and a nightgown. I grimaced at the touch of fabric against my sensitive thighs. Hobbling to the door, I opened it.

Sitting on the floor beside the entry, Marybeth had her hands clasped in her lap as she cried. "I could not stop him, miss. I tried."

"Shh. Do not cry. Did he hurt you?"

She rubbed at her arm, a hand print clearly visible and turning a dark shade of blue.

Repugnant beast of a man.

"He has passed out from the drink. Let us go until he wakes."

"But, miss, your wedding dress—"

"Let him wear it. Come now."

We rounded the corner, reaching the top of the staircase.

My father was approaching from the opposite direction, candlelight flickering over his scowl. "What is going on? Why are you out of bed?"

Marybeth and I turned to each other. I drew in a breath, squaring my shoulders. "The earl is currently asleep in my bed. He felt the need to force himself upon me prior to making me his wife."

"I beg your pardon?"

"See it with your own eyes if you do not believe me. Witness the blood on the bed and in the washbowl. See the bruises on my face and wrists. That is the doing of the man you have chosen for me."

I could not contain my disdain. How could the man forsake his own child? Given the opportunity to atone for his sins and remedy the injustice, would he take it?

With a fierce expression, Father hurried to the room while Marybeth and I huddled on the landing.

"What have you done?" His voice roared through the deserted corridors, chasing away my terrors.

Was it possible that my father had not known of the earl's penchant for brutality? Had he simply been blinded by the lure of a business merger and glossed over the grimmer details of the man's character? My mother had known. Perhaps Father had been ignorant. If so, he had failed in his duty to protect his daughter from such fiends. Though he certainly made up for it now. The sounds of him delivering a beating and the earl begging for mercy spread like cracks along the walls.

"Come." I took my friend by the shoulders and urged her down the stairs. "I cannot bear witness to any more barbarity tonight."

And in the morn, I would remain unwedded. Hell would freeze over before I would ever let that man call me his wife.

———

Sebastian

En route
13th of December, 1867

After two months in the wretched conditions of prison, life aboard the Hougoumont seemed almost bearable. The vile stench below deck played havoc with my stomach, but the moments above deck when the sea breeze flushed my lungs provided a brief reprieve. I made sure to pause from my chores every now and then to take in the sway of the sails. The ship had three tall masts with six rectangular sails on each, and several more triangular canvases at the bow and stern, and between masts. The power of the wind drove us east across the Indian Ocean, bound for the penal colony in Western Australia.

As far away from Emmeline as they could possibly send me.

My future stretched out before me, as bleak and unfathomable as the endless sea.

I'd imagined jumping overboard almost every day, just to see how deep the ocean went. How far would I have to go to find a resting place to keep me from living a life without her in some godforsaken primitive land.

The last glimpse of my father, moments before our failed escape, had revealed a mask of shock and disappointment. I hoped my actions had not cost him his position, but I feared Emmeline's father would have had no choice but to release him from his duties given his association to me. There was no way of me knowing Emmeline's fate. Wondering what happened to her twisted my stomach one hundred times more than the roughest seas ever could.

Had she been killed for her defiance, her betrayal?

In truth, our only crime had been falling in love.

It was a cruel fate that had put us across each other's paths.

The chance presented to us, a barbarous ruse.

Chapter
21

Ben

Brisbane, Australia
1st of January, 2017

Searching through the baby bag for the third time, I made sure Sebastian had everything he needed. Today I was taking him home.

Just me and my boy.

Happy fucking New Year.

My throat burned with trapped anger. *Ah, fuck. Pull your shit together.* I scrubbed a hand across my cheeks, the feel of my full beard foreign under my palm. The last time I'd grown a beard was the last time I'd lost her.

I'd vowed never to do anything to lose her again.

I hadn't counted on pregnancy being our greatest threat.

Stuffing the bag in the basket underneath the pram, I checked the straps holding a sleeping Sebastian in place. He loved to wriggle. And he was so tiny, the straps didn't sit over his shoulders, landing somewhere in the vicinity of an inch above his head instead. As long as he lay flat, we were okay. I scanned the room giving it a final farewell, and hoping I hadn't left anything behind.

But I was leaving something behind.

My wife.

I could close the door to this room. There was no closing the door on this chapter of my life until she came home to me. One way or another.

Alive or ...

I swallowed past the knot of emotion lodged in my larynx, and reached for the door handle.

My head reared back at finding Lee and Ronnie standing on the threshold. Lee with his fist poised to knock, Ronnie eclipsed by the biggest bunch of flowers I'd ever seen.

"Hey. We heard the little guy was breaking out. Thought you might need a support crew to escort the two of you home." Lee stepped in, his palm slapping me on the back as he bent to have a squiz at Sebastian. "They're angels when they're asleep. Not when they're hungry though. *Jesus*." He shook his head, whistling.

"Don't wake him." Ronnie pressed the flowers into my arms and gave me a hug. "How are you holding up?"

"Hangin' by a string."

"Understandable." She stood back. "Ready to go? We ubered here so you could sit in the back with Seb and Lee could drive."

I nodded dumbly, clutching the bouquet.

Lee took charge of the pram while Ronnie rested her hand on my back, steering me to the exit. "Where are you parked?"

"Third floor." I dug out my keys and the ticket to get out and gave them to her.

Hopping out of the elevator, Ronnie led the way to the ute like she knew exactly where it was. She probably did. She'd likely been scoping my memories through her touch on my shoulder, or however she did it. All I knew was that I was grateful. Numbness infused my veins with every step. I was leaving my wife behind in a coma. I kept my eyes on our sleeping baby to remind me why I couldn't fall into a heap.

I stared at him the whole way home, not saying a word. Ronnie and Lee talked quietly in the front, the radio on in the background. I'd spent hours staring at him already, trying to work out which bits were from whose gene pool. His tiny fingers were long like mine. His toes curled under the way Andy's did. Mini earlobes mimicked the way Andy's sloped into her neck, rather than curving around. She could barely fit one earring with the lack of lobe she'd been given.

"Here we are."

My gaze flitted to the front. My bloodshot eyes stared at me in the rear-view mirror. I rubbed a hand over my face.

Lee unlocked the house and went back to help Ronnie bring the bags inside. I carried Seb in and put him in his cradle next to my bed. He was having a decent sleep, and well timed, too. What a brilliant baby.

After switching on the baby monitor, I checked him once more, snapping a picture before I left. I had to capture all the moments Andy was missing. She'd want to see them when she woke up.

If she woke up.

The back of my throat burned with tears and I gulped them down.

Tossing the keys on the kitchen bench, Lee made a beeline for the dining table. "I hope you don't mind us being here. We won't stay long. Your mum cooked heaps of meals and left them in the freezer. She said she'd be back later to mind Seb if you wanted to go to the hospital."

Thanks, Mum.

Ronnie busied herself in the kitchen, getting lunch together. "The couch has been professionally cleaned."

The couch. Fuck. I'd never be able to look at it again, let alone sit on it. "I'm getting rid of it."

"What?" Lee squawked.

"Fair enough." Ronnie glared at him. "She's coming home soon." She poured dressing over a salad and tossed it through.

"Who? Mum?"

She shook her head. "Andrea."

I gripped the back of a chair and pulled it out, landing my butt down before it hit the floor. "You *know*?"

"I just received confirmation, yeah." She grabbed a plate of cold meats and began to dish them out. "She's a little worse for wear, but she'll be okay." Ronnie paused and aimed her gaze at me. "I foresaw this happening. I'm sorry I didn't tell you, but that would've been worse. Knowing something is going to happen and you can't do a damn thing to stop it—believe me, it sucks."

She knew.

I couldn't sort through the barrage of emotions pummelling me in that moment. I didn't know what to think. Was I glad that I hadn't been aware? Yes. The forewarning would have been fucking torture. Did I believe Ronnie when she said my wife would come back to me? I wanted to. So badly.

Brad blinked at her. "Is that why you were acting so weird when I wanted to talk about starting a family?"

"You guys wanna have kids?" *Now? After what Andy and I have just been through?*

I wanted to be happy for them. In truth, I was scared. Andy and I were in the minority of horror stories, but if my friends had to go through any more loss in their lives it would crush them. The risks could be high. That was the reality of pregnancy and childbirth. It could be a nightmare, just as much as a miracle.

Aren't I just the happiest camper?

He crossed the distance to put his arm around her and kiss her temple. "I'm in no rush. And if it never happens, I'll be fine. I just wanna enjoy life with you."

Smart man.

They didn't stay for long, and I was grateful for that. When Mum came back, she gave me a hug and went in to check on Seb. She'd been a godsend, making me meals and dropping in clean clothes to the hospital. Now she could add babysitting services to that list.

I needed to figure out how to split my time between the two loves of my life.

I hoped Ronnie was right. I understood enough about psychic abilities to realise that accuracy depended on the person's ability to interpret the cryptic messages.

Could I believe Ronnie's interpretation?

Maybe. But my heart wouldn't let the hope swell to any level of significance.

What if she was wrong?

______

Ben

Rockhampton, Australia
3rd of August, 2009, 1:22 p.m.

My phone vibrated in my pocket. I ignored it, shooting the nail gun to secure some skirting. Half a minute later, it buzzed again. I put the gun down and slid the mobile from my pocket. Four missed calls from Lee. And a text message. He hadn't shown up to work this morning. I'd sent him a text asking if he was okay. He'd finally replied. I opened it.

Andy was right.

About what?

Dialling the number for my voicemail, I listened for messages. He hadn't left any. What the hell was going on?

Gripping the phone, I brought up his contact and hit the call button.

I heard a click like he'd answered, but no other sound came through the speaker. "Hello? Lee?"

"Yeah."

"Mate, what's going on?"

"My parents died in a plane crash yesterday afternoon. Andy was right."

Oh, fuck.

"Jesus. Are you at home?"

"Yes."

"Is Midget with you?"

"Yes."

"I'm coming. Stay put." I hung up and went to find the foreman. "Rob. I gotta go, mate. That was Bradlee. I wouldn't expect him in for the rest of the week. He just lost his parents."

"Shit. Yeah, you go. Send him our condolences." He slapped a palm on my shoulder.

I packed away at record speed, dialling Andy's number before hanging up. She'd still be in school. I couldn't tell her yet. That was if she took my call at all.

Turning into Lee's street, I almost had the ute on two wheels. It was pointless and stupid to speed, but they didn't have any other family around, apart from a grandmother in Brisbane somewhere. I didn't have a clue if she was still alive, or capable of travelling to be with them. A mate needed a mate so I got there ASAP.

Lee opened the door before I reached it. He looked like death warmed up, with dark sunken pits under his eyes, and hair sticking out at all angles.

I didn't say anything. Instead, I pulled him in for a hug right there on the doorstep.

He shut the door and sat on the small step to the entry. "How did she know?" he choked.

"Andy?" I joined him.

"Yeah."

"She knows things. She might not get all the details, but she gains enough to make a person stand up and listen."

"I didn't." His eyes glazed over as he stared ahead.

I bent my knees, hooking my arms around them. "Don't beat yourself up. Don't do that. How could you have stopped them anyway? Do you think they would've listened?"

"No."

"There ya go."

"But I should've tried." His voice faded as tears flooded his eyes.

Hooking an arm over his shoulders, I brought him in close. He was my brother by choice. I shared his pain. The whole fucking situation ripped me to shreds. I couldn't imagine having to face the black hole that had opened before him. But I wasn't going to let him wrestle with it alone.

"What's done is done. Maybe it was just their time. I know it's fucked, but I kinda believe everything happens for a reason. And if there's one good thing in this, it's that they went together."

I was talking out of my arse. There wasn't anything good about this. Two kids had been orphaned. Lee was only nineteen and Letitia, thirteen. He was gonna have to raise his sister now on an apprentice's wage. I hoped they had insurance to pay off any debts and cover the funerals. Fuck, he'd need help planning those.

"Have they recovered the bodies?"

He straightened, wiping his face. "No."

Ah, fuck. My head went loose on my neck. He wasn't going to get any closure until they'd been found and put to rest. If there was anything left of them. The ocean could be violently unforgiving.

"How's Midget?"

"Passed out on the couch."

"Is Larissa with her?"

"No. She's working."

"Did you tell her?"

"Yeah. She said she'd be over later."

Wow.

The sound of gravel crunching under tyres approached. Stewart's car pulled to a stop outside the house, and Andy jumped out of the passenger side before running up the path. She squatted and caught Lee in a hug. "I'm so sorry. So sorry."

"How did you know? I haven't told anyone else."

"I had a feeling. I knew for sure as soon as I saw you sitting out here."

Stewart ambled behind her. "It's true?"

Lee bounced his chin once.

"Shit. I didn't believe her."

I locked Andy in my sights, willing her to return my gaze, but she was focused solely on Lee. And rightly so. This wasn't about my fuck-up, or needing her back in my life so bad I could hardly breathe.

"Is Tish inside?" she murmured.

"On the couch."

She patted him on the back "Do you mind if I go in?"

"Go ahead."

After pushing to her feet, she disappeared inside the house.

Stew joined us on the stoop. "Wanna get pissed?"

Typical Stew.

Brad rested his elbows on his knees, holding his head in his hands. "Actually, yes. I'd love to pass out for a decade and forget this ever happened, but I've got a little sister who needs me."

Stew pouted, nodding his head. "Does she wanna get pissed?"

My gaze shot to his. "Jesus, Stewart."

"What? It might help them both sleep." He turned to Lee. "I bet you haven't done much of that."

"None."

"I've got alcohol in the car. Me and Andy can stay over tonight. She can look after Midget. She's good like that."

Actually, that was a stellar idea. But if they were staying, so was I. Stewart and Lee needed someone to cut them off before it got ugly. Andy and Tish shouldn't have to deal with two drunken idiots. And the last thing Lee needed was to feel even more shitty than he already did.

I elbowed Lee's knee, making him raise his head. "Are you okay if we stay tonight? I'll sleep on the floor. I don't care."

"Do you guys mind?" He grimaced.

"Wasn't I the one who suggested it?" Stew heaved to his feet. "It's a great fucking idea. I've got beer and Bundy rum. I bags the couch."

"Where's Andy gonna crash then?" My brows dipped low.

I couldn't imagine what Stewart would be like had he been in this situation. Could he be trusted to look after his sisters and brother? The words, *fuck* and *no*, came to mind.

"That's her problem." Stew shrugged.

"We have recliners," Lee offered.

"There ya go. Ben and Andy on the recliners. Me stretched out on the couch. It's a done deal. Let's do this." Stew swaggered back to his car as Lee and I made our way inside.

We found Andy leaning on the couch with Midget tucked under one arm, a box of tissues in her free hand. They spoke in hushed tones, Andy asking questions and Tish responding numbly.

"Have you spoken to your gran?"

"No." Letitia hiccupped.

Andy smoothed the hair away from Midget's face. "Has anyone told her?"

Tish's hands clasped together. "I'm not sure."

Andy looked up and our gazes met for the first time in forever. I offered a sad smile and not just for the tragedy we were witnessing.

She reciprocated, her eyes a bit cautious, before turning her attention to Lee. "Do you need me to call anyone for you?"

"I spoke to Gran earlier. That was fucking hard. Telling a mother that her child is dead isn't something I ever want to do again."

"Aw, Lee." Her lip quivered, eyes glossy with tears threatening to spill. "Is she able to fly up here?"

"No. She's not well. I might fly us down once things get sorted. It'd be good to see her."

"I think that's a great idea."

He rubbed at the back of his head before averting his gaze. "I'm just going to go sit out the back."

He wandered off in a daze.

I tugged at the front of my shirt, suddenly conscious that I was filthy. "We decided it would be best if we stayed here tonight. Are you up for it?" I asked her.

"My bag is in Stew's car already."

My brows took a hike under my fringe. And then I remembered—*she'd known*. She'd been prepared to come running when the shit hit the fan. Because she was that sort of a girl. Unafraid to meet things head on. No one would ever catch her running with her tail between her legs. She was fierce in the way she loved. If she loved you, there was no question mark about it—you knew it.

I fucking knew it.

She was the something unpredictable in my life, the splash of colour in my black and white, the *special* thrown in to set me off balance. She was *perfect*. And I'd fucking lost her.

What a dick.

"Good. That's good." I kept nodding like a dipshit bobblehead before I backed out of the room and followed Lee to the veranda.

Stew busted through the door, holding his latest trophy—the grog. "Let's get shit-faced."

As far as coping mechanisms went, it wasn't a healthy one. But who the fuck was I to judge? If Mum and Geoff were to die, I'd probably get blind drunk, too. My father, on the other hand ... well, it wouldn't make much of a difference, would it? I'd be sad. But I'd get over that real quick.

It looked like we were all in for a night of drowning our sorrows.

Chapter
22

Andrea

Rockhampton, Australia
3rd of August, 2009, 9:38 p.m.

She's finally asleep.

Tish blew out soft even breaths as she rested her head on my shoulder. The poor girl was utterly drained. We'd spent the night watching cheesy rom-coms on the couch while the boys drank and did whatever they were doing out the back.

I eased from under her, putting a couple of cushions in my place before going to ask if her brother could carry her to her bedroom. I didn't even have to open the door to realise Ben was the only one remotely sober enough to do the job. Lee was leaning so far forward in his chair he was half lying on the table. One arm was stretched across the glass top, acting as a pillow for his head. Stewart was slumped on the opposite side with his feet on another chair, clutching a can of rum to his chest just like he'd done with his balls. Ben had a deck of cards set out in a game of solitaire.

I poked my head through the door. "Um, Ben?"

His head snapped up. "What's up?"

"Could you give me a hand for a minute please?"

He tossed the cards away and pushed his chair out before circling the table. I stood back to give him room, chewing on my lip as he faced me. *Oh, damn.* It was hard seeing him. I would've loved to crawl into his arms and cry. This was horrible. So, so horrible. These poor kids. I was trying to be strong for them, but I just wanted to dissolve into tears. It was so unfair. Life was so fucking unfair. The one person who I wanted to turn to for comfort was right in front of me ... untouchable.

"Tish has fallen asleep on the couch. Do you reckon you could put her in bed?"

He nodded, heading for the lounge room. Scooping under her knees and back, he made light work of the task. I didn't need to be reminded of how strong he was. I knew what it was like to be held by him. He was a gentle giant. My gentle giant.

I tucked the covers around her and switched on the fan for some air circulation. After making sure she had the tissue box and a bottle of water beside the bed, I left the door slightly ajar before going to find sheets for us.

Ben waited in the lounge, his arms crossed.

I swallowed against a dry throat. "Thank you. And thanks for getting dinner for us."

"No worries. I needed to pick up some clean clothes anyway."

I tossed a couple of sheets on the couch and two more on each recliner. "Which one do you want?"

"I don't care."

"Okay." Grabbing the sheet on the seat nearest to me, I unfolded it and flung it out to settle over the chair. "Are they still drinking?"

"No. I gave them tonic water and told them it had vodka in it."

"Nice one." I kept my eyes on my task.

"Andy." His voice cracked.

Nope, not looking. "That's my name."

"I know this isn't the right time to talk about us, but if you'll hear me out, I'd like to apologise for being a dick."

Why couldn't you have apologised two months ago? Why did you have to hurt me at all? I smacked at the creases in the sheet, making them worse rather than smoothing them out. *Whatever.* I was just buying time until my voice box untied itself. "You're right. Now is not the time. And yes, you were a major dick."

His mouth screwed up as he took his sheet and put it over his bed for the night. "I think you're an incredible friend."

I blinked, my eyes stinging in warning. "I think you are, too."

He did Stewart's sheet as well. That was how thoughtful he was. I might've looked like I wasn't paying him any attention, but I had him pinned in my peripheral vision. I'd had him in my sights since day one. I just had to trust my knowing that we'd be okay. Did that mean I'd make it easy for him to get back in my good graces? Hell, no. He'd hurt me bad. He needed to know I wouldn't tolerate any shit like that in the future. Boundaries.

I loved him, but I loved me more. And I deserved better. If he couldn't rise to the occasion, I wasn't going to drop my level to meet him. *Nuh-uh.*

Rise up, or ship out, Benny-boy.

———

Ben

Rockhampton, Australia
4th of August, 2009, 1:12 a.m.

Stewart and Lee hooked an arm around each other and aimed for the doorway. At the same time. Dickheads. They were never gonna fit. They ended up in a heap on the floor with bruised knees and egos.

Andy heard the ruckus and helped me get them in bed. Or to the couch, in Stew's case. She went back to her recliner as I did what I had to do in the bathroom. When I got to my recliner, she looked asleep. I didn't know how she could be with Stewart chopping down a forest just next to her.

Maybe I should tilt his head back?

I started to get up, but she beat me to it, adjusting his position until the chainsaw quieted to a snuffle.

"You're awake." I lowered the footrest and sat.

"I think the neighbourhood is awake." She pulled the sheet over herself.

"Is he always this loud?" I squinted, only just able to make out her features, the standby light on the TV casting a dull glow in the room.

"Only when he breathes." Her lips quirked. I think.

"Maybe he should've stayed home," I joked.

"Maybe you should've." She wasn't joking. Her tone had bite.

I expected nothing less. My heart thumped against my ribcage like it was beating me up all over again.

"Do you remember me telling you how I would wish on Venus?" Her hand brushed at her hair.

"Yes."

"I wished for someone who understood me. Who was secure and happy enough on his own that he wouldn't depend on me to make him happy. Because that's what I watched my mother try to do for my father, and fail. I knew that wasn't what a healthy relationship was about." Her arm swatted at the air before flopping back down.

"Whatever shit you've got going on in your brain, you've gotta deal with it. It's not up to me to fix you."

"I know. And I have." I huffed, rubbing a hand across my forehead. Standing, I crossed to her. "Come with me."

"No."

I held out my hand. "Come with me, please?"

"It's one o'clock in the morning."

"Do I have to throw you over my shoulder?"

"No. Jeez." She ripped the sheet off.

I grabbed my keys from the table on my way to the door.

"We can't leave. What are you doing?"

"We're not leaving." I swung the door open and waved her through, pressing the key fob to open the car. "Hop in. The back seat."

"If you think—"

"Andy. Just get in the car. I'm not going to touch you unless you tell me to."

She scoffed and yanked the door open. I retrieved my guitar before letting her in and closing the door. Rounding the car, I adjusted the driver's seat way back before sliding in, seating the guitar across my lap. It wasn't a full moon, but it was getting there. Enough that I could still see her beautiful face when the interior light switched off.

"I hate myself for what I did to you. It was inexcusable."

She crossed her arms and faced forward.

"Your first time should have been special, and I took you like an animal. I put you in a compromising position in front of your little sister. And then I left you. I'm no better than my scumbag father. A chip off the old block."

Her mouth dropped open as she stared wide-eyed.

"I want you to know that I've never experienced anything so amazing in my life. And I feel sick saying that because I treated you so roughly. I lost control. I'm sorry. I'd like to make it up to you if I can." I tucked the guitar under my arm. "I'm going to be the sappiest most clichéd idiot there is to prove to you that I want you back. So bad."

What was I doing? Her opinion of me was going to sink to the depths of sewer scum after this. Too late, my fingers were already strumming the tune I'd had in my head constantly for weeks.

I opened my mouth and closed my eyes, pouring my heart into the song I'd written for her.

You woke me up,

and I brought you down

Had me on cloud nine,

and feeling proud

I ran away,
from the one I love
Ruined chances,
I was dreaming of

You can depend on me
Baby, will you bend to me?
Don't be sending me
Away, away, away

So baby,
can you hear me out?
Or baby,
will you scream and shout?

'Cause there's no way,
this will go away
This love,
it is here to stay

You can depend on me
Baby, will you bend to me?
Don't be sending me

Away, away, away

Hangin' by a string,
What could possibly bring
You back to me?
My guitar apology?

You can depend on me
Baby, will you bend to me?
Don't be sending me
Away, away, away

I unclenched my eyelids to find her chewing on her lips, her eyes glossy with tears.

She sniffed, clearing her throat. "What's it called?"

"'Guitar Apology.'"

"It's good." Her mouth curved with a hint of a smile. "You say you took me like an animal. I loved it. I loved what we did. It was perfect. You made me feel desirable, sexy. I wanted you hungry for me."

Her words punched me in the gut and lifted me through the roof at the same time. *She'd loved it.* I was such a fucking idiot.

"Don't ever hurt me again." The words crumbled as she twisted away from me, swiping at the moisture streaming down her face.

I got out, abandoning the guitar on the front seats and joined her in the back. She'd curled in on herself. *Shit. Do I hug her? Will she let me?* Whatever hope I'd had deflated like a limp penis. That hadn't gone as well as I had planned. I banged my head back on the headrest, waiting for her to run from the car.

She didn't.

She crawled into my lap and sobbed.

I folded around her and breathed her in. "I will never leave you again."

Please don't ever leave me.

Chapter
23

Emmeline

Hampshire, England
9th of March, 1868

Marybeth wiped a cool cloth over my brow and held my hand as I bore down through another contraction. It had been eight months since my father had tossed the earl from the property. I only hoped the timing concluded the baby was Sebastian's and not an early delivery of Reginald Fortescue's offspring.

"'Tis crowning. Not long now."

"I am going to be sick."

She dropped my hand and ran to fetch a bowl.

I leaned over the side of the bed and vomited on the floorboards, unable to wait. "Sorry." Resting back on the pillow, I pressed a palm to my forehead. My head was threatening to split open and my vision blurred in and out of focus. "I cannot—" Bowing forward, pain ripped through my stomach. "Aargh!"

The overwhelming feeling that I had done this before settled in my chest. I had a son. His father's name was "Ben."

"Pardon, miss?"

"Ben. If it is a boy, name him Benjamin Sebastian."

"You can name him yourself."

I shook my head. *No.* I had to return. It was time.

Another contraction squeezed my insides. I screamed as my flesh tore, allowing the baby's head to enter the world. White spots danced across my vision. I fought for breath. With one more push, the body followed. I collapsed onto the mattress, fighting to stay conscious.

Marybeth gathered the crying baby in a towel and held it up for me to see. "'Tis a boy, miss."

Ben. Sweet boy.

"Look after him ... for ... m—"

My eyes drifted shut.

"Miss? Miss!"

My heartbeat sputtered and stalled.

———

Ben

Brisbane, Australia
8th of January 2017

I hummed our song, holding her hand, being careful not to mess with any tubes. My forehead rested on the bedrail as my eyes traced the pattern on the lino floor. This had become my routine over the last couple of weeks. Mum would look after Seb, while I came to visit Andy. I'd walk in with a question on my face. The nurses all knew what I was asking. The answer was always the same.

"No change."

Her hair had appeared greasy today. I'd have to remember to ask the nurses to help me wash it. There must be a way. Her skin was cold against mine. She smelled like Sorbolene cream. They must've given her a bed bath recently. The machine keeping her breathing gave me a beat to hum to even if it wasn't the right tempo. I slowed my song down to match her. And I would do it for the rest of her life.

The song came to an end.

"Seb smiled today. I think he may have had gas, but I'll take it." I raised my head and smiled at her. "He regained the weight he lost after birth, plus two hundred grams already." I rubbed my thumb in circles on the back of her hand. "He's doing great. He needs his mamma. Come back to us, Andy." I broke our connection and pushed my fists into my eye sockets. I was so fucking sick of crying. It didn't do shit. Didn't solve anything. Didn't make me feel better—just made it worse.

It didn't bring her back.

I dropped my arms, sighing. Maybe I needed a coffee.

Hauling to my feet, I wiped my palms on my jeans and turned towards the door. Making it three steps clear, I stopped when the beep of the heart monitor changed behind me. Her heart rate had hiccupped. Scanning her immobile form, I couldn't see any change. Must've been a glitch.

I spun away again, taking two more steps. Her pulse began to race, the machine going apeshit.

"Nurse!" I yelled, running back in the room.

Three nurses barged past me, blocking my view. I plastered myself against the window, hands clasped on top of my head. What the fuck was happening?

A doctor came in, voicing my question minus the curse.

"She's waking up," one of the nurses answered.

Fuck. I hoped to God it was true. I held my breath, mangling my bottom lip with my teeth.

"Andrea. It's okay. We're going to take the tube out and then you can breathe by yourself. Just relax." His elbows jostled as he worked.

I was glad I couldn't see what they were doing. Even if I did want to look, I couldn't. I was frozen, too petrified to inhale, let alone move. I focused on the *drip, drip, drip* of her IV, waiting for some sign that she was going to be okay.

"Okay. It's okay. Just breathe. You know how to do that. You've been doing it on your own for years."

I listened to the doctor's instructions like they were meant for me, ordered my diaphragm to help. My nostrils flared as I pushed air out. And then she coughed. My legs gave out and I slid to the floor. My arms felt like their bones had dissolved as they flopped at my sides.

I tilted my chin to the ceiling and mouthed a thank you.

Thank you to a God I hadn't believed in.

Until then.

———

Emmeline/Andrea

Somewhere. Everywhere. There.

Swirling ... spinning ... floating ...

The oppressive weight of carrying around a sack of flesh was gone. I'd released myself, and not for the first time. I'd done this before. But this was different. This time I was reuniting with the small part of me I'd left behind. And I was eager to go. I called in my energy, asked the fragmentation to heal and pull together again. It bubbled and vibrated like an oncoming earthquake.

But I couldn't get past a barrier.

They wanted to show me something before I went.

She wanted to show me something before I went.

Jess.

I felt her. Every soul had its own unique vibration. I recognised hers straight away.

A scene rolled across my consciousness. My energy dropped instantly. This wasn't a happy scene. Her spirit tugged my thoughts back, reminding me I was merely a spectator and that she was happy and free where she was.

I observed Jess laying on a bed. The frame was the old-fashioned wrought-iron style. Her mouth was gagged, hands tied above her head and secured to the frame, her feet tied to each corner of the end of the bed. Her body was naked.

I retreated, preferring not to witness this heinous crime. Jess's ghost reminded me she was no longer there—she was here with me. We were in another realm, our energies suspended in nothingness. No flesh to tie us down. No mind to fool us into believing a false reality. We were consciousness. Pure energy.

Jess's eyes blinked open as her head rolled to the side. Taking in her surroundings, she thrashed all her limbs, sheer terror in her eyes.

Why are you showing me this? I don't want to see this.

She planted a word in my awareness. **Watch.**

A man entered the room. He was muscular, like he did manual labour for a living. He wore nothing but a twisted smile. I knew that face. He was young. Only in his late twenties, maybe early thirties. Where did I know him from?

Johnno's party. I'd seen him. He'd been there when I'd picked up on the negative juju. Had I recognised him that night? Who was he?

For a fraction of a second, his face morphed into that of Reginald Fortescue the Third's. If I'd had a mouth, I would've gasped. I certainly recognised his acrid vibrational signature. But the young man was from a different time.

I pulled back again, feeling like a whisk had reached inside me, twisting me into knots. Reaching for Jess's energy, I tried to regain equilibrium.

I was from a different time.

Was this some sort of timeline warp? Had we crossed an impenetrable divide?

The scene continued to play out. The man climbed over her. Jess's eyelids peeled back. He beat her as he forced himself inside. Blood ran from her skin as his teeth sank in too deep. Vomit spilled around the gag in her mouth as her throat surged. Her face turned dusky pink before going a horrible tinge of purple blue. She choked on her own vomit. The dip at the base of her neck stopped pulling in with each breath. There were no more breaths. She was dead. And still he pumped in and out like an animal determined to get what he came for.

The scene changed. It was dark. The man had driven into ... where?

Mount Archer National Park.

The answer crossed my awareness.

He took Jess from the car boot and hauled her sheet-covered body over his shoulder. Tossing a lighter onto the seat, flames burst to life, spreading across the leather of the Mercedes. He ran through the scrub, surprisingly fast considering the weight he carried. There were no signs or walking trails around. This was a remote part of the mountain. The part cars drove through, giving no thought to stopping.

He travelled far from the road until he found a hollow tree stump a foot taller than he. Beside it was another truncated tree, this one much shorter. It was the perfect step. He heaved himself up, jostling Jess on his shoulder. Tipping her body into the log, her hair hung down to reveal that she'd been buried head first. Once he'd successfully stuffed her in, he gathered a pile of dry leaves and twigs and added the garnish to his creation.

Looking back towards the road, he watched the smoke rise and checked his watch. The fire spread quickly. He ran away from its advance, safely making it to a trail on the other side and jogging home from there.

I remembered the fire at Mount Archer on the news. It had burned for hours, incinerating a large section of bush. And most likely Jess's body. No evidence. No consequence.

The scene went blank. Jess was no longer with me. My energy became dense as I prepared to re-enter my body. Andrea's body.

The realisation of pain was the first thing to enter my mind. My hearing picked up sounds of a man humming. I knew that song. That was Ben's song. Our song.

Ben! My baby!

Air forced its way into my lungs and I struggled against it. My windpipe felt raw, like sandpaper had been dragged along its lining. Frantic beeping timed my distress.

People surrounded me, strangers talking at me. A tube slid from my mouth. I wanted to gag and cough, but nothing was working. The taste of plastic coated my tongue. Struggling to breathe, or make a sound, I attempted to lift my hand. The message didn't seem to travel from my brain to my muscles. I needed to sit up. Where was Ben?

"Okay. It's okay. Just breathe. You know how to do that. You've been doing it on your own for years."

The irritation in the back of my throat drove me mad until I managed to cough. I sucked in air and coughed again, doing this several more times before I could settle.

"Ugh." I lifted my heavy head. "Ben?"

"Yeah, baby?" He came into view at the end of the bed. "I'm right here."

"Seb?" I croaked.

"He's doing fine." He smiled a weary smile.

My head fell back and I let out a sigh. *Thank God.*

I had so much to tell him. And all of it was completely insane.

I decided to address something a bit simpler. "You need a shave."

He snorted and laid his head on my feet. "I know."

Chapter
24

Andrea

Brisbane, Australia
15th of January, 2017

Stepping over the threshold of our home for the first time in three weeks, my muscles practically sighed. Home. I was finally home with my family. Seb blinked at me before yawning as I carried him to the lounge room. This kid was love personified. Just looking at him had me walking a foot off the ground and my heart beating with purpose.

"Hello, honey. Welcome home." Mum came from the spare room to greet me.

"Hi, Mum." I hooked my free arm around her and gave her a squeeze. I hissed as my caesarean wound twinged, reminding me to take it easy.

"Sit down. Relax. You're going to be tired and sore for a while." Guiding me to the lounge, she made me do as I was told. "Let me cuddle my grandson."

"But I only just picked him up."

"Yes, but you'll have heaps of time with him. I've only got a couple of weeks."

I rolled my eyes, too tired to argue. She was right. I would have heaps of time to get to know my beautiful boy. She scooped him from my arms.

"What about me? I'm leaving tomorrow." Ben's mum joined me on the couch, patting my knee.

Hang on. Something was different. "When did we get a new couch?"

She smiled. "They delivered it a couple of weeks ago. Do you like it? I helped him choose."

I spun to question Ben. "What happened to the old one?"

All eyes turned on me, brows raised.

Ben scratched his chin. "Ah ... your waters broke all over it."

"Oh." My heart sank at the reminder of the blind spots in my life. The parts that I could never see in my mind's eye. Memories lost, or time spent in limbo while I was 'elsewhere'. I barely remembered the night I gave birth. I could hardly remember waking up after being in a coma. I did remember the doctor telling me I couldn't conceive any more children. That stung. But the fact that I was alive at all soothed the pain. And we had Seb.

The time between ... as Emmeline—I remembered all of it.

Jess. I'd seen Jess.

I gasped as the vision I'd been shown played back on fast forward. "Oh my God!"

"What?" All three of them crowded me, worry on their faces.

"I have to ring Stew."

"Why?"

"I know where to find Jess's bones."

––––––

Andrea

Brisbane, Australia
18th of January, 2017

Stewart's name flashed across the screen of my mobile. I snatched it off the coffee table and hit the answer button before wedging it between my neck and shoulder.

"Hey." Patting Seb's back, I waited for a burp.

"Hey, sis. How ya goin'?"

"Great. Tell me what you've got."

He laughed. "Straight to the point. Okay. We found the bones exactly where you said they'd be. They're doing DNA tests to identify the remains. I doubt they'll find any clues about the killer, or how she died."

"They might."

"Unlikely, given the fire damage and the length of time passed. They took the stump away for testing, too. The burnt-out car was removed long ago. We're still tracking where it was discarded."

Damn. "I saw his face. He was in his twenties, early thirties at a push. Muscle-bound."

"Hell of a lot of miners and sports nuts around here, sis. They all fit that description."

"Yeah, damn." I moved the phone and stretched my neck to release a cramp.

"Maybe we could hook you up with a police sketch artist?"

"Good idea."

"All right. I gotta go. Let me know if you remember anything else, ya weirdo."

"Hey, I'm helping your arse."

"Yeah, I know. Love ya."

"Love you too, Spew."

"Oi."

I hung up, giggling.

My brother, the cop. Still a bogan.

Rubbing Seb's back, I finally got a burp out of him. And it was huge, vibrating through my neck. "Ooh, Daddy would be proud of that one."

Holding him was *the* most amazing feeling, like I was full—overflowing with joy. I cherished him even more because I'd had to leave another baby boy behind. The loss of him and of my life as Emmeline was real and raw in the forefront of my thoughts. The thought of baby Ben made me hold Sebastian even tighter. The kid was going to get sick of me smothering him all the time. I wish I knew what had happened to Benjamin Sebastian Lovatt.

Why can't I find out?

I took Seb with me to the spare room, grabbing his bouncer on the way. Parking him next to the desk, I fired up the computer.

How the hell would I do this?

I didn't know the first thing about searching for a person born that long ago. I'd had trouble finding my keys every damn day since waking up—how was I supposed to do something like this?

Did I just type in his name?

At least I had his name, and his date and place of birth.

I typed in, *how to find a person born in 1868.* Google spat out heaps of suggestions about births, deaths, and marriage registries.

Of course.

With a little creativity and by following the strings, I found the record of his birth. But how did I track him from there?

"Oh, my God. I'm such an idiot."

I had a friend who was a librarian. Why the hell hadn't I asked her first?

I picked up my phone and dialled.

"Andy? You okay?"

"Hi, Ronnie. I'm fine, but I could use your help."

"I don't know how to change nappies."

"Luckily, I do. This problem is more in your comfort zone."

"What's up?"

"Do you know how to search for someone who was born in the eighteen hundreds?"

"Do you have a name?"

"Name. Birthdate. Birthplace. I want to know where he went from there."

"Ah, okay. Yep."

"Yep?" I sat up straight, clutching the phone.

"Yep. Give me what you've got and I'll get back to you."

"Oh my God. You're the best. Thank you."

"You're welcome."

After spilling all the information I could remember in a rush, I ended the call, giddy with elation. I would never be able to hold him, but knowing what had happened to him would mean the world to me.

There was someone else I needed to know about. Sebastian Lovatt. As Emmeline, I had been told that they'd sent him away on a convict ship. *To Australia!*

I typed in, *how to find a convict.*

There was a website made for what I wanted. *Convict.com.au.*

Perfect.

He'd left in 1867.

There were two voyages in 1867. The Norwood and the Hougoumont. But the Norwood left in April, and we'd run away in July, so that wasn't the one.

He must've sailed on the Hougoumont. The last convict ship to arrive in Australia.

I scrolled through the list of passengers. *Oh, God. There he is.*

Clicking on his name, another page opened with more details of his life.

Name. Aliases. Gender.

Birth. Occupation. Death.

My lips parted. He'd died on the 9th of March in 1883, aged thirty-three. What would have been his son's fifteenth birthday.

I slapped a palm over my mouth, leaning back in my chair as I lost him all over again.

Oh, Sebastian.

I trembled, my stomach twisting like rope.

As content as I was, the wound left by the loss of Benjamin and Sebastian Lovatt would never heal. A waterfall of tears kept me company and drowned my sorrow.

The website didn't say how he'd died.

The last bits of information were the details of his transportation and conviction.

Horse thief.

Twenty years.

Bastards.

I didn't want to search for the earl. I only hoped he was rotting in hell.

Unwillingly, I pictured his face. Seeing it stabbed a sharp blade through my heart. The image warped into that of a young man. Jess's killer. He stared at me with a crooked smile. *I know that face. Where the fuck do I know it from?*

I held the profile in place, an image on pause burning into the screen.

My eyes peeled open as my jaw dropped.

I lurched forward to punch in another search, this time going to my high school's Facebook page. I clicked through the photos from when I was a student.

Seb started to cry, so I picked him up before resting him against my chest. "Shh, sh, sh. It's okay."

I kept clicking.

Whoa. Hang on. Go back.

There was an album of photos from a sausage sizzle fundraiser. In the background of one photo, a guy wielded a pair of tongs, cooking sausages on a barbie.

Fuck, that's him.

He wore a high-vis, fluorescent yellow shirt, and a wide brim straw hat.

I made one more call.

"Hey, sis."

"It's the fucking groundsman."

Chapter
25

Andrea

Brisbane, Australia
20th of January, 2017

Ushering Ronnie in, I hurried back to a screaming Seb.

"What's wrong with him?" She put her bag on a dining chair before tossing an envelope on the table.

"He's waiting for his bottle." I measured the scoops of formula and twisted the cap back on before shaking it up.

"Ah." Lifting her chin, she moved towards the blanket where Sebastian squirmed and kicked in protest. "Are you starving?" She pulled up her skirt before kneeling down.

Seb stopped, turning his head.

"Oh, who is this strange person?" Tickling his belly before picking him up, she made a funny face.

"You can feed him."

"Oh, no. I don't know how." She gritted her teeth, frantically shaking her head.

"It's easy. Sit on the couch. Put him in the crook of your elbow."

Her mouth twisted as she frowned, hesitating. Unleashing another scream, Seb convinced her to follow my instructions. I stacked a couple of cushions under her arm to support his weight.

"Now put the teat in his mouth. I already tested the temperature. It's ready to go."

"Okay. If you say so."

Sebastian sucked his milk, eyes rolling back in his head.

"Ooh, you *were* starving." She laughed at him before looking up at me. "Go read your search summary. I didn't do a full report. I can if you want though."

"Thank you so much for helping me find him."

"You didn't tell me you were researching Ben's family history."

What?

My gaze shot to hers before I sat, grabbing the envelope and ripping it open.

Benjamin Sebastian Lovatt

Born - 9th of March, 1868 in Hampshire, England

Mother - Emmeline Louisa Beauchamp, seventeen years

Father - Sebastian William Lovatt, eighteen years

Guardian - Marybeth Amalie Hutch

Marybeth, you beautiful woman. She'd done as I'd asked, surpassing her role as loyal servant. She'd always be my friend.

No formal education

Worked as a stable hand on Beauchamp Estate until July, 1888

Farrier for Holdsworthy Stud from August 1888 to December, 1896

December, 1896 to September, 1897. A period of nine months where he didn't appear to be employed.

Travelled to Sydney on The Iris, September 1897, arriving January, 1898

Settled in Rockhampton, August, 1898

Oh! My baby had come looking for his daddy. My muscles tensed and I slid forward to the edge of my seat.

Worked as a jackeroo on Lewis Station, August, 1898 to 1915

Married Geraldine Martha Hunter, May, 1900

Two children - Henrietta Martha Lovatt, born 6th of February, 1901, and June Louisa Lovatt, born 12th of April, 1902

Died 13th of August, 1915. Cause of death: crush injury (trampled by bull stampede)

"Bull stampede. God, how horrific." My baby. Nausea curdled in my gut as I blinked away tears.

"Yeah. I didn't add in the rest of the family history because you only asked for info about his life specifically. But I can tell you his girls went on to marry. The youngest one married a Locke and gave birth to Ben's grandfather.

"So Benjamin Lovatt is Ben's great-great-grandfather?"

"Yup."

"Holy shit."

I'd slept with my husband's great-great-great-grandfather.

My eyes sprang open even wider when I realised something else.

Emmeline was his great-great-great-grandmother.

But that wasn't all. I'd recognised Ben when we'd met. I'd *known* him because we'd been in each other's lives before.

Ben Locke and Sebastian Lovatt were one and the same.

Our souls wove through time in a loving dance, drawn together again and again.

As I scanned Ronnie's features, I understood that Ben wasn't the only soul I'd crossed lives with.

Marybeth.

Whoa.

Epilogue

Sebastian

Rockhampton, Australia
18th of December, 1882

The *clip-clop* of the horse's hooves announced my arrival into Rockhampton. The day was mine to do with as I pleased. A weekly occurrence I rarely took full advantage of. Today, I'd chosen to borrow my fellow worker's steed to travel into town from Ironstone Mountain. Rockhampton post office was the address I'd listed on a letter sent to my father upon hearing of my employment at the mine. I decided to check if he'd replied.

A bell rang on the door as I entered the small office.

"Good day to you, sir." The postmaster wiped a hand along his counter, watching me approach.

"Good morning. Would you have any mail for a Sebastian Lovatt?"

"Let me have a look for you." He bent behind the counter and papers and boxes shuffled before he stood, holding an envelope. "I remember this now. It came about a month ago."

He placed the letter on the wooden surface. I picked it up. It was from my father. *Fifteen years.* It had been fifteen years since I had seen him.

"Thank you, kindly. Have a good day."

"You are welcome." He nodded before turning away.

I held the envelope, crossing the street to the nearest establishment serving liquor. Finding a table at the rear, I fell into a seat. Hands trembling, I opened the envelope.

Dear Sebastian,

I cannot tell you how happy I was to receive your letter. Not knowing of your fate has been incredibly draining on my spirits. I miss you terribly.

Gold, you say? I pray that you find what you are searching for. I am glad that you have secured work and that you are finally free to live as you choose.

I remain here at the Beauchamp Estate, although I find it hard to keep up with the physical work.

Memories of you surround me and that brings some comfort in my old age.

To answer your questions, Miss Emmeline never married the earl. He was escorted from the property just hours before the wedding was to proceed. I cannot tell you the reason why. Just know that Mr Beauchamp put his daughter's needs ahead of any arrangement he had procured. For that, he deserves respect.

I dropped the pages on the table.

Why had he not put her needs first from the beginning? What could have caused the earl to be removed so abruptly? Had he hurt her? Had Mr Beauchamp discovered that the earl was embezzling money or stealing from him? No, Father would have told me something like that. It could only mean he had hurt her in some way. My hands clenched in my lap as I ground my teeth.

I picked up the letter again.

She gave birth to a little boy on the ninth of March, 1868. His name is Benjamin Sebastian Lovatt.

You are a father, Sebastian.

Gripping the paper tightly, I read that line again. And again. Ten times I read it to make sure I had it right.

I am a father.

I have a son.

I blew out a breath. Would I ever get to see him? My mind spun a thousand scenarios, all of them involving embarking on a journey across the seas. Would I choose to endure the voyage again? Yes. Only this time as a free man.

I continued reading.

Marybeth, Emmeline's former chambermaid, is raising him alongside her own child. He helps me in the stables. He is just like you were, but a little more free-spirited like his mother.

Emmeline's parents do not acknowledge him as their kin, but they have allowed him to stay. For that I am grateful. I suspect they have not forgiven him for being the cause of his mother's death. I am sorry to be the one to break the news to you.

No. My head dropped as I crumpled the papers in my fist. Resting my elbows on my knees, my shoulders shook as I broke into sobs. I'd thought I'd known what it was to have my heart crushed. News of her death pulverised any remains left in my chest cavity. I had comforted myself, believing that she was with her family, living a charmed life. I had dreamed that she was happy witnessing Miss Modesty's foal grow to an adult. I'd fantasized that her parents had changed their minds about the earl. That she had been spared from a life with the insufferable ratbag. That bit I had right, at least.

I had never imagined this.

A world without her in it was unimaginable.

To finish reading his letter would be an impossibility. I slid off the chair and stumbled for the exit, collapsing in the alleyway between buildings. My elbow captured my guttural cries of agony as I flicked through all the possibilities of the life we could have had. A blessing that was never meant for me. I sobbed until I had nothing left and for many hours beyond. I lay in my filth, my tongue as dry as the autumn leaves. I stayed there, unable to do much more than breathe and acknowledge the movement of the shadows across the wooden cladding as the sun tracked through the sky, once, twice.

I wanted the sun to take me as it sank below the horizon.

Wherever the sun was, that was where I would find my Emmeline.

We would be together again.

Acknowledgements

I finished it! Thank you so much to my beautiful readers. You keep me going when I'm not sure I have it in me. Your faith is fuel for my tired imagination, painting my sketchy character outlines into bold colour and pulling their 2D frames from my mind and into vivid life. Big hugs to you all. Thank you for the feedback—it helps me more than you know. I'm so thankful to have shared something from my vulnerable insides and have you embrace it as your own. Thank you, thank you, thank you.

To my reader group, JM's Gems—you are definitely a highlight in my life. You're all such strong, inspiring people in your own right and have been so welcoming and tolerant of my weirdness. Thanks for being weirdos with me. ;P

Special mention goes out to Kat—fellow misfit and blurb/cover critic. Plus, repeated signing assistant. I'm so damn lucky that you put up with my distracted, stressed, weird self. Thanks for coming along on so many adventures. Some of them questionable, but whatevs. Keep livin' large!

Jane! Thanks for bringing Vicky into my life. Thanks for the writing crawls and the chai teas. Thanks for the vines in my hair and the chicken on a spring. That poor chicken. No thanks for the internet dating. O.o

Vicky—master juggler. Thanks for pimping the heck out of my books. Thanks for taking the strain off my back. Thanks for laughing at my lame jokes. Thanks for keeping in touch, because we know I'm shit at doing that. Just, thank you!

Lauren and Anna—the CREATING ink ladies. I love working with you! Thank you for all the smiley faces when you tell me off. Lol. #repetitionandfiltersforthewin

In all seriousness, thank you for being so encouraging and understanding. And tolerant. Let's not forget that. You see the things that I don't, and I'm forever grateful for your invaluable input. ~~Up, down. In, out.~~

Who puts the finishing sparkle on all my projects? Fiona from Fiona Dreaming. Thanks so much for being so patient with me and for spotting the sneakiest of errors. Much love to you.

To my cover designer, Ben. No, I did not name the main character after you. Sorry about that. Thank you for taking on a newb and for being so understanding of the unforeseen delay. Your work is beautiful. I love what you've done with my covers! You're stuck with me now.

Every one of you who signed up to share, and/or review my book—a billion thank yous go to you guys. Getting the word out is the hardest part for me. Being an introvert and dealing with a busy life makes the social media game an unscaleable wall sometimes.

As always, I left my boys until last. My preciouses (not Gollum's). We have had some year, haven't we? You've got no idea, but sometimes I watch you doing the simplest of tasks—chewing, breathing, watching TV— and I marvel at your perfection and how freakin' lucky I am to have been blessed with you. Despite all our challenges, I wouldn't change a second. I looooooove you all ridiculous amounts.

Thank you. <3<3<3

————

Read on for an excerpt from *Sensing You*, book one in this series.

Book Three, Indulging You (Felicity's story) will be coming soon. :)

Excerpt From Sensing You

PROLOGUE

My mind wandered to that place where my dreams flee, replaced with vaporous intruders and penetrating horrors. My body twitched and jerked, struggling to find consciousness as the misty form of a woman drifted into my room.

Not again.

She wore a floral, summer dress. One strap was torn and hung loose from her shoulder, and dark bruises circled her neck. Reaching out her hand, she wrapped it around my foot. My body stilled. Inside my chest, my heart froze while my stomach threatened to prolapse. She pulled on my foot, imploring me to listen. I knew she couldn't really drag me away, but I felt the icy touch, the drag of her fingers on my terrified flesh. I wondered if I would somehow disappear. My hands reached desperately for the pillow.

"Stop," I pleaded.

"You have to help me. You have to stop him."

My whimpers turned into sobs. "Please … g-go away."

I felt another presence. Heard the shaky rumble of his voice as he told the lady to leave.

"Daddy," I whispered, relieved. He smiled at me with sad eyes.

But the spirit refused to budge.

"I'm sorry, honey bunch. I love you," my father's voice whispered, heavy with regret.

The wretched fingers of loss clawed their way into my chest, pulling apart my ribcage as if just learning of his death.

I dropped the pillow, and reached out to him. "Nooo! Daddy!" My screams were useless. He was gone.

Wrenching my sweat-soaked body upright, my throat ached as the scream continued to escape the depths of my chest. I pressed my lips together to cut off the sound, but that only lasted a second. My mouth opened wide again as I gasped for much needed air.

A hammering sound filled the room. My muddled brain mistook it for the pulse in my ears, but it was the beating of a fist on my bedroom door.

"SHUT UP!" My housemate screeched as she continued to pound.

I was definitely awake now. My hand circled my throat. I needed to check for myself if my screams had stopped. *Yup. All good.* "Yeah, keep your skin on!" I tried to shout back, but my voice came out hoarse.

"Fucking freak," she mumbled before I heard the shuffle of her feet on the tiles.

Again, frozen fingers grasped my toes and pulled. I snapped my foot back, leaving her hand suspended and empty. I watched my stubborn, unwanted visitor through narrowed eyes, and a whole lot of false bravado.

"He's coming. He's going to take another."

"Okay got it. You can go now. You're not wanted here. *Leave*." My voice was low, but firm.

Her face went blank, and her hand dropped from its raised position. The holographic image of her faded, but the chill running up and down my body remained.

I liked to think I could run from this, but there's no hiding from things unbound to time or matter. My stupid sixth sense was telling me the proverbial shit was going to hit the proverbial fan … soon.

Fuck my life.

About the Author

Author of smart, sexy characters, J.M. Adele loves to flit between the dark and light sides of romance. Somewhere along the way, an almost constant procession of imaginary characters settled into her thoughts and she picked up a pen to share their stories.

She lives in Queensland with her three greatest loves—her children. When she's not writing or being a mum, you might find her hiking up a mountain, singing in the car when nobody is looking, or curled up with a good book.

Follow J.M.

www.jmadele.org

www.facebook.com/authorjmadele

@JMAdeleBooks

@j.m.adele